YOUR MONEY OR YOUR LIFE ...

Standing up, Packer addressed the aircraft's passengers.

"One dozen," he said, "I give them a dozen of you, and I get a new engine for this bird!" He laughed, luxuriating in the changing, mobile features presented to him. He saw the selfishness of each look, saw the side-glances, the obscenity of sudden hope on each face. The silence was mounting to a pitch of audibility. It was this he wanted.

At last a man spoke, obscene with grooming and money. "A thousand dollars, feller, if you count me in!"

There was a surprised, disgusted murmur, the last reaction of communal identity. Packer knew what would follow, and called out, "You heard the man – I'm bid one thousand dollars for his fat hide! How much are the rest of you worth?"

Also by Craig Thomas in Sphere Books:

FIREFOX
WOLFSBANE

Rat Trap

CRAIG THOMAS

SPHERE BOOKS LIMITED
30/32 Gray's Inn Road, London WC1X 8JL

First published in Great Britain
by Michael Joseph Ltd 1976
Copyright © 1976 by Craig Thomas
Published by Sphere Books Ltd 1977
Reprinted 1977, 1978 (twice), 1979

Set in Linotype Garamond

Printed in Great Britain by
C. Nicholls & Company Ltd
The Philips Park Press, Manchester

Contents

the first one is for

JILL

Acknowledgements

I wish to acknowledge the assistance given to me by T. R. Jones so helpfully and freely during the writing of this novel which he read so enthusiastically. His help was invaluable in the flying and airport sequences. I also wish to thank A. R. Handley from whose intimate knowledge of the modern army I borrowed immodestly.

Craig Thomas
Lichfield

All men dream: but not equally. Those who dream by night in the dusty recesses of their minds wake in the day to find that it was vanity: but the dreamers of the day are dangerous men, for they may act their dream with open eyes, to make it possible.

T. E. Lawrence:
Seven Pillars of Wisdom

1: Occupational Hazard

British Airways Captain Burgess, on the flight-deck of Speedbird 5106, glanced across at his second pilot, then over his shoulder at his number three, placed behind the two more senior pilots on the folding jump-seat, monitoring both of them on the approach to Heathrow. Hislop and Simpson. Beyond and behind Simpson, and out of his range of vision as he concentrated ahead, were the navigator and the engineer, making-up the flight-deck complement of the Boeing 707. The two pilots with Burgess were both a lot younger than himself, at fifty-two, and a world away from him in experience. There was the void of two wars, Europe and Korea, between them and himself. Both of them had flown only civil air routes since leaving the College of Air Training at Hamble. Simpson was a cheerful imitation of young men who had died over southern England and northern France, while Hislop . . .

Burgess sniffed in audible disdain, catching sight of his second pilot again from the corner of his eye. Hislop was a man with a problem; the problem was politely referred to as his wife. Only that morning at Kennedy International, at five-o-clock Eastern Seaboard Time, he had bawled Hislop out for spending a sleepless night unsuccessfully trying to contact that same wife by transatlantic telephone. Wives who drank or who were unfaithful, and Ruth Hislop was both, played hell with pilots' reflexes. As for his own wife – with Marjorie he had little more to worry about than her failure to cut the lawns. He hated Ruth Hislop, he realised – for what she was doing to the young man next to him. The feeling was pure, vitriolic, satisfying.

The VHF crackled in his headset and the random thoughts flicked away as if a hand had wiped his mind clean. It was the control tower at Heathrow, supplying the next of the careful sequence of instructions designed to land him safely at the airport.

'Speedbird 5106 – London. Further right now, on to a heading of One-Nine-Zero.'

'London – 5106. Turning right onto One-Nine-Zero, flight level at three thousand.'

'Roger.'

Burgess checked his speed, noting that it was satisfactorily stabilised at two hundred and ten knots, and wondered what the runway visual range was at Heathrow, since he had not yet received the information from London Approach.

He glanced sideways again at Hislop, at the handsome, dark features set in their habitual frown, the mouth pouting with an obstinate, childish cheerlessness. Burgess, as the vitriol flowed, decided to make a manual approach rather than rely on the autopilot. The manual approach would be useful practice – the British Airways *Manual of Flight Procedure* laid down strict regulations for such practices at regular intervals, and Burgess never despised regulations designed to make air travel safer. Yet he knew, with a pleasing touch of malice, that he had made his decision to try and shake Hislop out of his petulant, moody, transatlantic silence.

He watched the second pilot tidy away the charts, then he said: 'I'm going to make a manual approach on this one, John. Would you handle the throttles to break-off height?'

He lifted his head, turned it slightly, and said to the number three: 'Peter, call my height and range once we're established.'

The R/T came on.

'5106 – London. Further right now on to Two-Four-Zero, descend to two thousand feet, intercept the ILS for runway Two-Eight Left, and call established.'

'London – 5106. Turning right onto Two-Four-Zero, leaving three thousand for two thousand.' Burgess turned to Hislop, and added: 'Wheels down, please.'

The second pilot's hand moved to the central console, then he said: 'Wheels selected down, sir.' His eyes moved to the indicators and three green lights glowed comfortably on the panel. He gave Burgess the required confirmation. 'Wheels down and locked. Three greens.'

Burgess had already noted the dull thump of the wheels locking and had checked the slight pitch change as they dropped into the gale of the slipstream. His eyes studied the Instrument Landing System dial in front of him and, as he watched, the localiser needle which showed the beam down which he would fly to the runway eased off its stop on the right hand side of the dial. He maintained his heading for the moment. He registered his height established at two thousand feet and felt the first injection of adrenalin he always felt, and needed, as he started his final approach. It was a pure excitement, a routine tension that never disappointed, which no machine could ever emulate, or spoil.

He scanned the instrument panel and noted that everything showed in the green; the irrelevancies of Hislop's private life and the length of his lawns disappeared from his mind. He was simply and totally a pilot landing an aircraft. Only the panel was real to him and the awareness, coming almost through the fabric of the shirt stretched across his broad shoulders, of the other members of the flight crew .

Burgess levelled the wings as the direction indicator steadied on two-eight-zero degrees. He noted that the two ILS needles now formed the only true cross which interested him. He was in the slot, meshed on to the path that would take him unerringly to the end of the runway.

The second pilot was completing the pre-landing checks as Burgess pressed the transmit button, and said into the R/T: 'London – 5106 is established.'

'Roger,' came the reply from London Approach. Then: 'Call Tower, One-One-Eight, decimal Two.'

Hislop's hand went to the change-over switch of the VHF, then moved to the flap lever, selecting fifteen degrees.

'London Tower – 5106.'

'5106 – London Tower. Continue your approach, you are number two in the pattern. Surface wind Two-Seven-Zero, five knots.'

Simpson's voice cut in, level and mechanical: 'Four miles outer marker, thirteen hundred feet.'

'Tower – copied the wind,' Burgess said into the R/T. The outer marker light on the panel flashed its two-per-second

13

agreement with Simpson, and Burgess heard in his earphones the confirmatory bleep of the panel light.

At the same moment, cutting across the comfort of the noise, he heard Hislop's urgent call: 'Christ! Fire warning, number one!'

Then Burgess saw for himself the red chatter of the warning-light, the indication that there was a fire in number one engine, slung beneath the port wing. Even as his stomach surged, his mind spewed out an amalgam of data, response, guesswork, procedures . . . Was it for real, or simply a spurious warning light? Visual check? Close down the engine? Pull the extinguishers . . . and have British Airways climbing up the wall over the repair bill if it turned out to be a spurious signal? He needed a visual check. It didn't cost anything – except time.

He leaned forward and round in his seat, felt the shirt come away from the back, sticky with sweat, felt the slight tremor in the control column as Hislop monitored while he made his check. Anticipating the sequence of his responses, a part of his mind admitted that Hislop was doing his job as he had been drilled to do. Burgess was aware of the sharp, hot animal smell of fear-sweat in the confined space around him. Already one and a half seconds had elapsed since Hislop's warning cry. There was nothing untoward to be seen beneath the port wing, no flare of orange, no thin streamer of smoke. Number one engine looked perfect, innocent.

He swung his gaze back to the panel, noting first that the aircraft was still firmly on the ILS. On the engines panel, located in the very centre of the instruments, the jet-pipe temperatures registered normal, the fuel pressure and flow were normal, rpm normal . . . He completed, with a dead feeling, the only checks he could make. Which of the alternative explanations should he accept? He could consider that the light was spurious, and continue on all four engines – the fire tenders would be ready for them when they landed. Or should he assume that the emergency was real, and cut out number one?

For the first time in the eternal few seconds since Hislop's warning and the appearance of the red light, he was aware

14

of the seventy-two passengers in the bulk of the 707 behind him. There were no alternatives, he decided.

'Stop-cock number one.'

Hislop's breath exploded with relief, even as his hands moved swiftly. He closed the throttle on number one, then closed the high and low pressure fuel cocks. The engine, on fire or not, was isolated, without fuel.

Burgess heard the whine-down, and registered the quieter note produced by the three remaining Conway engines. Simultaneously, he trimmed out the swing of the aircraft towards the shut-down engine, and wondered how many of his passengers had detected the change in engine note – and of those who detected it, how many had recognised its significance? None, he devoutly hoped. As it was, the stewardesses would be aware immediately that the landing had moved out of the pleasant category of the normal, the routine. They were good girls, he reflected. No panic. Six seconds had now elapsed since the appearance of the warning light.

'London – 5106. We have fire warning, number one engine, which is shut down,' he said into the R/T. 'Continuing approach, two mile final.'

From the corner of his eye, he saw Hislop looking at him with something approaching envy. If the younger man envied him his calm, then the boy's nerves were in a poorer way then he had suspected. He cursed Hislop's wife as a rider to the thought.

'5106 – London. Roger. Emergency services are waiting.' Then Burgess heard the Tower instruct the captain of the aircraft ahead of him in the landing pattern. 'Clipper 4655 – overshoot. Repeat – overshoot. We have an emergency.' There was a brief pause, and then he heard: 'Speedbird 5106, you have priority clearance, number one on approach.'

Burgess smiled at the incongruous thought of the 747 captain ahead of him now directed to overshoot the runway and already climbing out of London on the correct overshoot procedure; no doubt he was cursing vociferously and anticipating the number of passengers who would call down the wrath of their gods on the head of Pan-Am.

Simpson called out: 'One and a half miles, eight hundred

feet.' His voice betrayed the uncertainty of the moments after Burgess's decision to stop-cock the engine. The engine was shut off, made as safe as it could be, but Burgess knew that for Simpson the aircraft had become a duralumin enemy.

He turned to Hislop and said: 'As soon as we're down, stop-cock number four, and give me full reverse on numbers two and three.'

'Roger.'

Burgess smiled briefly in encouragement, but Hislop's features were a stony mask. The instructions he had been given would enable Burgess to bring the plane to a halt as quickly as possible, and get his passengers down the emergency chutes as fast as they could move. He had no intention of playing games with an uneven reverse thrust from one engine on the port side and two to starboard.

Burgess began to feel the sense of relief welling up in him, premature though it might be. Another thirty seconds and they would be touching down on runway Two-Eight Left. Unless something totally unexpected occurred, they would get away with it.

'Tell the stewardesses to prepare for emergency evacuation as soon as we stop rolling,' he said.

He heard Simpson's sudden, incongruous obscenity, but he dared not turn his head.

'What the fuck . . . ?'

Burgess saw the threshold lights of Two-Eight Left through the haze and called the Tower. 'Runway in sight.'

'Roger. We're ready for you.'

Simpson's voice was still mechanical, yet at the back of his mind Burgess registered the flat urgency of fear.

'Skipper – a man here with a gun says we're being hijacked.'

'Stop pissing about, Peter!' Simpson was merely expressing his relief at completely the wrong moment and in completely the wrong way, Burgess thought angrily. Yet there was that tenor beyond play-acting in his voice, wasn't there?

He heard the screech of the tyres on the runway, felt the tremor through the column as the 707's total weight of one hundred and fifty-three thousand pounds settled on to Two-Eight Left at one hundred and forty-five knots. From the corner of his eye, he saw Hislop stop-cocking number four engine with one hand, while with the other he pushed numbers two and three to full reverse thrust. The deceleration thrust him against the restraint of his straps. At the same moment, he felt the sudden cold pressure of the gun barrel against the angle of his jaw.

The Senior Air Traffic Controller (SATCO), Heathrow, released the breath he had been holding for interminable seconds as he saw the twin puffs of smoke from the tyres as British Airways Flight No. 5106 from Kennedy International touched down on runway Two-Eight Left. The engines opened up to full reverse thrust and their whine drowned the noise of the crash-wagons, fire tenders and the ambulances, as they pulled away from beneath him like furious insects, scarlet and white, to parallel and intercept the aircraft's course.

He was standing behind the padded seat of the Ground Movement Controller, in the 'Greenhouse', the topmost floor of the control tower. The balding man on his right, the Local Controller, at that moment in contact with 5106, bent forward to speak into the R/T.

'5106 – contact London Ground, One-Two-One, decimal Niner, and acknowledge when convenient.' Then he sat back in his chair having handed over the aircraft, and its problems, to the man seated in front of the forbidding figure of SATCO.

As far as the half-dozen men in the 'Greenhouse' were concerned, everything was normal, except for the noise of the 707, which might have been an audible expression of the stretched nerves SATCO felt around him. He was aware that the hands gripping his binoculars were white at the knuckles and, inspecting the eye-pieces, he saw that they were rimmed with perspiration. He looked through them once more, following the apparently-innocent passage of the 707 across his field of vision. The wagons dashing to meet it, more insect-like than ever at that distance, pursued it, then gradually overhauled it.

He could sense the relaxation, premature but not unexpected. He became aware that the collar of his hastily-donned jacket was turned up, and smoothed it down. The aircraft was on the ground, where they could get to it, rolling to its expected stop. It hadn't been a real emergency, by the look of it – probably a bare wire at the back of the instrument panel. . . .

Then he realised that 5106 had not acknowledged. Perhaps the man had his hands full, after all? He leaned forward involuntarily, his breath hot, ticklish, on the neck of the Ground Movement Controller in front of him. There was another thing – the plane was taking a long time rolling to a halt, as if the captain were treading on egg-boxes rather than his brakes.

The 707 bowed forward over its nosewheels as it finally stopped. SATCO recognised the signs of severe braking. He rubbed at his jaw with one long-fingered hand. The Ground Movement Controller's voice was perfunctory, as if discussing the weather.

'All surface traffic to clear south-west of airfield – suspected fire emergency, Block One-Oh-Two, runway Two-Eight Left. Senior Fire Officer, report back this frequency soonest.'

SATCO raised his binoculars to his eyes, expecting to see the emergency chutes billowing from the belly of the plane, the first of the passengers unkemptly tumbling down them to safety. The 707 sat with seeming indifference on the runway, a superior species surprised by the attention of the emergency services. The small, bright spots of the vehicles had pulled into a circle round the silent plane, like an impotent swarm.

The voice of the Ground Movement Controller disturbed his thoughts.

'5106 – London Ground . . . ?' It was as if the man had felt SATCO's impatience transmitted through the hand that gripped the back of his chair. The voice of the pilot, strained after the certain calm of the controller's voice, shocked him.

'All engines shut down . . .'

SATCO said swiftly: 'Ask him if he needs assistance with the emergency doors?'

'5106 – do you need assistance with the emergency doors?' It was a polite, necessary enquiry. The voice of the pilot sounded like a snub.

'Negative!' It was almost a shout from the R/T. The

18

Ground Movement Controller turned involuntarily to look up into SATCO's face. Then the pilot's voice continued, the words dropping like heavy stones into the silence he had created: 'We have an armed man on the flight-deck. I repeat – there is an armed man on the flight-deck, who insists that all emergency vehicles leave the immediate area of the aircraft.'

'5106 – wilco. Are you satisfied with the condition of number one engine?' The controller's voice almost maddened SATCO with its unchanged, mechanical calm. The temperature inside the air-conditioned 'Greenhouse' seemed to rise involuntarily. He felt perspiration prickle his forehead. He craned forward, leaning heavily on the man's chair, his mouth open, body taut, willing the R/T to supply him with more information. The captain's words drummed in his mind – the hijack; the nightmare of every SATCO, every airport, every government. The fanatic on the flight-deck.

'London Ground – we can see no sign of fire at the moment, but we would appreciate a visual inspection soonest – if we can persuade our friend to allow it.'

SATCO shook himself like a wet hound, or a man awakening with difficulty from a dream, and turned away from the window and the R/T. He was prompted by his training, by the drills he had rehearsed *ad nauseam* during recent massive security exercises at Heathrow. He knew what was required of him now, though he was reluctant to move. A great part of him wanted to go on looking out towards Two-Eight Left, to the far end where the 707 had rolled to a halt – rabbit-like at the snake he had glimpsed out there.

He felt himself sweating freely, knew he looked shaken, bemused, as he snapped in the direction of the Deputy SATCO, standing behind him: 'Rat Trap – Situation Beta! Transmit the call on Security Channel E'

The Deputy, who was a well-fleshed younger man, usually bland and irritating in manner, a front-office type, as SATCO had often reflected, nodded but made no move. He opened his mouth into a round, dark hole.

'Do it, man – don't simply register the fact! Rat Trap, Situation Beta!' He added, as if to himself: 'The bad one . . .'

He took half a step towards his deputy and the man nodded again, swallowed, and turned away, heading for the second floor of the tower and the Telex Room. SATCO watched him go, and felt his stomach churn. In a sudden human insight rare with him, he understood what was in his deputy's mind.

The simple transmission of the code identification would alert the airport police, the Met., Special Branch, and the Home Office and the Ministry of Defence. It would establish the fact of a hijacking aboard an incoming aircraft at Heathrow with each of those bodies. It would bring into action the massive security machine that the Home Office, the Ministry and the Commissioner of the Metropolitan Police had created. He had seen the faint tic about his deputy's eyes, the drawn pallor of the skin. Dawlish had seen himself setting in motion a chain-reaction whose destiny and power he could not conceive or control.

SATCO shook his head and turned back to his view of the runway, deserted except for 5106 as other planes would continue in the holding pattern until the emergency was over. 5106 bulged in his vision, as if some inward lens had flexed in his eye.

He had to do something, now. It was difficult to remember what it was – then it came to him. His first priority was the airport. 5106 might have an engine fire. He could not wait for the arrival of the Executive Officer, Civil Emergencies (Hijacking) – it would be too late to deal with any fire by that time. It was with a curious gratitude that he concentrated on the fire as his own first priority.

He spoke, suddenly, in an abstracted murmur that carried to every man in the 'Greenhouse': 'If that thing's got a bomb on board, I want it towed as far from the cargo terminals as possible – and bloody quickly!'

Detective Inspector Philip Bracken, Special Branch, squinted in the bright sunlight that dazzled and gleamed from the metal surfaces and the windows of Heathrow, staring towards the tiny, gleaming cigar of the 707. He understood, with a certain intimation that came from his stomach, that something was wrong. Something beyond, that is, the circle of bright spots that were the emergency services. He was standing next to Detective Inspector Hollis of the Alpha Group, that permanent section of the airport security staff designed to police the airport, and all passengers boarding outbound flights. Hollis's function was press relations. Bracken had known him, briefly, when he had been part of the Met. – before he had moved into the more subterranean world of the Branch.

Bracken was waiting for his wife. She was a passenger aboard British Airways Flight No. 5106 from New York. Hollis, who knew why Bracken was at Heathrow, was silent, glancing from time to time in his direction. Bracken had removed the polaroid sunglasses, as if their pallid, sepia image of the scene dissatisfied him. His eyes were clenched tight, as though to squeeze out the sight rather than to focus upon it.

He sensed that the plane carrying his wife had been hijacked. There was no evidence to suggest that this was the case. Yet he knew it. It was no fire, no normal emergency. . . . He smiled at the idea of a normal emergency, despite his own edginess. The passengers had not appeared via the emergency chutes, scrambling away from the scene of a possible explosion or fire. The plane was like a coffin – a tomb. Nothing moved out there on the runway. The scene was frozen.

It was what he had trained for, what he had anticipated for three years as assistant to the senior civil servant who carried the title of Executive Officer, Civil Emergencies (Hijacking). Hilary Latymer, his superior, had also waited since 1972 and the drafting of Directive 316 by the Home Office, M.O.D. and the Commissioner of the Met. . . .

He hardly felt the irony of his situation. His job was to assist the man known as 'Ratcatcher', the man who ran the whole 'Rat Trap' operation to prevent, or counter, armed hijacking at Heathrow. Now his wife was on a hijacked plane.

He thought, detachedly, as if the mind floated above the churning stomach and the muscles which threatened to go into spasm, of Alison his wife. It had been six months since she had left him to spend an extended holiday with her father, Dr William Fosse, Visiting Professor of Medieval History at Princeton – a holiday that was, in reality, a trial separation. He had written once in that time. Then she had written announcing her return. He had been almost blithe, arriving at the airport in good time. One of her complaints had always been his unpunctuality with regard to her. He had thought his prompt arrival would, perhaps occasion a lightness of mood, one that might have lasted at least until they reached the large, old semi in Wimbledon.

It was difficult to think, as if the sun dried the brain, slowed it. There was little direct emotion, he thought. There was a sense of possession, masked by protectiveness . . . something that belonged to him was being threatened. There was naked fear, but for someone apart from himself. There was the sense of unreality, despite the perspiration, the weakness of the bowels and the pumping heart; it was celluloid reality, or a training exercise.

The 707 sat on the gleaming tarmac, wrapped in the haze flung up by the stretch of concrete. He noticed the bare, burnt grass in patches, the slanting light from windows, heard voices murmur behind him on the observation-gallery, like a nearing tide. Then he heard Hollis's words distinctly.

'You – know what it is, Philip?'

Bracken turned to him. Hollis saw the bleak withdrawn face, as if the skin had dried out, bleached, in the sun. Bracken nodded. He looked at his watch. It was two minutes after four. Without speaking, he moved past Hollis. He was heading for the control tower.

'I told you, man – get those damn people away from here!' The voice was American, loud and harsh in the hot, confined space of the flight-deck. The heavy Smith & Wesson revolver with the full chamber that Burgess seemed to have been staring into for an age, waggled threateningly a foot from his face. 'You heard me – do it!'

Burgess opened his mouth as if to speak, but he felt his whole system working as if he were at some great depth in the ocean, fighting terrific pressure merely to move a muscle. He felt the cold dribble of sweat beneath his arms, sharper than the general wetness of his shirt, darkly-stained across chest and back.

'I – can't . . .' he managed to say.

'You think this is some kind of joke, man?' The voice seemed capable of only one tone, the urgency of fanaticism, the cry of the omnipotent.

'Look at that bloody light, *man*!' It was Hislop, his hand waving at the control panel while his eyes never left the American's face. 'What do you think *that* is – a bloody fairy-light?'

The American raised his free hand, the left one, and slapped Hislop across the face, back-handed, with terrible speed and force. Then he grinned as Hislop fell back in his seat, clutching his bleeding mouth.

'Who do you think I am, man – Santa Claus?' For a moment, the gun had wavered aside from its level bead on Burgess's temple but now it snapped back, and the American glanced round him swiftly, as if he felt himself menaced by the animal of physical violence that he had suddenly released. Only Hislop and Burgess remained with the American on the flight-deck.

Burgess's stomach was still churning from that initial confrontation with death, death boring into his jaw. He was too old, and it was too many years ago, the last time he had seen death leap over his shoulder like that. The American had been thrown off-balance, and forward, by the impact of touchdown and he had restrained himself only by a hand on Burgess's seat – the other hand carrying the ultimate insurance.

Hislop, Burgess noticed as his eyes left the American's face for a moment, was dabbing at his mouth with a damp handkerchief bright with blood from his swelling lip.

The temperature of the flight-deck was rising steadily now that the aircraft had stopped, and the cabin warmth was influenced by the heat of the brilliant August afternoon outside. Yet the rise in temperature seemed accelerated by their situation. Burgess looked down at his hands. They were still trembling, an insane tremor he had fought all the way down Two-Eight Left, holding the 707 to the centre. Now there was no column to grip, he could not control the spasms of his body. He felt ashamed, as if he were incontinent.

'Now, man – are you going to give the order, or do I?' the American said.

Burgess raised his eyes from the shameful hands in his lap

and looked into the white, drawn face, and the grey, expressionless eyes. The American's hair was fair, long, and unwashed. He was dressed in a leather jacket and light-coloured slacks. His frame was tall – he stooped – and thin. Burgess returned to the eyes. They frightened him.

'We must have someone to make a visual check of that engine – we have a fire warning-light . . .' Burgess's voice became calmer, stronger. He was dealing with a situation of which he was the master, for the moment. 'You heard me tell the tower – you must let them look at it!'

'Hell, man – the engine's not on fire!'

'Are you an expert?' Hislop snarled, and the gun flickered in his direction for a moment, then returned to Burgess.

'How many?' he asked after a moment.

'Two.'

'Clay!' the American yelled, seeming to have reached a decision, and the cabin door opened. A thin-faced, suspicious negro put his head into the cabin. He possessed fine features, caucasian rather than negroid, and he was dressed in a light, elegant suit. His hair was frizzed into an afro style.

'What you want, Packer?' he asked.

'Go outside, tell two of those guys out there they can inspect the engine – tell them to send for a ladder, or whatever they need – then bring them inside when they've finished. Everyone else gets clear – understand?' The negro appeared about to question the decision, then he nodded his head and ducked back out of the cabin.

Packer said to Burgess: 'O.K. – talk to the man. Everyone else gets the hell out – get a ladder so we can get those two aboard.' He glanced at his watch. 'Two minutes to pull back – five to inspect the engine. Then someone dies, unless we're obeyed. . . .'

'You can't check an engine in five minutes . . .' Hislop began, and Packer turned towards him, a mirthless grin on his face.

'Leave it, John,' Burgess said. 'I don't think we have much part in the decision making process aboard this plane – do you?'

'That's more like it – captain,' sneered Packer. He waved

the gun in the direction of the R/T. 'Tell them.'

'You've got to let the passengers off . . .' Hislop began again. Packer grinned openly.

'Would you like the gun, too? Then you can spread my brains all over the wall, and go get something to eat!' He returned his gaze to Burgess, who was waiting to speak to the tower, and said: 'When you've passed on the good news, tell them I want to talk to the fuzz – someone big, not just one of your wonderful British policemen – understand?'

Burgess nodded and began to relay Packer's instructions. He could visualise the scene in the 'Greenhouse' away behind him. SATCO was probably chewing his nails down to the quick, worrying about the possibility of an explosion. And the passengers, naturally. As he spoke to the Ground Movement Controller, he began to wonder what demands the hijackers would make. What did Packer want? With a sinking feeling in the pit of his stomach, he considered his own danger – not the danger to passengers or aircrew, but to himself. These men, when they got what they wanted, would demand to be flown out of the U.K., without a relief crew. If anyone was really trapped in this duralumin coffin, it was himself. He shuddered.

'The Senior Air Traffic Controller wants to speak to you – I've told him who you are,' he said. 'I'll switch on the cabin speaker.'

'I said the fuzz, man – I don't wanna talk to the man who parks the airplanes!' He bent forward to the mike, and snapped: 'Get me someone I can talk with – I need to talk to someone who can make deals!'

Burgess heard SATCO's offended tones. 'Senior police and governmental officers have been informed of your – action. My concern is with the efficient running of this airport. You are sitting on one of our main runways, holding up a great deal of traffic . . .'

'Is this guy for real?' Packer asked, looking into Burgess's face.

'He has an important job to do.'

SATCO continued, 'We shall have to tow you to a parking block, which is quite near your present position . . .'

'To hell with you, mister! This plane stays where it sits!'

'That is impossible – you must understand that.'

'It's you that has to understand, man! I'm holding a gun on your two pilots here – there are five other people back in the plane, covering all of your passengers. This plane has taken root until I say it moves!'

There was silence for a moment, and then Burgess heard the noises of the fire-tenders and the ambulances pulling away. He felt suddenly deserted, abandoned. Probably there was no fire, no emergency. He smiled thinly at the irony of that idea. He looked at Hislop, who had retreated into a profound, frightened silence, as if Packer's last remark had finally winded him, knocked the last of the bravado of disbelief out of him. Hislop obviously felt exactly as he did himself.

Burgess had not heard whatever SATCO's reply had been. It was not dangerous for him to be sitting at the end of Two-Eight Left – merely very inconvenient for half the world's airlines, and upsetting for the method-worshipping SATCO in the tower. The involuntary smile disappeared from his face. What if there were a bomb on board. ... SATCO was afraid for the cargo terminals, away to port of the aircraft. Burgess had a sudden, chilling sense of being in some way already dead, and being forced to watch his own demise, its mechanics, from some olympian high place. SATCO wanted the world to go on turning as normal, despite the fact that the world had stopped for 5106.

Packer's face was suffused with anger. He yelled into the mike: 'You complacent bastard! I don't give a speck of shit for your arrangements – you just tell the fuzz to hurry it up, man. Tell them to bring Shafiq Nasoud with them when they come, if they want to do any deals with me!'

Burgess looked at Hislop, and knew that his own face registered the same surprise-becoming-doubt he saw in the features of his second. Shafiq Nasoud, Arab terrorist, picked up at Heathrow two months earlier, attempting to smuggle small arms through Customs in a suitcase – a desperate move the BBC had called it at the time. What would they call the attempt to release him from custody, Burgess wondered.

* * *

Detective Chief Superintendent Clarence Seaborne of Special Branch stood at the high window of his office, looking down at the traffic in Victoria Street below him. The dusty road was busy at four-fifteen in the afternoon, with the earliest of the commuters on their way home. He was waiting for something. Then he saw it. A police car pulled out into the traffic, its siren's noise reaching him thinly. Its flashing light was almost invisible in the brightness of the sunlight. He watched it down the street, out of sight of his craning head, and then turned from the window, rubbing his huge, rasping jowl thoughtfully.

Lucas, his assistant, was on his way to Battersea Heliport, thence to Gatwick and the slightly run-down offices of the Flying Fish Charter Company, to board a light aircraft which would take him to R.A.F. Chivenor, on the north Devon coast, where he would collect the Arab terrorist, Shafiq Nasoud.

As if in tribute to the gloominess of his internal narrative, Seaborne shook his massive head, then rubbed his hand through the thinning sandy hair. Nasoud was being held in custody awaiting trial at H.M. Prison, Dartmoor – a security measure which normally applied to Provos on whose behalf rescue operations might be mounted. He had been there for more than a month. Already, he would be on his way to Chivenor under police escort, and a dummy Arab, also under heavy escort, would be beginning a car journey to London as a decoy operation. Seaborne, incongruously, wished the blacked-up policeman and his escort luck in the holiday traffic on the west country roads.

Seaborne was still angry at the peremptory telephone conversation he had had with the Home Secretary a few minutes earlier – the call that had sent Lucas dashing for a waiting car, and Battersea. As Commander, Special Duties Group (Hijacking), his was the police responsibility for Beta Group operations at Heathrow, under the overall direction of Latymer. To Seaborne's mind, the Home Secretary was on the point of caving in before anyone in authority had spoken to the hijackers – why else the unseemly rush to have Nasoud, the price to be paid for the passengers, transferred to London?

Seaborne eased his large frame into the cramped swivel-seat behind his desk and loosened his tie. His heavy features expressed irritation at the temperature of the room, the resistance of the knot in his tie, and the situation he found himself in. He felt little of the sense of challenge, of surging adrenalin, that others might have felt in the situation. Seaborne was basically a humane man, and he feared for the safety of the people aboard the plane. More than that, however, he was angry at the glimpse he had already received of political nervelessness in the face of terrorist action. Seaborne was an unforgiving man, a man who hated criminals – particularly the political criminal who had been his concern since his appointment to the Branch. He had never met Nasoud – yet he felt he wanted to do physical damage to the man, in some sort of reparation.

Det. Supt. Morgan was the man who commanded the Alpha Group which was responsible for security at the airport and permanently based at Heathrow. Now he would subordinate his group to the shadowy Beta Group, commanded by Seaborne – a group of Special Branch experts who were called into action by the hijacking of an aircraft incoming to the airport. Morgan's team was commanded by men from the Branch, but it comprised, largely, men from the Met. Seaborne's own Beta Group comprised only men from the Branch. Morgan's men, from the time that Seaborne himself arrived at Heathrow, would content themselves with controlling public and press, patrolling the perimeter, handling passengers, and the like.

Seaborne briefly wondered why he delayed his own departure for the heliport. Some reluctance seemed to seize him, pressure him softly into remaining where he was. He suspected his own nerve might be failing him – the actor pausing a moment too long in the wings, seized by a cramp of the intelligence, feeling insecure as he envisaged the performance unrolling before him. . . .

It was Latymer, he recognised. Hilary Latymer, 'Ratcatcher'. Hilary Latymer, civil servant. Seaborne sniffed audibly. He did not, he admitted, trust Latymer. He belonged to the Home Office, to Whitehall. Academic, clubman, widower – reserved, aloof, assured. Seaborne sniffed again. In the three years during which he had had increasing contact with Latymer, the Executive Officer, he had failed to understand him, failed to penetrate the bland, urbane surface the man used in his dealings with other human beings.

Seaborne tugged himself, hands thrust into pockets, out of his chair and returned to the window. Where was it they had to give the traffic police oxygen every couple of minutes – Tokyo?

'Why the hell isn't this bloody hijacking taking place in Tokyo?' he suddenly said aloud.

According to Civil Emergencies Directive 316, dated November 24th, 1972, there were to be three stages to any response to an armed hijacking at Heathrow. Stage one – negotiation. Stage two – counter-threat. Stage three – the shooting-match. Seaborne shuddered. Only the P.M. could initiate stage three. Latymer was responsible for the other two stages, in consultation with the Home Secretary as to the details of stage two. Directive 316, Seaborne thought, was a nice, tidy document. And, the pretty thing was, he added, no one yet knew whether or not it would work – so Whitehall assumed that it would.

Stage one was really his pigeon. The general alert to the Beta Group had gone out, and it only remained for him to get to the airport before his men arrived. Almost savagely, he tugged his tie straight and tight. Then he pressed the switch on his intercom and proceeded to order his transport to Battersea Heliport.

The Home Secretary was pretending, with an admirable determination, to be looking out over St James's Park, his hands clasped behind his back, his narrow shoulders hunched, the excessive formality of his dress making a dark patch against the brilliant sunshine from the tall windows. His head was almost bald, fringed with the remnants of his grey hair. The atmosphere in the room was subtly electric, though enervating rather than stimulating, like the heavy, oppressive moments before a storm breaks.

Hilary Latymer was content to wait until the Minister should wish to continue the conversation. He did not glance at his watch as he sat in an armchair on the other side of the Home Secretary's desk. It had been four twenty-six when he had knocked on the door and been summoned to enter. He knew, to within a minute, that twelve minutes had passed. Latymer had time to spare before he needed to be at Heathrow, to begin the negotiations that might lead to seventy-two passengers and the aircrew walking away unharmed from the British Airways 707 now sitting on the end of one of the runways.

Latymer's own feelings had submerged beneath the bland, assured aloofness before he had reached the Minister's office. All that remained was the uncomfortable knowledge that Bracken's wife was a passenger on the plane. Latymer had never interfered with his assistant's private life, though he had been aware of the separation. He had met the woman – Alison? – once or twice, and found her mildly attractive. What disturbed him now were the possible ill-effects on Bracken's performance of fears for her safety. He might resist or challenge Latymer's decisions, his conclusions and recommendations. That would not be comfortable.

The Minister remained silent, snubbed by Latymer's implicit condemnation of his premature summons that Nasoud be brought to London. The man, promoted to his office in the last months of the present government because of a retirement through illness, would not, should his party be returned at the impending election, be returned to Cabinet office. He was not a success, and he knew he was not. Which made him, Latymer knew, a dangerous superior to have in the 'Rat Trap' situation.

Latymer had ordered his car to take him to the heliport, and he had ordered the file on Nasoud to be brought to his office. All he waited for now was the Home Secretary's dismissal, his good wishes. The man seemed reluctant to let him go as if, by retaining him in Whitehall, he could postpone the outcome of the situation at the airport. The Home Secretary, a liberal man in private life, was hesitant, diffident, inclined to meet challenge or suggestion with inflexibility, dogged certitude. Latymer found him difficult, cold and unimaginative in office.

Latymer spent little time considering the motives for the

hijacking, except to reflect that Nasoud hardly seemed to warrant such dedicated and thorough attention from former associates. He was a member of Black September, but out of the limelight since his suspected involvement in the assassination of two Israeli diplomats in Cyprus in 1972. Then he had turned up on a flight from New York, with a suitcase full of small arms and ammunition – like a salesman at the door with wares for display. It had been naïve, silly and desperate.

As far as Latymer knew, the SIS and MI5 both had concluded that Nasoud was now a loner, a chip broken from the terrorist block. Nothing had been turned up by the FBI with regard to his American contacts, though he was known to have spent more than a year in the U.S. There had been no further attempts to smuggle in arms, and no Arab activity within the U.K. The last couple of months had seen a decay of interest in the Nasoud affair, and the security services were inclined to write him off as a desperate attempt to transfer guns and ammunition from Arab hands to the Provos – some half-hearted kind of international terrorist co-operation.

As to his new-found friends and the reasons why they should go to such complete lengths to obtain his release, Latymer was prepared to postpone such speculation until he reached Heathrow.

The Home Secretary turned away from the window and seated himself behind his desk. The toothbrush moustache that obscured the thin upper lip still seemed to bristle with affronted dignity. The pale blue eyes, which gave the face such a washed-out look during television appearances, were narrowed and gleaming. Latymer sensed the man's air of personal affront. This affair at Heathrow had arrived in his last days of high office, as if merely to plague his political sunset. He placed his hands in front of him, fingers linked, and returned Latymer's polite stare. He did not dislike Latymer, despite the air of the pedagogue the man always wore. In fact, Latymer's appointment as Executive Officer, made by his predecessor, was daring beyond his own imagination and one he envied.

Latymer was responsible only to himself, the Cabinet and the P.M. in the event of an armed hijacking at Heathrow.

31

He had been a Research Fellow at Cambridge before his present appointment to the Home Office; he was a distinguished academic, a career which had followed a period of important, if discreet, service in wartime and post-war Intelligence, and a subsequent and unsatisfying sojourn in Whitehall. More than anything, Latymer looked like a diplomat – tall, grey-haired, vigorous, with aristocratic features and an air of imperturbability. A handsome man, the Home Secretary admitted – impressive in appearance and intellect.

The Minister cleared his throat. Latymer's expression remained unchanged.

'The first priority is time, Latymer – you must buy us time. We cannot, at this juncture – whatever you may think of my action with regard to this Arab...' He cleared his throat again, smoothed the irritation from his voice. 'We cannot consider agreeing to their terms for his release.'

'I understand that, Minister,' Latymer said quietly.

'The Prime Minister has called a special Cabinet meeting for later this afternoon – of all those ministers he can reach at such short notice ... We have to have time for that meeting to take place and for the Cabinet to reach its conclusions ...' He leant forward, as if to impress the other man. 'Conclusions, Latymer, which will be based upon your recommendations, as the man on the spot.'

Latymer stroked his aquiline nose between finger and thumb, then said: 'What, might I ask, Minister, is the P.M.'s feeling at the outset?'

The Home Secretary appeared abashed, then said: 'I am authorised to tell you that you must buy this man Packer and his accomplices off – at any price *below* the one they are asking.'

Latymer's features, which had begun to darken, expressed his relief. He nodded. 'I understand.'

'Your first consideration must be the safety of the passengers – this is *not* an exercise, and it must not be treated as such, under any circumstances. Seventy-two innocent lives are involved, as well as millions of pounds of aircraft, and a highly-trained crew.'

'And – the final eventuality?' Latymer asked.

'Outside your authority, and mine,' the Home Secretary said with a slight shudder. 'Perhaps we ought to be grateful for that,' he added, inviting Latymer into a conspiracy of relief. Latymer merely nodded. The Minister continued, his face suddenly more serious than before: 'Just remember your brief, Latymer – and its limitations. You are empowered to board, or immobilise the aircraft, if either proves feasible – if you can achieve either without endangering the passengers.'

'I don't see how . . .' Latymer began.

The Home Secretary lifted his hand and said portentously: 'Identification – assessment – decision, Latymer. You'll be the man on the spot, you'll be able to assess what you can or cannot attempt. . . .' Latymer sensed the resentment in the Minister's tone. He understood its origins. If anything went wrong, it would blow up in the Home Secretary's face. His would be the face muddied by resultant adverse publicity. Latymer was protected by his very anonymity. That was what the Minister resented.

Then the Home Secretary added, in a voice he intended to be conversational: 'Is Seaborne on his way to Heathrow?' Latymer nodded. 'You'll be able to work with him, on the real thing?'

'If he is able to work *for* me,' Latymer replied drily, making the emphasis clear.

'I'm sure he has read Directive 316 and knows who is in command, Latymer,' the Home Secretary replied acidly. Then, his face darkening again, he added: 'Buy us the time we need, Latymer.'

'I'll get you your time, Minister – if these people are open to reason,' Latymer said in a voice that suddenly sounded weary. 'I am, after all, merely an executive, and I do as I am bid.'

The Home Secretary's reply was high-pitched, rather too loud, because he was stung by Latymer's tone and because he was suddenly afraid, again, of the myriad things that could go wrong, the myriad ways in which opprobrium could be heaped on him.

He said: 'This must be held at stage one, Latymer – it has to be!'

2: *Security Exercise*

Alison Bracken looked again at her watch, a process that had developed into something resembling a nervous tic, as if prompted by the irrational idea that her situation had a defined limit in time. It was four-forty. She shifted in her seat unobtrusively, careful of her bulk since she was six months pregnant. She felt grubby and untidy. The thin cotton dress that she was wearing was stained with perspiration beneath the arms, and the high neckline chafed her throat. Her mouth was dry with smoking – a habit she had promised to rid herself of when she discovered her pregnancy, but which she had not managed to renounce. She had chain-smoked her way through a pack of toasted American cigarettes during the flight and since the hijacking had occurred. She had seen the blond and the negro, together with the girl, move from their seats up the gangway, and then the blond had pushed his way past a stunned stewardess and through the door to the flight-deck.

What had terrified her, precisely, was the thought that her death would be instantaneous, that the aircraft would crash on landing and cheat her of life. Now her bulk, her dampness, her dry mouth, irritated her – and that irritation was uppermost in her mind. Nerves, she realised, can only be stretched for so long before they lose their elasticity and loosely subside into a dull, depressed sub-shock, where the unfairness of the situation is all that appears to matter. She thought of the people on other planes, in departure lounges, selfishly wishing them in her place.

She brushed her auburn hair out of her eyes, and her gaze returned to the gangway leading to the flight-deck, and the two hijackers standing in front of the door. Packer, the tall, thin, fair-haired leader, was out of sight, returning to the flight-deck after the two fire officers had been violently brought on board. A passenger gangway had been driven out from the terminal for the purpose. The driver had casually been allowed to go free — Alison envied him deeply, bitterly.

The negro stood at the head of the gangway like a carved figure, expressing no weariness, no sign of tension. The girl — Alison studied the girl again — was thin, with blonde hair that was untidy, and deep, piercing eyes. She was holding a gun on the three members of the flight crew, the stewardesses, and the fire officers, all of whom had been gathered together in the front rows of seats in the first-class compartment. There were two other hijackers, she knew, behind her in second class.

The airport had ceased to whine with the noise of aircraft taking off and landing. It had seemed that there had been a flurry of activity from the other main runway, as if aircraft and their passengers were fleeing the scene of a horror they dared not contemplate. An added, whining note of urgency from their engines; and then, nothing. Distant insect figures had moved away, out of sight, mute witnesses of a tragedy that had already occurred. There was silence now, as if the 707 were parked at the end of a deserted runway, one belonging to a wartime aerodrome, with grass pushing insistently through cracks in the concrete. It was all, somehow, unreal. Her eyes flickered between the view from the window and the faces of the hijackers. Unreal. Even terror had that capacity of distance, so that she felt a spectator in another's drama.

She had no idea what they wanted, what demands they would make. They had issued their orders, which had consisted of demands not to move, not to attempt anything stupid, in the classic formula of fiction. The mood of the twenty-eight passengers in the first class — she had had no idea how many there were before the plane had rolled to a halt but now she had counted them . . . how many times? The mood of the compartment was subdued, the tension that had filled the place with a sharp, stinging animal scent had died, replaced by the same dull, bestial immobility, the mute acceptance she felt herself.

She did not know whether or not she was going to die, or when, and it was becoming increasingly hard to care. There was no focus of action, nothing except the mute figures of the captors, the mute figures of the captives. A tableau.

She thought distantly of her husband. A policeman. Attached, with an appreciable irony, to the office of the ... what was it? The Executive Officer, Civil Emergencies ... training, waiting, even hoping, for just this eventuality, a hijacking at Heathrow. She recalled her scepticism with a bitter smile, and began flicking through the pages of *Harpers* as it lay on her lap; another nervous tic.

She thought of her father, and her reasons for travelling to America. It had seemed safe, a safe place to run from a marriage which had teetered on the edge of breakdown for years. A police widow. She had never learned to accept the way in which he brought his work home with him, the way it invaded their lives. Finally, when he had said they would have no real holiday that year because of pressure of work, she had chosen to see it as a breaking point – and had left.

Finishing her sightless inspection of the glossy unreality of the magazine, she began to study again, like a tongue returning to a hollow tooth, the three terrorists in the first class. It was an unconscious habit, her scrutiny, one she had acquired from her husband. The negro, the one called Clay, was flamboyant, expensive, incongruous. She did not know what to expect from terrorists in sartorial taste – but somehow, not this.

The girl's face was hardened, rather than given distinction, by high cheekbones and a lack of make-up. She wore flared pants, a black blouse belted at the waist, and a band across her forehead. A student? She, somehow, was understandable, like the Arab. He was dark, swarthy and had a shock of black hair and a thick moustache hiding most of his features. He, too, looked like one of those figures glimpsed in the footage of television film, and the poor photographs which appeared in newspapers, of hijackings, trials, exchanges. He was dressed in a woollen shirt, a bush-jacket and light slacks. The remaining two, out of sight in the second class – she had glimpsed them once or twice – had the appearance of minor business executives. Packer, the leader, could have come from any campus in the western world. Except for his eyes, she reminded herself. They were chilly, fanatical.

She looked out of the window again. Studying those faces,

closely for perhaps the first time, had made her afraid. Very afraid.

There was a car waiting at the Heathrow Helicopter Terminal to collect them. Ducking under the slowing rotors, his grey hair blown awry, Latymer felt the urgency he had tried to control on the journey from Battersea overtake him. He had arrived at the scene of the crime – the battlefield. The whine of the rotors died away and he smoothed his hair and looked about him. Heathrow was a landscape, from his vantage point. A silent landscape and he knew the cause of the silence. Directive 316 laid down, and his own rules of procedure enforced it, that all aircraft within the London approach pattern would have been allowed to land, and all taxi-ing planes at the threshold, poised for take-off, would have been instructed to do so – Runway Two-Eight Right being used, take-off and landing being performed alternately. All aircraft in the terminal control area, the airspace outside the approach pattern, would have been diverted to Luton, Stansted and Gatwick, and all aircraft on the ground not in immediate readiness for take-off would have been held, and shunted as far from the 707 as possible.

Yes, there it was – a distant speck, gleaming in the brilliant sunshine, shrunken in the haze – British Airways Flight No. 5106. His gaze swept the airport perimeter, taking in the massive inactivity, the silence. He had a sudden memory of nights spent standing on the edges of aerodrome runways in southern England, watching planes lumbering skywards, carrying his agents to France.

Bracken, waiting by the car, said, 'Almost eerie,' His voice sounded small, and when Latymer turned to look at him, he saw his eyes fixed on the distant speck of the 707. Latymer had a sudden, immediate sympathy for him. He knew Bracken's marriage was not a particularly happy one, that his wife had left him, at least for a time – that had been Bracken's affair, his private life. Now – now it was something that invaded the strategy, the objectivity of the situation.

'Come on,' he said rather brusquely. 'We'll do nobody much good standing here.'

He ducked his frame into the waiting car and Bracken slid into the passenger seat next to the Special Branch driver.

The 'Greenhouse' was a scene of suppressed tension, tension that somehow dissipated as Latymer entered, as if the occupants had suddenly thrown their cares on to him. Latymer recognised the tall, spare figure of Greenwood, the SATCO, and beside him the shorter, more rotund shape of Scott, the Airport Commandant. There was also Dawlish, the Deputy SATCO, and another man, presumably Scott's number two. The resident airport officials had already left the room and only Seaborne occupied the central island in the middle of the circular room. The diversionary instructions to incoming planes were being made by the traffic controllers from the floor below the 'Greenhouse', from the room which contained the tower radar complex and the control back-up system.

Latymer wanted to be rid of Greenwood and Scott as quickly as possible, though he understood that there were polite preliminaries to be gone through before he could reasonably ask them to leave. Seaborne began to unroll himself from a chair placed before the central console on the raised dais, but Latymer waved him back to his seat. He shook hands with Scott and Greenwood in turn, sensing rather than seeing the deference in their eyes. They were confronted by an individual who possessed power such as neither of them had ever possessed – nor, perhaps, wanted. There was a distance between the two men and himself.

Latymer noticed that Scott was wearing light slacks and a woollen shirt. Probably he had been playing golf when the 'Rat Trap' alert had reached him. Yes, Latymer noticed with a smile, there was the betraying bulge of a golf ball in his right pocket.

'Afternoon, "Ratcatcher" – bad show, this,' he said rather pompously, obviously relieved that Latymer had arrived and determined to show him due deference.

'Indeed – a very bad show,' Latymer said.

'You'll be wanting a progress report,' Scott continued. 'Chief Superintendent Seaborne has been keeping us up to the mark!' Scott smiled and Latymer knew that the man was pretty well out of his depth, but that he had unquestioningly followed the rules of procedure. A man without too much imagination, thankfully.

'You have the full passenger manifest, Commandant?' Latymer enquired evenly.

'On its way, sir. It's being sent up from passenger control. Of course, it won't contain any last-minute bookings, but we've been in contact with Kennedy. They'll be sending the full manifest over the telex any time now, together with their usual passenger-security photographs.'

'Good. Have them sent to me here as soon as they arrive.' He nodded, and Scott beamed like a puppy that has been patted. Latymer turned to Greenwood and said, taking the two men with him to the window as he spoke: 'You've spoken to them, SATCO – what's your opinion?'

Greenwood coughed and seemed to shrug away the school-boy deference in his gaze. 'I – can't really say, you know ... He seemed very – determined ... ?' SATCO dropped his gaze, as the uselessness of his words struck even him. The situation was beyond him, and he had no delight in realising the fact.

'I see,' Latymer murmured. He looked down for a moment, as if deep in thought, and then said: 'Thank you, gentlemen – for good or evil, this thing is in our hands now.'

Scott understood that he had been dismissed. He said: 'Right – we'll get over to my office, Charles – I think we both need a drink!'

Greenwood looked hesitantly in Latymer's direction, then at Scott, and nodded reluctantly. Then he looked slowly round the 'Greenhouse' and shrugged abruptly, the captain of a surrendered vessel. He resigned himself to the inevitable.

'Yes, Commandant. I don't think there's any need for me to stay.' He looked again at Latymer, who absently shook his head. He was already studying a sheaf of notes handed to him by Seaborne. Greenwood scowled in reply to the dismissive nod, and he and Scott left the room.

Without looking up, Latymer said, 'Very well, Philip – let's have Mr Seaborne's team in here, shall we?'

Bracken went out and Latymer crossed once more to the window. He looked out across the baking expanse of concrete towards the stranded fish of the 707, and then down at the notes again. Seaborne's bulk joined him at the window.

Latymer said, 'As soon as that complete passenger manifest arrives, I want all the passengers checked out – people waiting to meet them, addresses in London, New York – anywhere.'

'Sir,' Seaborne said.

'Good. Now give me your report, before I have to talk to our hijacking friends.'

As Seaborne began his account of security measures already effected, the Beta team began filtering into the bright glass bowl of the 'Greenhouse'. Swiftly, and in almost absolute silence, like morticians arranging the limbs of a huge corpse, they established cameras on tripods, their telephoto lenses staring like beaks towards the 707. Telephones were plugged into the sockets which led down the special landlines that had been installed, and recording equipment was wired into the R/T and the telephone system. Latymer appeared unaware of the activity as he listened to Seaborne.

'All remaining planes grounded, sir – despite protests from Lufthansa, Alitalia and El Al that they were prepared to take the risks involved in an explosion while they were in closest proximity to the 707.' Latymer nodded. It probably would not have mattered had those flights taken off – but they would take no unnecessary risks

'All incoming flights diverted to the other three airports, except for those on final approach . . . All observation galleries cleared and the passenger lounges with windows facing Two-Eight Left informed that passengers must vacate them. . . . The airport approaches are being patrolled and all traffic turned away, except for taxis and coaches collecting passengers. . . . West London Air Terminal has been security-telexed to postpone all departures for Heathrow – indefinitely. We've alerted hospitals to prepare for possible casualties – and the special medical team is installed downstairs to supplement the first-aid facilities. . . . We've got the perimeter patrolled – men and dogs – and houses near the airport are being investigated, as well as the airport hotels. . . .'

Latymer held up his hand.

'Now – tell me about the lounges and the cargo sheds,' he said.

'Mr Morgan's Alpha Group are on that now, sir – thorough search, and the questioning of everyone in the passenger lounges, especially foreigners . . . in case of any back-up operation from here.' He added, as if sourly disappointed, 'We've found b-all so far, sir.'

'Good – in one way.'

Seaborne sniffed. A couple of tame terrorists, as a bargaining-point, would have been useful at that moment.

'Owing to the aircraft's present position, we've had a bit of bother placing the marksmen,' he went on. 'I've got men in positions 15, 16, 22, 30 and 34, as well as some on the perimeter beyond the runway.' He looked directly at Latymer, taking his eyes from the distant plane for the first time in his recital, and added: 'You'll get no joy out of them, sir. They've got the range – just. But they can't guarantee to be accurate at the distance. If one of them showed himself we might, just might, be able to guarantee his sudden demise, with a lucky shot. . . .'

Seaborne looked back towards the 707. It complicated things, that open sunlit expanse bathed in late afternoon light. He went on: 'Men from all the required Beta units have reported in, except for one fearless duo who crashed their car near Staines and are waiting for a lift. Bomb-disposal are here, photographers and recorders, as you can see . . .' He waved his hand around the room, and Latymer took in the humming scene apparently for the first time. He nodded, as if satisfied, plucking at his lower lip with finger and thumb.

As he turned back to the window his face seemed, to Seaborne, to adopt a sombre expression. There were lines on the high, clear forehead. He sat down on the wooden bench running round the circumference of the 'Greenhouse' beneath the windows, as if deliberately turning his back on the single, immobile white bird out on the runway. Bracken, Seaborne saw, remained like a stone figure, a little apart from them, staring out of the windows.

Latymer felt a shiver of tension run through his frame. He knew that as the men completed their preliminary tasks, more and more of them were turning towards him, as a kind of focus, a still centre. He knew they required visible action,

41

firm command. More than anything else, as activity slowed and ceased, Latymer sensed the hot and sticky atmosphere turn subtly into a flagging weariness, a sense of a long process hardly begun. He was briefly aware of himself as a runner at the beginning of a gruelling race – and then discarded the image. He was a soldier, at the outset of a war, the beginning of a battle. And he meant to win, at whatever cost to himself. He had been designed other than as a political animal by the wartime friend and colleague who had appointed him as Executive Officer. He was selfless, in a real and profound way. He had heard all the polite excuses for urban revolution at Cambridge. None of them had ever persuaded him of the necessity that the innocent should die. He looked up and saw only Seaborne's face, looking down into his own.

'We are ready, then – are we not?'

Seaborne nodded. To him, the sober, elegant figure in front of him was an enigma. Seaborne felt uncomfortable near him, working for him. He was too smooth, too perspicacious, for the policeman's taste. And yet, as he said those words, Seaborne realised that the man was afraid, nervous of what lay ahead. Now, for the first time since his appointment he had to face the present moment, and the unknown moments ahead of it. Seaborne admitted to himself that he was glad to hand over command to Latymer, if it was a command that frightened the man.

'Yes, sir,' was all he could find to say.

Latymer stood up – reluctantly, it seemed to Seaborne. Seaborne allowed himself the luxury of one more qualification – he had no idea, none at all, of Latymer's real, private attitude to his work. He had no idea whether the man would stand up to threat and blackmail – or buckle. The enigmatic Latymer worried him.

Latymer crossed to the R/T, forcing himself to stand very upright, to walk with a measured, calm tread. He sensed the others watching him, except perhaps for Bracken. Latymer knew he was already making an important impression upon the Beta team. This would be the first time some of them had had more than a fleeting impression of him. It was an entry, as on to a stage. There was a breathlessness in the atmosphere

42

of the 'Greenhouse', not to be explained by the sunlight and the closed windows. He paused for a moment before the R/T console, and his mind held an image of an oil-slick, of turbulence quelled by an effort of will.

'Recording equipment,' he said without turning round. Behind him, he heard machinery switched on and the hissed running of tapes. Then he bent to the R/T, and said: 'Control tower to aircraft 5106 – are you receiving me – over?'

He flicked the switch and waited. There was a silence at the other end of the channel. Then he heard Packer's voice.

'You got someone to talk to me at last?' he drawled. The voice was confident, merely irritated at delay. 'No wonder your country's becoming the ass-hole of the world, the time it takes you to organise a conversation! I been waiting here more than an hour, man.'

'I take it I'm in communication with the armed man on the flight-deck?' Latymer enquired conversationally. He saw from the corner of his eye the slight flicker of Bracken's brief smile. He hoped his tone was carrying to the rest of the room.

'Right on, baby – who are you?'

'Someone in authority.'

'What power of decision do you have, man?' The voice was hard, insistent.

'I am empowered to listen to your demands and to negotiate with you for the satisfactory outcome of – our mutual problem.'

'It's your problem, man – I got no problems. Can't you see the sun shining – that's for *us*, man!'

'I see. However, if you are assured that you want to speak to me, then perhaps you might reiterate your demands?'

Bracken watched the fine beads of perspiration along the line of Latymer's grey hair and sensed what the man's inward control, the effort his relaxation of voice and manner was costing him. Latymer was suddenly at a distance from him, a man alone in the room with an audience. He was alone on a stage. Latymer, he saw, was tense, even frightened, now that he had heard the hijacker's voice. Bracken's own emotions boiled at the casual, arrogant voice from the R/T.

'What rank do you hold in the fuzz, man? You tell me you got authority – who are you?'

43

A slight frown of irritation creased Latymer's brow for a moment, then he said: 'My name is Hilary Latymer – I represent the Home Office in this matter.'

'You're not a pig?'

'No. The police are, in this matter, under my control.'

There was a silence, and then Packer said: 'We want Shafiq Nasoud, man. Him, and a free and clear passage to the Lebanon. That's what we want you to arrange.'

'I can assure you that Her Majesty's government will not consider any of your demands until the passengers and flight crew are released. Unharmed, I may add. . . .'

Latymer heard Packer's harsh, braying laugh. 'Oh, brother – you ought to be in vaudeville! You want us to hand over the passengers and the crew? What then? You *starve* us out? Sorry, soul-brother – we keep the aces here!'

Latymer was some time in replying, then he said: 'Without conceding your point, of what importance is this man Nasoud to you – you're an American, not an Arab?' His voice suddenly sounded tired and defeated.

'You never give up, do you? The hell you don't! Let's just say – we look after our friends, man. Nasoud – he's a friend.'

'A somewhat extreme demonstration of your affection.'

'On the button, man. We're extreme, you said it. And we mean what we say. Nasoud has to be here by midnight – and everything cleared for take-off, including a hostage that the Lebanese will respect. If not, you can watch our captive audience disappear in a loud blue cloud!'

'What do you mean?'

'A bomb, man – a bomb. The supreme trip. We'll put this wagon in orbit, baby!'

'You have a bomb on board? I – do not believe it.'

There was a derisive snort from the R/T. Packer said: 'I could leave you playing guessing-games – but I won't. Speak to the captain of the ship, he's seen it. And don't try to make him say more than I want, or he's dead. I can hear every sweet little word you say.'

'Hello – Captain Burgess?' Latymer looked down at the sheaf of notes Seaborne had slipped beneath his gaze.

'Yes.'

'Are all the passengers and crew unharmed, Captain Burgess?'

'Yes.' The man's voice was monotonous, somehow bereft of humanity.

'Good. We're doing all we can. Now, tell me – is there a bomb on board your aircraft?'

'Yes.'

'How big?'

'Too big.'

'I see. . . . Where is it?'

There was a slight pause, as if Burgess did not understand what was required of him, then he said quickly: 'The girl has it – in the first class . . .' There was an audible grunt through the R/T, and then Packer spoke, his voice a snarl.

'Now you got a captain with a headache, man! I don't expect he'll thank you for your stupid little trick when he wakes up!'

'Yes. That was most unfortunate. Very well, Mr Packer, or whatever your name is – I shall be in touch. Midnight, you said.' Latymer flicked off the transmitter, brushed his manicured fingertips along his hairline, and turned to Seaborne and Bracken, motioning them up on to the central dais. He said, in a low voice: 'Well, gentlemen – you heard our friend from the colonies. What do you think?'

'Christ!' was Seaborne's first comment. 'Six of them – and a bomb! What the hell is security at Kennedy coming to?'

'Quite,' Latymer observed. 'Things must be getting quite slack. Perhaps they only bother with incoming flights, or internal travel? The American failing – they expect only demands for money. Who would board an aircraft to this country, in order to ask for money?' His smile was thin and humourless.

Bracken observed: 'They've taken out an insurance policy on the piper's music, sir. Six of them. Two of them, and we could consider rushing the plane if everything else failed. We might lose a few men, a few passengers. But six – we could trigger slaughter before we got half-way across the tarmac . . .'

He tailed off, as if possessing a too-vivid inner image.

'Your wife is travelling . . . ?'

'First class – sir.'

'Quite. Now, tell me about Packer, Philip.'

'Cool. I don't know – violent. He enjoyed hitting Burgess. He's enjoying the whole thing . . .'

'Indeed. You agree, Mr Seaborne? He's not a frightened man?'

'No, sir. He's clever. It's highly-organised, planned . . . and he means what he says.'

'Yes, perhaps so. As you say, he's not frightened . . . but then, perhaps he's not desperate either?'

'I wouldn't want to put my shirt on it, sir,' Seaborne replied, sniffing.

'I hope not to ask you to do so, Mr Seaborne. However, the question is, at the moment, a nicety. There is a bomb, and presumably it will be armed at this moment, or capable of being armed and detonated at the blink of an eye.' Latymer pushed his hands into his pockets and patrolled the edge of the dais. Suddenly, he stopped and addressed them. 'I don't hold out much hope of the Cabinet deciding to shoot this one out – not with an election in the offing. Already the Home Secretary has sent post-haste for Nasoud . . .' He paused, then added, 'If we only had someone inside that aircraft – or could get someone inside . . .'

He waited, as if for inspiration, and then said, 'I pause for a reply. . . .' Bracken looked merely grim and Seaborne remained glumly silent. 'We'll pass, then – for the moment. Now, Mr Seaborne – what about the matter of FBI help in preparing a dossier on this man Packer?'

Seaborne brightened and said, 'They've promised to give it top priority, sir. A matter of another hour or so.'

'Good. Then we shall have to deduce from the passenger manifest who else we are dealing with. With six of them, we have to build up a picture of six psychologies, of their movements and behaviour, and we need an assessment, by an expert, as to what they might do. . . . To help us decide how far we can go – do I make myself clear?'

'Yes, sir.'

Latymer paused, then said, 'Very well, Mr Seaborne – start listening to my recent conversation. I want a psychological assessment from you to compare with anything we get from the States. And get a large cutaway chart of a 707 in here.'

Seaborne nodded and moved away. When he had gone there was a silence which lasted for some moments. Latymer noticed how hot and bright the room was. He brushed a hand through his hair.

'I'm very sorry, Philip. Do you want – to stay on the scene?'

Bracken looked at him, puzzled, and then said, 'Yes.' He sighed and scuffed his foot along the floor, looking down at it all the time. 'I – you know my marriage wasn't exactly roses all the way, sir . . .' He looked up at Latymer, who was holding out a gold cigarette case. Bracken took a cigarette and produced his lighter. The gas spurted audibly in the hot silence of the room. Bracken went on, exhaling deeply: 'I know you never enquired, sir – it was none of your business, as long as I did my job. But she went to America to see her father – it was a short of trial separation. Then I had a call the other day – saying she was coming home and she had some news, and were we going to try again . . .'

'And your feelings?'

'I said yes, but I didn't know what I wanted . . . until I realised what was happening out there on the runway.'

'And now?'

Bracken's eyes were bleak. He said, 'I only know that I'd do anything, agree to anything, as long as she would be safe.' He looked unblinkingly at Latymer, and added: 'It's a hell of a way to discover you love your wife, sir.'

'Mm. The airport lounges are filled with people who think the same, about someone on that aircraft, Philip.' He coughed. 'Which doesn't make my job any easier. I – hope you never have cause to hate me for anything that happens here.'

'So do I, sir. You – would you rather I transferred to something – some other work?'

'Would you rather?'

'No, sir.'

'Good. Now get off and make a tour of inspection, as my staff officer. Make contact with Morgan – let him know I'm leaving Alpha entirely in his hands. I know he and Seaborne are both good men – but you understand the way my mind works. I want to know for myself the extent and efficiency of our security here.'

Bracken nodded and turned to go, a slight smile revealing that he understood Latymer's intention.

As he reached the door, Latymer added: 'Send Barbara in, would you, Philip? And make sure that all the sightseers who will be arriving are kept *out* of the airport – that means away from the perimeter fences, as well as the gates.'

'Sir.'

It was a hot and humid day at R.A.F. Chivenor. Detective Chief Inspector Lucas, in the company of the Station Commandant, Group-Captain Mallory, stood looking out over the estuary of the Taw, across at the Appledore shipyard. There was the slightest breeze blowing, but it seemed neither to cool nor relax either man. The Beech Baron, in whose slight shade they stood, was silently in position on the main runway, gleaming in the scarlet and gold of the charter company's colours. Two armed men stood stiffly to attention in their blue uniforms on the other side of the small aircraft.

Lucas turned his squinting eyes from the pastoral scene before him and looked at his watch. It was a long drive from Dartmoor to Chivenor, allowing for holiday traffic. Yet security demanded that Nasoud be delivered to an R.A.F. station rather than a small, unprotected civilian airfield. Apart from which, Lucas admitted, there was sea-fog on the south Devon coast and they would not have got into a civvy airfield anywhere near Dartmoor.

'Your chaps late, Chief Inspector?' Mallory asked. Lucas tossed his head.

'Bloody holiday traffic!' he said.

'Quite. Hell of a scramble at Heathrow no doubt?'

'Yes.'

Mallory looked at his companion, the tall, dark-haired policeman, noticed again the tiny bulge of the holster and accepted the silence he seemed determined to maintain. He smiled slightly at the atmosphere of security that had flown in with the small civilian aircraft. Mallory, an honest man in private, wished whoever had command of the operation at

London airport the very best of luck. He was a man who had never considered a switch to civil flying from the service – a fact of which he was now extremely glad.

His mind wandered over a mental landscape which included the crew of the 707, the armed men bristling in the airport shadows, the scene of controlled panic in the tower. It was a bad business – very bad. There were no winners in a game like that. And even on a beautiful day on the Devon coast – Mallory intended to play a round of golf later that evening – the tension was apparent. A cold hand had reached out and touched him. He saw the pilot of the Beech Baron coming across from the tower having paid his landing fee and, no doubt, got himself something to drink, and then he heard the screech of tyres on hot concrete. He turned his head and saw the black police car scuttle past the tower, followed by two attendant motor cycles, then a second car, then two more motor cycles. He sensed a new alertness in his companion.

'Ah – here we are,' he said.

Lucas waited, tense, stiff, as the car carrying Nasoud pulled up alongside the plane. Lucas stared intensely into the back of the car. The Arab's features were expressionless, dull and sullen – yet for Lucas, whose first view of Nasoud this was, they held a fascination. The man's thin frame was jammed between the bulk of two enormous CID men. The door of the car opened and a short, red-faced detective stepped out.

'Chief Inspector Lucas?' he enquired as he joined them, holding out his ID card.

Lucas nodded, handing his own ID card over for inspection. He glanced down at the other card.

'Superintendent Wharton?' he said.

'That's it. Got your man here.'

'Thank you, sir.' Lucas passed him, bent down and spoke into the car. 'Get him aboard, will you, as quick as you can.'

He stepped back and watched Nasoud bundled out of the car.

Wharton said, 'Do you want the cuffs left on?' He held out the key, but Lucas shook his head.

'No,' he said. 'He won't be a silly boy at ten thousand feet.'

'Very well.' Wharton unlocked the handcuffs. The Arab

was then forcibly assisted into the Beech Baron.

Wharton murmured to Lucas, 'Pretty bad at Heathrow?'

'I haven't seen,' Lucas said. 'I expect so.'

'They going to exchange this wallah for the passengers?'

'I – don't know, sir. Just insurance, at present.'

'Wouldn't have thought he was worth the fuss, would you?'

'Perhaps not.' Lucas turned in the direction of the approaching pilot, a young man with a red face and carrot-coloured hair, and a carefully home-aged flying-jacket.

Lucas grinned and yelled, 'Come on, Ronnie – time to be off!'

Ronnie Whitaker, junior pilot of the Flying Fish Charter Co. based at Gatwick, waved cheerily in reply, and put on a little extra pace for the last few yards to indicate his good intentions.

Lucas turned to Wharton and nodded. 'Thank you, sir. I take it the dummy's on his way to London by very slow car?'

'Yes. One of my men, complete with burnt cork and indeterminate costume – escort of three cars and motor cycles, as requested. God help them in the evening traffic, that's all I can say!' He held out his hand, which Lucas briefly shook, and added: 'Good luck – all the way.'

Lucas nodded, his lips pursed, and then rejoined Mallory who was staring up at the Arab inside the plane. He looked down as Lucas joined him.

'Thanks for all your help, Group-Captain,' Lucas said.

'Don't mention it. Sorry about the circumstances. We'll call Heathrow direct and let them know you're on your way. Good luck.'

'Thank you. But I'm only the messenger boy. I don't have to make the decisions.'

'Lucky man.'

Lucas climbed into the cramped cockpit of the Baron, settled himself next to the pilot, with the silent, glum Nasoud behind him, and turned in his seat.

'Now – you be a very good boy, Shafiq, or I'll blow your brains out of the tail of this nice little aircraft – savvy?'

Nasoud nodded and Lucas grinned. In less than an hour,

he would be safe and sound in the armed hands of the Alpha Group at Heathrow. Nasoud did not respond to the grin, or to the words, and Lucas turned back to the pilot, and said, 'Right-oh, Ronnie, my boy – Heathrow next stop!' Whitaker grinned at him and continued with his pre-flight checks. Lucas slipped on his dark glasses and gazed out over the estuary of the Taw again, envying the life of the servicemen on that particular station.

As Bracken stood on the observation gallery, hands clenched on the top rail, the marksman lay alongside him on an inflated airbed, with dampened sandbags at its head for steadiness of aim, the slim rifle at his right elbow, the walkie-talkie to his left, and his eyes glued to the binoculars on a squat tripod in front of him. There was a flask of coffee and a packet of half-eaten sandwiches at the foot of the airbed. The 707 was a small, distant white shape – slim, aerodynamic, its British Airways markings hard to distinguish with the naked eye. Near it was a single fire tender, ladder extended, which had been used for the inspection of the engine, and a passenger gangway up which the Fire Officer and his assistant had been taken into the plane after they had made their inspection.

The heat haze smoked around the plane, seeming to remove it further from accessibility. It was at something approaching the maximum range of the slim rifle. And against hijackers there was only one kind of effective shot. From where he lay, that was impossible. Other marksmen were slightly closer, in the lee of the cargo sheds away to Bracken's right – but they, too, were far away from an ideal situation for snap-shooting.

The light of late afternoon was blinding – splintering off glass and metal surfaces. The silence, Bracken noticed again, was almost sinister, certainly depressing. He fiddled with the strap of his binoculars, as if to lift them to his eyes again. Then he shrugged his hand to the rail once more, observing the sludge of conflicting emotion and memory that swilled through his consciousness. What he had said to Latymer was true – he would give anything, agree to any terms, just to get Alison off that plane. She had been coming home but he had felt little, burying anticipation in work. He suspected that she had no great hopes of a new beginning, coming rather to inspect the corpse and ascertain the cause of death. He had been early arriving at Heathrow, mostly, he realised, to appease his own sense of another likely failure.

Now, it could all be too late. Bracken's feelings for his wife, now that she was trapped in a duralumin coffin, stewing and fearful on an airport runway, close to a bomb and six desperate people. All rather too late to make any difference . . . he might never get the chance to tell her he loved her. He hadn't heard from her for six months, except for the one call from the States and a single brief letter.

He turned away from the persistent, obsessive image of the 707. The observation gallery was empty – not even a solitary cameraman or reporter. Hollis had control of them in the sweaty, confined space of the airport press room.

Bracken had completed his check of the security arrangements and now there was nothing to stop the flow of personal narrative. The gates were closed, the lounges constantly patrolled, the perimeter secure. Traffic had idled to a trickle of departing cars and coaches, and the ghouls who had begun to arrive had been stopped and turned away at a barrier erected a couple of hundred yards from the main gates. A traffic control group from Alpha had moved in and the thick, congealing stream of vehicles had begun to melt, move again on the main roads around the airport.

Heathrow was sewn up tight. Bracken wondered, for the first time, what Latymer would do. The first movement of stage one was complete. Figuratively, Heathrow had been dug up and taken away for inspection under a microscope. Except for the landlines which linked them with Whitehall and Downing Street, the outside world had gone away, been cut off. Now what would the man do?

Bracken, like Seaborne, had never been able to fathom Latymer's personal feelings towards his job. The man was a true civil servant in that; his feelings never projected themselves like awkward fractures into his conversation, or his planning. His role was defined for him, and he seemed content with that. With an academic enthusiasm, it seemed, he had thrown himself into the intellectual problems of the office of Executive Officer, Civil Emergencies (Hijacking). Yes, Bracken decided – that was the problem with Latymer. One didn't *know* anything about him. He *was* his job – or had been, up till now.

Bracken began to walk away from the rail of the gallery, heading for the stairs. He felt suddenly chill. For all he knew Latymer was a man who might use the power that had been given into his hands, and be damned to the Home Secretary. He forced himself not to look at the 707 again before he descended the steps.

The Beech Baron was climbing steadily towards 6,000 feet, to level at 7,000. Ronnie Whitaker's view was limited by the haze. He was on top of the inversion at his cruising height. The visibility did not worry him as he studied the instrument panel. He was in a good mood. Without being in the least inattentive to the task of flying, he mused gently.

His passengers had retreated into their separate silences – the thin, bony Arab, sullen and captive, and the tall frame of Lucas slumped into the seat next to him, as if the man were dozing. His hand rested lightly inside his jacket, near the gun in the shoulder holster. The flight, Ronnie reflected, was certainly a doddle. Despite his lack of flying hours on the Beech Baron, he felt himself to be in control of the aircraft, felt that quiet confidence induced by the weather, the cockpit routine. He wondered vaguely about Nasoud, the man seated behind Lucas. Lucas had been uncommunicative on the subject. Presumably, Ronnie thought, he was part of some deal with the hijackers on board the 707.

There was a single, abrupt bang from the starboard engine, like the noise of a backfire. Lucas stirred, opened one incurious eye. Then he sat upright as he registered the change in the engine note. The aircraft swung viciously to the right, and Ronnie stamped his foot down hard on the left rudder pedal to counteract the swing, even as he expressed the single expletive:

'Shit!'

'What the bloody . . . ?' Lucas began, even as Ronnie's eyes flashed to the fuel gauges, checking contents, pressure flow, tank selectors, the exhaust-gas temperature dial, the temperature and pressure gauges, the mixture levels, and the fact that the lights showed that the filters were in auto, and the switches were in the 'Both' position. Everything was reading normally. And the starboard engine had cut out.

A second bang, and then a third overlapping it, cut off Lucas's question, and the starboard engine began to run again, the engine note returning to its throaty, comforting normality. The rpm on the starboard engine slid up to the set 3,600, and Ronnie eased off the rudder pedal. A fourth bang from outside the cockpit caused the engine to cut again and the needle on the rpm dial slid down. The aircraft pulled again to the right and Ronnie stabbed his feet down on the left rudder pedal.

'What the hell are you playing . . . ?' Lucas began again.

Ronnie, his eyes finishing their check of the fuel mixture switches, all of which registered maddeningly normal, said, 'Either fuel or ignition – I can't spot anything.' His voice was a flat monotone. 'It could be a bit of grit in the injectors.'

'Don't you know anything about this bloody plane?' Lucas yelled.

'Yes,' Ronnie replied, his contempt for Lucas's massive ignorance obvious in his voice. 'Low mileage, one owner from new – a snip!'

The starboard engine banged, started up, and he eased his foot off the rudder pedal. The rpm climbed again to normal; then the engine banged again and the needle began to slide down. He banged his foot down on the pedal. Lucas's eyes were wide as he stared at the wobbling nose of the Baron through the perspex in front of him. He was suddenly in an unstable, tiny, ineffectual machine a long, long way from the solid earth.

Ronnie, more by instinct than analysis, switched on the booster pumps, the engine note roared, steadied, and the two engines of the Baron resumed their characteristic note.

Ronnie sat back in his seat, smiled, forebore to wipe his hands on his trousers, and said, 'Sorry about the rough ride, gents – we're all right now.'

'Are you sure?' Lucas asked suspiciously.

'Yes, I *am* sure!' Ronnie snapped at him. 'I'm not asking you if you've got the right man there, am I? Don't tell me how to do my job!'

Lucas nodded, accepted the justice of the remark, straightened his tie in a reflex action, and said, 'Sorry, Ronnie, old son. Don't let it happen again.'

'It won't,' Ronnie said darkly, catching his breath – then, more forcefully repeating himself, 'It won't!'

The radio crackled and London Airways, with its routine enquiry concerning the Beech Baron's height, restored normality to the cockpit.

Ronnie flicked a switch, and replied, 'Passing through flight level Six-Point-Two. Position approximately fifteen miles west of Cheltenham.'

'Roger. Call Seven-Zero.'

Lucas, settling himself, feeling the wateriness in the pit of his stomach disappear, turned to Nasoud and studied the Arab's features. They remained set in their sullen expression.

Irritated by his apparent unconcern, Lucas grinned and said, 'Had you worried there, did we, Shafiq? Get a touch of gyppy tummy, then?' Lucas laughed at his own joke but the Arab remained unimpressed. Lucas turned to Ronnie, who had begun to whistle through his teeth. Lucas wondered whether he was being ridiculous, remaining unsettled by the fireworks in the starboard engine.

'We're all right, then, are we – Ronnie Ronalde?'

'Sure. You're in the hands of the fearless, the intrepid Toad,' Ronnie replied, apparently pleased by Lucas's continuing discomfort of mind.

The aircraft was trimmed to level flight and Ronnie set the boost and rpm to cruising speed. The engine nagged at the back of his mind. He was not nervous, like Lucas, because he was a professional. Yet professional interest caused him to be curious, alert. An unexplained engine cut-out could happen again, at any time. . . . The booster pumps had sorted it out, apparently. He recalled that he still had the boosters switched to 'On', and flicked them off. There was no change in the engine note.

Glancing from his side-window, he saw Cheltenham sliding towards the port wing and realised that, in tinkering with the erratic movements of the Baron while the engine was playing up, he had slipped north of the airway. He would have to alter his heading slightly and slip back into the comfort of his allotted airspace. He listened to the starboard engine again, was comforted by the sound, and began to feel contented once more, recapturing the mood of the early part of the flight.

He called London Airways to establish his flight level at 7,000 feet and then, as he switched off the radio, the starboard engine banged, spluttered and died. His eyes roved the dials in front of him, his left foot stamped the rudder pedal, bringing the nose swinging back onto course, and he registered that every reading was normal, except for the rpm needle dying away. Lucas, turning to him with mouth open, was ignored, and he cut in the boosters again. The engine picked up, the needle slid up the dial and the aircraft settled to normal flight.

'You said it was all right,' Lucas said accusingly.

'It is!' Ronnie snapped. 'I'll just have to use the boosters all the way.'

'You're not carrying a couple of sheep to market, or a jockey to a race-meeting!' Lucas yelled.

'No – just one shit-scared detective!' Ronnie replied.

Ronnie, whatever his bravado, had felt his familiarity with the aircraft slide away from him. There was one rule, and one only, in such a situation – to put the aircraft down and have the engine inspected. He had flown the Baron before, in worse weather – but he just didn't have sufficient hours to feel confident. He could no longer see the rest of the flight unrolling with the simplicity of the topography beneath him. His eyes flickered to the map resting on his knee.

Had Ronnie Whitaker but known it, had he read the pilot's notes published by the Beech Aircraft Corporation more thoroughly, he would have noticed a singular amendment, relating to the Baron aircraft type alone. This stated that when a Beech Baron has been standing for some time in hot sun, there is a possibility of engine-bay and fuel lines becoming warm and the fuel evaporating which could, for a short time, conceivably cause engine misfiring and cutting. Beech's recommended SOP (Standard Operating Procedure) was to select booster pumps 'On', and to leave them on.

Ronnie, however, was unaware of this. Looking at his map, he realised he had a choice of airfields open to him. Without consulting Lucas who, whatever his feelings, accepted that the pilot was in command of the aircraft, Ronnie decided an R.A.F. station would be best. Aston Down, Kemble, Little Rissington and Fairford were all in his immediate vicinity. Even Brize Norton. The landing should, he knew, be made sooner rather than later, and that narrowed the choice to R.A.F. Little Rissington which should, at his height of 7,000 feet, be visible to him.

He turned to Lucas and said curtly, 'I'm taking her down.'

'Like hell you are!'

'I'm not landing in a field, you silly bugger – R.A.F. Little Rissington is just up ahead of us.'

Lucas looked as if he wanted to continue the argument and then he shrugged his shoulders.

'You're in charge,' he admitted.

'Too bloody true!'

Ronnie switched on his radio. He called London Airways, giving height and position, and then explained his engine problem. London Airways agreed that Heathrow be advised. The conversation was couched in the flat, unindicative monotone of an ordinary civil flight. Lucas sat silent, a bullying presence, requiring that Latymer be informed of what was happening. The confirmation of Ronnie's request took what seemed little more than seconds.

The controller at London Airways said, 'Your details passed to Heathrow – advise you call Little Rissington direct to request landing clearance.'

'Roger, London Airways. Have you any conflicting traffic for my descent?'

'No conflicting. Your flight plan cancelled and Heathrow advised. You are cleared to QSY Little Rissington. Call leaving Seven-Zero.'

'Roger. Thank you, sir. Leaving Seven-Zero this time.'

Cheltenham slid alongside them, to Lucas a very long way down and away to port, and Ronnie began to seek the airfield in the haze. It ought to be visible already, at his height – and it wasn't. . . . Then he saw it, directly ahead.

Ronnie, suddenly screwed up into an unfamiliar tension, reduced power. The aircraft's speed began to drop. He lowered the wheels and acknowledged with a nod the three green lights which told him the undercarriage was down and locked. He selected fifteen degrees of flap, and called R.A.F. Little Rissington.

He turned to Lucas, and said, 'I'll switch on the cabin speaker, so you'll know what's going on.'

Then he concentrated his attention on his call. 'Rissington Approach – Golf-Bravo-Kilo-Foxtrot-Oscar. Have slight engine malfunction, starboard engine. Request landing clearance. Over.'

The voice of the Rissington controller came over the R/T. 'Roger, Foxtrot-Oscar. What is your position and height?'

'Just south of Cheltenham – leaving five for four.'

The dialogue was comforting. The airfield was in sight. Ronnie fitted himself like a cold hand into the warm mitten of the pre-landing routine. All he had to do was to land the aircraft – hoping that the starboard engine did not play up again at a critical moment; or, if it did, that it cut out above one thousand feet. This would at least give him time to cut the engine fully, feather the prop and set up the Baron tidily for a single-engine landing.

He sensed Lucas, beside him, was tense, but silent – as he should be. Ronnie smiled to himself. Lucas's faintly patronising attitude had not really got under his skin – nevertheless, it would be nice to land the Baron like a feather.

The controller at Rissington acknowledged his statement.

'Roger. Stand by for further instructions. Are you ready to copy the weather?'

'Ready to copy, sir.'

'No cloud – visibility four miles in haze. Wind light, variable. QNH One-Zero-One-Five, QFE Zero-One-Two. Which runway would you like to use?'

Ronnie glanced down at the map on his knee, at the pattern of the station's runways, checked visually against the airfield he could see ahead and said, 'Copied the weather. Will take Zero-Eight, for a straight-in.' There was, after all, no point in messing about, he reflected. Straight down.

'Roger. Do you require any assistance?'

'Negative. I have the airfield in sight.'

'Roger. What is your height?'

'Three-Six-Zero-Zero feet.'

'What is your type?'

'Beech Baron.'

'Thank you, sir. You're still cleared number one.'

Ronnie felt his system calming down, felt the edge taken off his hearing as he strained it to the note of the engine. Boosters off, and the engine was running sweetly. What he had failed to notice, however, was that the pattern of runways below him did not exactly correspond to the pattern the map ascribed to Little Rissington. As he put the Baron into an orbiting descent, he spotted the hangars and runways – but failed to register the absence of married quarters or an administrative block. What he failed to register, since his attention was glued to the runways as a metaphor of safety rather than as a physical reality, was the curious dereliction of the airfield he was approaching.

'So far, so good,' Lucas observed, sensing Ronnie's growing confidence.

'Piss off!' Ronnie replied blithely. 'I expect they're brewing a nice cup of tea for you now. Bring the colour back to your cheeks!'

Ronnie spotted the north-south road that bordered the airfield, without realising that it was the wrong road; what he registered as the village of Little Rissington was, in fact, the village of Little Colesbourne, still some twelve miles away from the R.A.F. station. The airfield below him was Chedworth, abandoned for years. As the altimeter registered seven hundred feet, he called the Rissington controller.

'Foxtrot-Oscar – long finals.'

'You are not yet in sight, Foxtrot-Oscar, but still number one for landing, Zero-Eight,' the controller replied.

Ronnie attributed the fact that the tower could not yet see him to the omnipresent haze. He said to Lucas and the Arab:

'Check seat belts clipped and tight – and make sure that Omar Sharif understands!'

'Why can't they see us, Ronnie?' Lucas asked.

'Shut up.'

Ronnie proceeded with his pre-landing checks and selected full flap and booster pumps 'On'. In so doing, he made his final, and fatal, error of judgement. The booster pumps had been set at 'On' since the last time the starboard engine had cut out and Ronnie now, inadvertently, switched them off. At one hundred and ten feet above ground level, and nine hundred yards from the end of the runway at Chedworth, the starboard engine cut out for the final time. The aircraft was now at a low speed, with full flap and the wheels down.

Everything happened for Ronnie in a frozen slow motion. As the Baron began to swing to the right, he stamped on the left rudder pedal and smashed open the throttles in his panic. By doing this, he compounded an already-dangerous situation. The aircraft turned turtle.

Lucas saw the trees of Withington Woods above his head, he saw dark green and a rushing sea of leaves as the aircraft rolled on to its back. Then there was the terrifying impact, the horrendous noise, as the tree tops ripped off the port wing and engine at the roots. Even as the cry of tearing metal flooded his awareness, he was flung against the bulkhead and struck his forehead. He thought he could hear Ronnie screaming in terror as he blacked out.

The scream that had penetrated Lucas's drowning consciousness became part of a weight on his chest and shoulders and at one with a rush of cool air and the distant lapping of the cries of alarmed birds. It caused him to open his eyes. It had been only a matter of seconds, perhaps – that scream had obliterated time. There was still a weight on his chest and he struggled with it like a drowning man. He sensed he had hold of a limb, a foot, then the sensation was gone. He rolled in his seat and the dead, terrified face of Ronnie Whitaker stared into his eyes. Lucas was sick across the dead pilot's flying-jacket as he saw the ugly angle at which the head was limply hanging, and the spreading, livid bruise on the temple. Ronnie's neck was broken.

Lucas seemed to recollect that there was a second passenger – perhaps he had screamed? Something connected with the seat behind him, one of the passenger seats. He shook his head, wiping a dribble of bile from the corner of his mouth. His mouth was slackly wet. His head felt wet, too, and ached a great deal. He touched his forehead with his fingertips and inspected, through foggy vision, the redness he found, the wet redness he knew was blood.

The other person in the aircraft . . . ? He formed the thought with what seemed incredible slowness. The smell of his own vomit was strong in his nostrils and a fly, entering through the open door at his side, buzzed loudly round the blood on his forehead. The door was open . . .

He turned in his seat, with difficulty since his belt was hampering him. There was no one there, no other person . . . he saw the dark, swarthy features, connected the name – Nasoud had flown!

He tugged at the harness trapping him in his seat, freed it, stood up dizzily in the cockpit and leaned out of the door. Dizziness suddenly overcame him, he lost his balance and tumbled out of the fuselage, landing with an explosion of breath on a tugging, ripping cushion of bushes. His weight bent the already-broken branches, and he toppled to the ground. The aircraft had lost both wings, both engines. It was nothing but a skeletal, motionless fuselage. The bright paintwork, scarlet and gold, was smeared and gouged. It was a desecrated tomb.

Nasoud was hobbling away from him, across the clearing in the wood. The dark, limping shape was moving swiftly.

Lucas shouted. 'Halt – or I fire!'

The Arab looked back, perhaps frightened as he might have been by a ghost. Lucas tugged the gun out of the shoulder holster and tried to extend his arms to keep them steady. It was too much of an effort. The Arab, realising he was threatened, crouched lower and scuttled for the trees. Lucas tried to focus, but the blood from the cut on his forehead was like a red curtain across his vision. He squeezed off the whole clip of ammunition, the shots echoing in the green stillness, rousing the cries of offended birds. But the Arab, apparently unhit, disappeared into the trees.

As the thunder of the gun died away, Lucas could hear him blundering through thick undergrowth, the sound fading as he moved further away. Lucas tried to move after him and pain, noticeable for the first time, shot through his ankle. He toppled over, unable to support his own weight without the fierce concentration on his target that had brought a temporary oblivion of his broken ankle.

He sat awkwardly on the ground, thrusting a fresh clip of cartridges into his gun, and cursing like a child who has been cheated or robbed, tears streaming down his face.

Nasoud was half a mile away before Lucas realised that he had to attempt to get some message, some warning, to Latymer. His wet eyes focused on the shattered fuselage and he hoped to God that the radio was undamaged. He had to get off a message, at least as far as Little Rissington. He began to drag himself upright against the fuselage, ignoring the excruciating pain in his ankle as he tried to swing himself up to the open door. His efforts were so concentrated that he did not hear the approaching beat of helicopter rotors.

The time was six-ten in the evening.

3: A Search is Mounted

Packer turned away from the VHF set, ignoring Burgess and Hislop who were cramped, sweating and weary with nagging fear in their seats, and turned to Clay who stood looming behind him on the flight deck. Asif, the Arab, had bundled the Senior Fire Officer back to his seat in the first class. Clay's face was faintly amused, the whites of his eyes seeming to challenge Packer, to comment on his failure to work a miracle in the matter of the engine replacement. Packer, against all the expert advice, and his own nerves, was unable to deny that the suspect port engine would have to be replaced. Latymer had gained that much of a victory over him, and Packer did not like it.

'You, baby – you're the one who's gonna be sittin' out on the runway!' he snarled. Clay shrugged, as if he did not care, increasing Packer's sense of temporary impotence.

'I ain't gonna fry out there, man. I got the right skin for this weather,' Clay observed, smiling in the manner that always irritated Packer.

Packer turned to Burgess and Hislop. Hislop's face, he noticed with satisfaction, had swollen from the blow.

He said, 'O.K., move it. You join the rest of our house-guests in the first class.' He waggled the gun in his hand. 'Don't try anything.'

Neither Burgess nor Hislop looked as if they were contemplating any sudden move – neither of them looked in the least interested in escape. The captain had become old in the hours that had limped by since Packer had appeared on his flight-deck – shrunken, his large frame now looking merely middle-aged, out of condition. Hislop had returned to the sullen figure of the transatlantic crossing. In both of them, the high-water marks of fear had left their stain, but the tide

63

had now ebbed and they were left spent and deadened.

They passed Packer's gun, and then Clay's gun, and left the flight-deck. Packer watched them down the narrow corridor, then called out:

'Asif – Joanne! Get in here – I wanna talk.'

He watched as Rice and McGruder changed positions, so that one of them covered the first class and the other the second. There would be no trouble, not with their guns on automatic. Packer correctly sensed the mood of the aircraft. There would be no trouble. The Arab and the girl came down the corridor to the flight deck.

When they had squeezed through the door, Packer said, 'They gotta replace the engine. Asif agrees, so does Clay.' His voice was challenging, yet defensive. It was as if he feared the girl in some way. 'I got them down to four men and four hours' work. Clay has to be on the runway, and one of you others at the door nearest the engine. The men will have to be searched before . . .'

The girl interrupted him. There were two livid spots of colour on her white face. 'What d'you mean, Packer? You're gonna let men walk up to this bird and take away one of the engines?'

'Listen, soul-sister,' he snarled in reply. 'You want outa here when we got Nasoud? O.K., we gotta have a new engine. I don't wanna come down in the sea, baby – I got no reason to commit hara-kiri!'

'All right – all right – so we have a new engine! What about Nasoud – they agree?'

Packer appeared relieved. His anger increased, confident now, and bullying. 'Don't give me that bullshit you learned from your Senator daddy! I give the orders on this plane – me, not you!'

'Packer – you don't give me anything except the creeps! You didn't organise this hijack . . . Mr J. organised this little outing for all of us!'

Packer seemed disquieted by the reminder, but he bluffed the feeling away. 'Forget the fixer, baby. Right now, and until this bird flies – I'm the man on this trip, I call the shots!'

The girl subsided into an angry silence, and it infected the others around her, until Clay said, 'What you think, Packer man? They gonna give us Nasoud?'

'They must do. We have threatened to destroy the aircraft. They dare not let that happen, not in the middle of London Airport – especially since there will be a General Election this year.' The speaker was Asif, talking, it seemed, from some inner assurance. Packer scrutinised the swarthy, moustached face.

Asif had entered the U.S. more than twelve months previously, by an indirect route from the Middle East. He had never left the group since their first meeting. Packer knew as little about him now as he had done then. He was a cousin of Nasoud, but that was not why he was there.

Nasoud was important – to Mr J. in New York he was very important. He had talked to Peabody before Peabody had died, and he had heard the names, the addresses . . . at the moment, the British didn't know what they had in Nasoud. It was Packer's job to make sure they never found out. Packer suspected it was Asif's job to kill Nasoud – Asif was, after all, Mr J.'s link with Arab groups in Europe and the Middle East. Asif was important, Packer knew. He wasn't along just for the ride.

Packer had argued that the attempt to smuggle in arms in a suitcase was a crazy idea – Mr J. had told him that a preliminary gesture was important, perhaps vital. So Nasoud had been sent. Only after he left did Mr J. discover that Peabody had, for some reason, talked to Nasoud, revealing names, addresses in the U.K., revealing parts of the strategy – more than that, Packer suspected. Nasoud knew who Mr J. really was. Mr J. wanted the Arab dead.

'You sound damn sure, Asif,' he said thickly.

'Mr J. is certain, Packer – which makes me certain also. The Arab lapsed into silence once again.

'Mr J. ain't sittin' here with the pigs breathing hard all round him, Arab!'

'Mr J. employs people like you and me for that, Packer,' Asif replied.

*   *   *

65

Barbara Martindale no longer listened to the conversation between Latymer and Lucas over the telephone. She had heard the first words, the escape of Nasoud, and had sat ever since staring at the now redundant notes in the pad on her lap. Only minutes before, she had been sitting with Latymer in the tiny office one floor below, listening to his conversation with the Home Secretary, listening to the daunting news that the President of the United States considered that the lives of seventy-two passengers were less important than the future of the Middle East. Washington was not prepared to jeopardise Kissinger's initiatives by taking action against, or supporting action against, Arabs – wherever and whenever. On top of that, the Lebanese government was showing a great reluctance to admit the hijacked plane into its airspace, let alone allow it to land at Beirut. As to supplying a high-ranking hostage, at present it was out of the question.

She had left the hot, oppressive little room without windows in a mood of shocked incomprehension – her only outward-looking feeling being for Latymer. As his secretary, she did not have to be in love with him. It was simply that she was so in love. A fact which had no significance in her relationship with him.

Latymer, despite the distressingly negative news, had gone straight to the R/T and spoken with Packer. He had forced the man to accept an engine replacement, and intended to extract a bargain from it – passengers for the new engine; perhaps, later, more passengers for fuel. Latymer seemed to have accepted that eventually Nasoud would be turned over to the terrorists, and his task was to ensure against a double-cross on their part. He had narrowed the limits of his vision and his task. It was to save as many of the passengers as was possible.

Then the telephone call had come from Lucas, routed via the Ministry of Defence. Nasoud had escaped from the wreckage of the light aircraft bringing him to Heathrow. Barbara Martindale had seen the drawn flesh beneath Latymer's eyes, the sense of pain alive in his face. It was the unforeseen, the ruin of his plans. He had felt, as she had done, that seventy-two people out on the runway had just died.

Around Latymer, the activity of the Beta team had come to a halt as each man listened to Lucas's voice over the speaker which amplified it. The Beta team had been in the process of collating and sifting the data regarding each of the passengers aboard the 707. Scott had delivered the full passenger manifest, including photographs of every passenger, taken by the automatic camera as they passed through customs. They had been transmitted to Heathrow direct. Now the long process of deciding who among the names and faces were the six hijackers had begun. Men listened to telephone reports, marked off names on the list as police on both sides of the Atlantic checked addresses and occupations.

Elsewhere in the 'Greenhouse', other men checked with the world's police and security organisations on Nasoud and Packer. All possible links were being investigated. The Special Branch, the SIS, the FBI and the CIA, the security forces of the Common Market countries, and even the headquarters of the Mossad, in Tel Aviv – all were linked to the 'Greenhouse' by permanently open lines.

But now the activity had ceased. Its futility seemed evident. Barbara looked up from her shorthand and saw the vein throbbing high on Latymer's pale forehead. He was hunched over the telephone, his whole body strained with the effort of listening. The receiver was pressed to his face, even though the amplifier was working. Tapes hissed, the only other noise in the room. Barbara saw Bracken standing near Latymer, his face white and strained in a more obvious way.

'The map reference is 136 029,' Lucas was saying and Latymer, as if emerging from a trance, snapped:

'Clarence, get me OS map 163, Cheltenham and Cirencester – quickly!'

Seaborne waved a hand at two men stationed near the door and one of them disappeared.

'And you were airlifted to Little Rissington by an army helicopter?' Latymer said into the receiver.

'Sir,' Lucas replied. 'There's some sort of exercise down here – a tactical something-or-other . . .'

'A Tactical Deployment Exercise,' Latymer confirmed.

'Yes, sir.'

'Good. That means there are already men on the scene – if we can use them. Very well, Lucas. You mustn't blame yourself for what has happened, however unfortunate. Hang on there, would you? We'll be in touch as soon as I can organise something at this end.'

'Sir.'

Latymer put down the telephone and turned to confront the room. He studiously ignored the atmosphere of defeat that appeared marked on every face.

'I want the Ministry of Defence on the line – now!' He looked round at them. 'I need not stress the – *absolute security* of what you have just overheard. No one, *no one* must get wind of this . . .' He looked out of the windows, towards the 707, now a pinpoint of white in a gathering gloom. A storm was approaching, the air outside heavy with thunder. Darkness, he realised, would come early to Heathrow. He uttered a silent prayer that the weather was better in the Cotswolds. The plane looked like a white storm-gull. 'Especially our friends out there!' he added.

'What the hell do we do, sir?' Bracken asked in a thick voice.

'Do? We recapture Mr Nasoud, with the minimum of delay – that's what we do!'

'He could be anywhere by now.'

Latymer's patience snapped. 'Our friend is a stranger in a strange land – he's got nowhere to go, and no one to help him. The army's on exercise in the Cotswolds at the moment. What more, pray, do you require?'

Latymer felt his own stomach churn as he spoke, and realised that it was now that he had to establish his personality with these men. Even his own assistant was wavering. Complacency and routine had suddenly been transmuted into panic. A great fear possessed him, on which all his earlier calculations foundered. What if they could not recapture Nasoud . . . ?

'Ministry of Defence, sir – office of the Deputy Chief of the Defence Staff (Intelligence) on the line,' a voice called, cutting across his doubts. He stood up and strode across the room, consciously acting a part. Already, there was the clatter of a typewriter, the clicks and splutters of dialling in the room. Forced by his projection of efficient urgency, the Beta team was returning to work. Seaborne, knowing his role, crossed to a second telephone extension.

'Peter?' Latymer said.

'Hilary, old man – just caught me, I'm sorry to say. On my way to the club. What can do?'

'Something very urgent.'

'I gathered that, old man.' Lt.-General Sir Peter Crashaw, K.C.B., D.S.O. was Latymer's liaison with M.O.D., the man on the other end of the 'Rat Trap' line from Heathrow.

'Our party seems to have mislaid its bargaining-power, one Shafiq Nasoud. . . .' He let the words sink in, heard the surprised whistle, and then added: 'In the Cotswolds. From my man, I gather you have a T.D.E. down there at the moment – is that correct?'

'Ah. Strategic Command. Postponed from earlier in the year – now being held in the middle of the tourist season . . . just like the army, I suppose. "Exercise Stroller", that'll be the one you want.'

'*Want* being the operative word, I'm afraid.'

'Mm?'

'The whole shooting-match – I shall need to take it over.'

'You don't want much at short notice, old man.' There was a brief pause, and then: 'Very well. I'll clear that here – as long as you can clear it with the Home Office, and *you* appoint someone as G.O.C. Assume the thing is on from this moment – O.K.?'

'Thank you, Peter – I'll keep you informed.'

Latymer put down the telephone and looked around him. The faces of those nearest to him expressed a kind of wonder. Hearing only his end of the conversation, they had seen him take over an army exercise with the minimum of fuss. He smiled in satisfaction, for their benefit.

Seaborne, at the other line, put down the telephone and said, 'Gloucestershire Constabulary – all the help you need, under the personal supervision of Assistant Chief Constable Maxon. I've told them nothing but roadblocks, car searches, et cetera, so far – but the special duties groups are on alert, as are the road patrols and the dogs.'

'Thank you, Clarence.' Latymer crossed the room with long strides, exuding a sense of purpose he was barely beginning to feel. He stood before Bracken, and as Seaborne joined them, he said, 'You will take effective charge of the manhunt, Philip.'

Bracken's mouth sagged, and then the sense that Latymer was dealing from the bottom of the pack showed in his eyes. He looked suspiciously at him and said, 'Why me – sir?'

'If you want me to be brutally honest, Philip – you, because you have a greater desire than any of us to see Nasoud back in custody, in the shortest possible time. Also, you know the area – you were once on the strength of Gloucestershire CID. And . . .' he paused, calculated his tone, and added, 'furthermore, you're little better than a spare part hanging about here!'

Bracken looked hurt and angry. He blurted out, 'I *can't* leave, sir!'

'You can, and you will. You will take a Jetranger helicopter, the property of the Dragonfly Charter Company, from this airport in less than ten minutes and get down to . . .' He looked at Seaborne, who was crackling open the required OS map. Latymer found his bearings. Looking up after a moment, he said, 'This is where the Beech Baron came down – this deserted airfield at Chedworth. You'll make for that and rendezvous with Stratco Field HQ, wherever that is at the moment.'

'Stratco Field HQ?' Bracken echoed, genuinely puzzled.

'The headquarters for this exercise – a group of dark-green caravans probably hidden in some woodland, which is why you'll need the chopper. The exercise will be at brigade strength – it'll have choppers, amphibious craft, scout cars, infantry – all linked by a complex communications system, perfect for our purposes.'

'How can you be sure?'

'I can't – but I can make an educated guess. Peter Crashaw will already be asking Stratco Field HQ to call us direct. Whoever is in charge, and it'll be no one below full general, wouldn't be wasting his time watching a couple of Land Rovers go through their paces. This is a Tactical Deployment Exercise, one that intends to test methods and systems, not weapons. That means it's big.'

'I'm to be in charge – of all that?'

'Yes. They do what you want them to do.'

'Your authority extends that far?'

'You know it does. And also to you, my designated officer in this situation. You give the orders. What will happen will be that you won't work with the G.O.C. Stratco, but with the man under him – a brigadier, no less. And you must co-ordinate the police effort with that of the army. Clear?'

'Yes.' Bracken seemed frightened by his new powers. Latymer smiled encouragingly, and then turned to Seaborne.

'Your job, Clarence, is to order the police to close off this section of country.' His hand swept in a circle over the OS map. 'All roads and tracks, question all drivers, search all vehicles and be damned to the holiday traffic! And they'd better start making a list of all buildings within a ten-mile radius of the crash. That's here.' He took a slim gold pen from his pocket and drew a red circle around the reference point verified by Lucas. 'Get on to that, would you? And tell the A.C.C. that I shall want to employ a double-circle search in this area – I know it's wasteful of manpower, but with police and army we have the numbers to cope. Warn him I may need a house-to-house in Cheltenham, Cirencester and the villages in the area.'

Seaborne, half-way across the room, his subordinate already dialling the required number, nodded and continued on his way to the telephone, mentally a trifle breathless from the scale on which Latymer was prepared to think.

'Do I keep in touch while I'm flying down?' Bracken asked.

'No. A resumé of what has been done and what needs doing will be in the army's hands by the time you rendezvous. Maxon will join you there. Do you know Maxon?'

'Yes, sir.'

'Don't think much of him?'

'Not much – stuffy to the point of pomposity. He'll be difficult to work with.'

71

'Get him to do what you want,' Latymer said levelly.

'Sir.' He turned to Barbara and said, 'My chopper ready yet?'

'Just warming up – they're a bit worried about the weather, sir,' she added, speaking to Latymer.

'Damn the weather! They've got to get off. So have you,' he added to Bracken, taking his elbow and walking him to the door. When they reached it, he said, 'With all this help, he's already in the bag, even if he doesn't know it. Make sure he stays there, Philip!' He looked hard at Bracken, as if demanding a reply.

Bracken seemed to be looking beyond him, towards the windows. Then his eyes focused on Latymer, and he bobbed his head. 'I'll try as hard as I can,' he promised grimly.

For a few moments Latymer stared at the door which had closed behind Bracken, and then Barbara touched him on the arm.

'A call from G.O.C., Strategic Command, for you,' she said.

'Good.'

The telephone conversation with General Sir Stephen Cornfield, K.C.B., D.S.O., M.C. and bar, was brief and to the point. Cornfield temporarily resigned command of the exercise, placing his aide Brigadier Spencer-Handley at Bracken's disposal. 'Exercise Stroller' was as big as Latymer had hoped, at full brigade strength, almost one thousand men and seemingly endless varieties of equipment. Cornfield had already put foot-patrols into Withington Woods, and choppers were beating the area of the crash. His men had been ordered not to shoot. Cornfield agreed that Stratco Field HQ could be moved to the airfield at Chedworth within forty minutes.

When Latymer put down the receiver, he retained the smile of satisfaction on his features. The men around him seemed to draw a comforting sense of urgency from his solidity, his driving purpose. They did not see the doubts already beginning to infect his mind, could not guess the sense of impotence he felt as soon as Cornfield's breathy confidence had left him. From an entirely unexpected quarter, from Nasoud himself the catalyst had appeared which could heat the situation to the point of explosion.

He knew he had to force Packer to exchange at least some of the passengers for a new engine and fuel. It was six-thirty, and darkness probably would come early because of the storm. Cornfield had told him the weather appeared thundery in the Cotswolds.

Shafiq Nasoud slumped at the base of a tree, his shaking, heaving shoulders pressed against the rough bark, and tried to calm his breathing. He wiped the flecks of foam from his lips with a shaking hand and felt the weakness, the palsy, of his tired body. His ribs began to ache again and he surmised that he had broken at least one of them in the crash. Carefully, wincing and grimacing, he hoisted his wet shirt, and inspected with dabbing fingers the dark stain of the bruise low down on the skin above his left rib-cage. He winced, cried out with the pain of his finger-pressure, and knew that he had broken a rib. It was that which had slowed him up, caused him to pause to catch his breath so many times as he had fled through Withington Woods in a north-westerly direction; on and mercilessly on until now, if he turned his head, he could look down from the edge of the wood at the mossed remains of an ancient building – and beyond that the road, a narrow road running south-east to north-west, and beyond that again, almost hidden by the haze, the narrow gleam of a river which a map would have informed him was the River Coln.

Nasoud had no idea where he was. For security reasons he had never been told which prison held him. He had arrived there in a small aircraft and been brought away from it by car, with a hood over his head, and he had been kept under constant surveillance in solitary confinement during his entire residence. From the scenery that had surrounded the prison, he had wondered, from his inadequate knowledge of England, whether it might not have been Dartmoor, a prison of which he had heard. They had flown east that afternoon, presumably towards London, but not for very long after leaving the airfield on the coast . . . then had come the crash and his escape.

At first, Nasoud had been amazed that the policeman had not pursued him – but then assumed that he had been badly hurt in the crash since he had been unable to move him out of his seat and had had to climb over him to the door.

As his breathing decreased in audibility and his pulse ceased to race madly, he began to think ahead to the remaining hours of daylight – that was as far as he would let himself think. He had no idea why he had been taken from the prison. It had seemed a sudden decision. Presumably, he was required for further questioning by the British secret service.

What he did know, however, was that there were people in London who would help him. He had never understood why fat, frightened Peabody had spoken to him as he did – perhaps to warn him off – but he had remembered all the names, the addresses . . . and he had not revealed them under questioning. Now, those people, out of fear that he might betray them, would be forced to help him. All that Nasoud had betrayed were the names of Arabs like himself. Initially, on the first night, he had wept to think he had betrayed brothers and saved people he did not even know, but then, gradually, he had contented himself with the rationalisation that those he had betrayed were sacrifices for the Palestinian cause. Nevertheless, it had been bitter giving those names away, while keeping others secret. Now those he had saved would help him. He would see to that.

Nasoud assumed he was an expendable pawn in the game of international terrorism. He had no ability to conceive of a rescue-attempt on his behalf. At first, it had been a pleasant delusion to believe that Asif and the others might help – hold a hostage for his release, hijack an airliner full of people. But now he knew that the 'Army of the Night', as the madman Packer liked to call the group, would do nothing for him.

What he had to do, he knew, was to remain in hiding, lie low while the search buzzed round about him like a swarm of desert flies, until he could make his way to London. Once there – well, there were ways of being smuggled out of Britain. He abandoned the problem – it was difficult to concentrate with the pain in his ribs. And the day was hot and oppressive, humid. He was soaked with perspiration; flies buzzed round him. All he could do, he realised, was to stay clear of habitation, of any kind, until after dark at least. And he had to stay away from all roads for the present.

Yet he could not stay where he was. The woods where the aircraft had crashed would be searched thoroughly, too thoroughly for him to escape discovery. Dogs would be used, undoubtedly, and the police would be armed, even though it was not the fashion in England. He pushed himself to his feet, grimacing with the effort, his breath coming in a painful wheeze between his teeth. He steadied himself, felt the hot sun on his face and the legs beneath him retreat to a vast distance, as if hiding from their threatened efforts on his behalf. He groaned and almost sank to his knees in despair. He was perhaps hundreds of miles from London – he had no map, no compass, no gun. He had no chance. . . .

He looked down over the ruined building only hundreds of yards away, and beyond it to the thin gleam of the river. Perhaps there . . . ? There was a village, like a settlement in a great painting, almost hidden in the haze away to the north-east of him. He had to stay well clear of that which meant he would have to follow the course of the river to the south-east. He wiped a hand across his eyes, and a dirty sleeve of his cotton jacket. He did not even know in which direction London lay. The awful loneliness that Latymer had predicted for him overwhelmed him, and it was many minutes before he could stand upright again, sniffing loudly like a lost child. For the moment, the river, he decided. He could act and think effectively in no other way. Merely as a hunted animal, with a hunted animal's limited perspective. He had to stay free – simply that. He was not hungry, though he was thirsty. He had to put distance between himself and the wreckage on the other side of the woods, even if that meant crossing open land. Therefore, he had to take the risk of being seen and head towards the river, keeping the village well to his left.

Suddenly, as if he had heard the pursuit of dogs, the cries of men, he launched himself from the trees and bundled breathlessly down the slope, the long grass brushing against his calves, the air stirred to a breeze by the swiftness of his flight. Many times he almost lost his balance, arms flailing in front of him to right himself. He felt his head and lungs would burst with his speed, and that his legs would run away with a motion of their own. Yet he also felt a light-headed elation. Almost as if he were a character in a film running in slow-motion, his arms spread wide in a glorious sense of joy, he careered down the slope towards the road and its low hedge. He was free, running and free, and the feeling sustained him, pumped the blood madly in his body, anaesthetised the pain in his ribs and lungs.

Then he was throwing himself down in the shadow of the low hedge, the grass stems biting his face, foam from his wide-open, gasping mouth flecking the green. He lay like a stranded fish, gasping in lungfuls of air, dying. For a while he indeed thought he was dying, and then the feeling passed away, leaving him wanting to stay where he was, motionless. The grass seemed to cool him, and the sweat was now pleasantly chill across his back, his body sated against the hard earth as if in the aftermath of copulation.

When his breathing had stilled and his heart beat had died away to a faint pounding, he lifted himself painfully so he could see over the low hedge. Nothing on the road. He rolled on to his back, searching the hazy, milky sky above and around him for signs of searching aircraft and helicopters. Again, nothing. The noises of insects were loud, crackling like burning wood in the grass around him.

Then the urgency of flight, the unthinking, desperate, almost passionate desire to run, overtook him again. He scrambled his way through and over the hedge, crossed the road, bending at the waist, and flung himself over the drystone wall on the other side. The river was little more than a couple of hundred yards from him now, and he hurtled towards it through the dark sea of grass. Thankfully, he slid down the bank and ducked his body into the cool stream. The river was narrow at that point and appeared shallow and inviting. He floated in it, eyes closed, face towards the sun like a fugitive plant, cooling himself. He wanted to shout, cry out, after the long, empty days in prison and the lack of hope. But he silenced himself, stood waist-deep in the stream and took stock of his surroundings.

It was then that he saw the bridge, further down the river to the south-east – a railway bridge, he gradually realised. Excited, he waded towards it. He kept in the river because he knew that he would leave no scent for pursuing dogs as long as he stayed in the water, and because the shallow bank of the stream afforded him cover from the road.

When he reached the railway he saw, to his desolation, the grassy track and the scattered sleepers that indicated its abandonment. No trains, no trains to London, would pass him here. He sat weakly against the bank, and wept.

Gradually, the animal emerged. He did not realise it, had no control over the process; but it occurred, inexorably. The animal – that asked nothing more than the refuge of a few moments, nothing more than the strength in tired limbs to drive it forward. Nasoud *was* a hunted animal. He wiped his face with cooling water and calculated with animal cunning that if he turned northwards along the course of the old railway he would undoubtedly end up in the village he had seen in the haze. And animals like himself kept clear of human habitation. So, climbing up the bank and on to the bridge, he turned south-east and began to jog along the grassy, uneven hollow that had once been a local railway line.

The dark green army caravans were being towed on to the deserted airfield at Chedworth as the Jetranger hovered and then began slowly to descend. Bracken, grimly silent throughout the journey from Heathrow, watched them pull into a loose circle reminiscent of the defences of a waggon-train. There was one caravan in blue R.A.F. paint. Five low buildings in all, contrasting with the dilapidation of the airfield. Bracken glanced at his watch. It was seven-fourteen. Nasoud had been running for an hour.

The Jetranger touched down and, bending low, Bracken scuttled from beneath the umbrella of the rotors. He straightened up, the wind of their declining speed whipping his hair, tugging the tail of his jacket. They had touched down a mere hundred feet from the caravans. Already they had been unhitched and other vehicles were pulling alongside them, like calves alongside their mothers; scout cars, a couple of 1½-ton lorries and an armoured personnel carrier. Bracken felt a momentary annoyance that these vehicles should be standing idle, until he recollected that they represented only a tiny fraction of the available forces. From the largest of the caravans a short, stocky officer with the insignia of a brigadier stepped down, as if welcoming a guest for the week-end. He held out his hand to Bracken.

'Spencer-Handley,' he said. 'Chief-Inspector Bracken?'

Bracken showed him his ID card, and the soldier nodded. Sensing that Bracken had no time to waste, he said: 'Better come inside, Mr Bracken and we'll see if we can't give you a picture of what's been done so far, and what's being done.' He indicated the steps and Bracken preceded him into the brightly-lit interior of the caravan.

There were a number of officers inside, assembled, Bracken guessed, to await his arrival. The man who was late, and conspicuous by his absence, was A.C.C. Maxon. Bracken shook hands with Spencer-Handley's team in turn.

'You'll need most of them,' the brigadier said, 'I'm sorry to say, Stanton especially, my signals officer.' Stanton was a tall, bespectacled soldier. 'He'll give you a direct link to Heathrow, to M.O.D., or Timbuctoo, if you ask him.'

'Would you outline what's already been done, Brigadier?'

'Certainly. Come over to the map.'

They threaded their way through the group of men, who fell in behind until they were facing a huge wall map, already well-populated with coloured pins. A sergeant stood to one side of it, lifted his headset to enquire as to whether there were any orders and then resumed fiddling with the pins in a cardboard box. He looked, Bracken thought, as if he felt them to be intruders, people about to spoil his careful handiwork.

Swiftly, without fuss or self-congratulation, Spencer-Handley outlined the area of the search. He had plugged as many gaps as he could in the outer ten-mile ring of the search, his vehicles retiring and reporting in as soon as they were replaced by police road-blocks. Traffic, he explained, was heavy on the main roads, especially the A.435, the Cheltenham to Cirencester road – the jams were piling up. His men had orders to search every car. Bracken privately regretted the necessity of having soldiers searching cars, thus alerting the media, but it was unavoidable. Spencer-Handley went on to outline the areas of intensive ground search, supported by choppers, Withington Woods being the focal point.

'This chap of yours didn't wound our friend by any chance?' he enquired, interrupting his flow.

'Not as far as I'm aware.'

'Pity. However, we've estimated his physical condition as being rather poor – delayed shock after the accident, something like that. Which places him . . .' He waved at the map, describing a loose circle, after Latymer's manner but smaller in radius, 'somewhere in here.' He went on to explain each of the coloured pins while the sergeant nodded, as if hearing him recite a lesson learned by heart by way of an imposition.

When he had finished, Bracken felt a creeping optimism lighten his mood. Nasoud, as Latymer had forecast, was in the bag already. All they had to do was to prevent him getting out of it.

The noise of a police siren interrupted a detailed explanation by Major Stanton of the capability and equipment of the neighbouring communications caravan.

'A.C.C. Maxon of the Gloucestershire Constabulary, if I'm not mistaken,' remarked Bracken.

Spencer-Handley smiled conspiratorially, as if Bracken had subtly joined their team and the newcomer were definitely an outsider. Bracken moved to the door of the caravan just as the police Jaguar drew up with a screech of tyres and a bucking of its springs. Maxon, a tall, thin-faced, austere individual, climbed out and on looking up seemed surprised to see Bracken – and not particularly pleased. Bracken came down the steps and held out his hand. Maxon's handshake was limp and damp.

'Welcome aboard, sir,' Bracken said.

'Hmm,' Maxon grunted. 'You, I take it, are in charge of this operation, Bracken?' Bracken nodded. 'Very well.' Bracken felt he had the look of a driving-examiner on his face. 'If that's how it must be, it must be so. I certainly don't intend to put any obstacles in your way. I realise that this operation is of the utmost urgency. Now, shall we go inside and get down to business?' He brushed past Bracken, who gritted his teeth. Maxon was certainly going to show the army that he outranked Bracken.

Swiftly, under Bracken's direction and with Maxon discreetly silent for most of the time, the army officers assembled the remainder of the ten-mile ring of searchers, the first of whom had began to move from their starting-points a little after seven. The sky had become overcast and threatened a storm, and the atmosphere was muggily close. They had to narrow the ring as much as possible before darkness. Within the closing circle were a number of foot patrols which had been ferried by choppers to likely hiding places analysed by Anderson, the staff Executive Officer, and Mayhew, the bridgadier's ADC. Other patrols continued on their lines of search, established before Bracken's arrival. Amphibious craft were out on the River Coln, patrolling its length as it edged Withington Woods. Police patrols, meanwhile, called at every farm and building within the area, warning local farmers and residents to keep careful watch for the fugitive.

The communications caravan had been staffed by police officers to supplement the army personnel. Stanton had disappeared early from the HQ caravan to supervise their work. Only important material filtered through to the main caravan, the remainder being documented, awaiting decision. Meanwhile, the remnants of 'Exercise Stroller' continued to play themselves out, like a stream drying up. There were Harriers up from Wittering, operating with one of the army reconnaissance teams since the brigadier had considered it too expensive, as well as impolitic, to have Harriers in the air and then not to use them, merely because the police had annexed his men and equipment. Thus the R.A.F. caravan remained firmly the scene of the flotsam of the exercise.

Bracken, after less than fifteen minutes, had begun to accept and employ the temporary godhead invested in him. The feeling of transience disappeared, as did the strangeness of issuing orders to army officers, from a brigadier down to a first lieutenant. Only Maxon, it seemed, had been incapable of accepting him as a temporary superior. Above all, however, it seemed that Maxon could not swallow the army's central role in the operation to recapture Nasoud. Eventually, when

Bracken argued that soldiers were more effective than dogs, he seemed unable to accept more and had excused himself, departing to set up his headquarters in the village of Chedworth, commandeering the village hall for his purposes. He was in direct radio contact with Bracken and the others.

When he had gone, Bracken said, 'I think we might go up in one of your choppers, don't you, Brigadier?'

'Nothing simpler, my boy. But – do you think it's worth it?'

Bracken looked at him, and said, 'I can't hunt a man from inside a caravan.'

The brigadier smiled, nodded sagely, and said, 'Very well. Sergeant, nip across to Major Stanton's hideaway and get him to call me up a chopper pronto. I don't want to take my flying castle up!' The sergeant disappeared.

'Thank you,' Bracken said.

As he turned to the wall map and saw the area shaded in blue, marking the countryside through which the first closing circle had already passed, he heard a high-pitched whine growing outside the caravan.

'Harriers,' the brigadier explained. 'Part of the exercise – the only part left, in fact.' He raised his voice in competition with the noise outside. 'They're bringing in their snaps of the targets they're supposed to destroy. Can't use ammunition in this part of the world – besides, it's not a tactical operation. So, they fly in, take snaps, and bring them here for analysis.'

Bracken looked thoughtful for a moment, and then said, 'Could that photographic equipment be of any use to us?'

'I don't see how . . .' The brigadier adopted a thoughtful look, rubbed his chin and added, 'You can get them to take some snaps, if you wish. But they won't be carrying any super-spy cameras, if that's what you're thinking!'

'Pity.'

'Have a look at them later, if you wish. Might give you an idea or two.'

Bracken nodded. The noise was dying down through the frequency range as the Harriers, safely at touch-down, cut their VTOL jets. Bracken's eyes gazed at the wall map. The ring of blue round the ten-mile circle was thickening. More to himself than to the brigadier, he mumbled, 'Where the devil is he?'

Ten minutes earlier, the Harriers that had touched down at Chedworth had screamed over Nasoud's terrified face at zero feet. The journey along the railway track had taken a long time. The elation of his mind from the edge of the woods to the river soon deserted him, leaving him desperately tired, with legs that constantly threatened to collapse beneath him, and a tearing pain in his ribs. His running had become a limping, halting progress, body bent as he clutched the bruise over his ribs. The mugginess of the evening, too, sapped his energies, evaporating the will at a frightening rate.

When he halted for perhaps the twentieth time, he could see a tunnel less than a hundred yards ahead of him. The tunnel, he realised, offered a hiding place, a shelter from the ground search and that in the air. Time after time, he had thrown himself flat against the bank of the track, pressing his shaking body to the grass, as 'Wasp' helicopters passed overhead. Once he had heard the voices of a foot patrol moving parallel to the railway line. By some miracle, they had not heard his ragged, stifled breathing, had not observed his crucified posture against the bank. When he was sure they had moved away, he had dragged himself upright and forced his weary muscles into the agony of a jog-trot. Then, some minutes earlier, the helicopter activity had ceased, as if the sky had been swept clean of them. He had stopped after another minute's running, stopped to rest within sight of the tunnel, temporarily unable to summon up the vestiges of strength to carry him to its blind, womb-like safety.

Then he had heard the distant roar of the Harriers, an alien, dreaded sound, but not entirely unfamiliar. All at once he was back in the Lebanon, and the Israeli Phantoms were screaming overhead, delivering their horrifying fire-power into the refugee camp – the crowded, stinking, hopeless place that their reconnaissance reports told them contained at least one Palestinian guerrilla unit.

He began to run, his mouth sobbing open, his legs driven by a terror oblivious of pain and weariness. It was no longer a deserted railway line; it was the hard-packed, fouled earth of the camp, and the smells and screams of the place were filling his senses. The tunnel loomed ahead of him, wobbling crazily in his vision. The terrible sound of aircraft at zero feet pursued him, overhauled him. He had to make it – he had to . . .

As he passed into the tunnel, he raised his face. The Harriers screamed over him, passing out of sight. He flung himself to the ground, the hard earth striking him a savage blow, winding him. He waited for the cannon shells, the rockets – but they never came. When he realised he was still alive, he began to cry with relief, oblivious to the noise he was making.

Hilary Latymer rubbed his fingers in pressing circles against his temples. The deep, oppressive twilight of the gathering storm had caused it – the hot, still atmosphere. He had a headache. He was angry with himself, because it was not the time to have a headache, to feel . . . He smiled, in spite of himself – to feel one degree under. He looked at his watch. Seven-twenty. Bracken had made his first report and had sounded optimistic. Latymer refused to consider the probability of success for the manhunt. It simply *had* to succeed. He had begun to doubt whether he could avoid the handing over of Nasoud in exchange for the passengers. He was afraid of Packer, afraid of what the man might do. He was afraid of his lack of information concerning the man. His ignorance was dangerous, potentially fatal. The FBI was dragging its heels in supplying information, despite his repeated requests and pressure from the Home Office – on orders from Washington obviously.

His own men had narrowed the field, were reasonably certain that four of the six hijackers could be pinpointed with the aid of Kennedy International passenger photographs. Packer, Clay – Asif an Arab was an obvious choice, and a girl. And he thought he knew the girl. Joanne Fender, fugitive from justice, the heiress kidnapped two years earlier for a huge ransom, who had been converted by her captors. Since when she was wanted for armed robbery, malicious wounding and drug trafficking. He knew Joanne Fender only too well.

She had been treated for hypertension and depressions for a period of time before her kidnapping. She was an unstable character – dangerous. Packer, too, Latymer was willing to wager, had a psychiatric record. Latymer was afraid to consider what the embracing of a credo of violence and desperation might have done to their unstable personalities.

Which made it all the more vital, he realised, that he should attempt to obtain the release of as many passengers as possible, as soon as possible. There was a bomb on the aircraft, a mechanical, stable thing. He had to deal with Packer – engine and fuel for lives. He had no idea how many he could release for those things; he hoped it was a considerable number.

The storm flashed and thudded across the tarmac before him as he gazed from the window. Vivid streaks of lightning lit up the underbelly of the lowering cloud cover, and the thunder boomed and rattled at the windows of the 'Greenhouse'. It was a meteorological landscape suited to the bizarre events of the day. Mad Packer, wrapped in storm, had come to demand a lunatic justice.

Then he heard Packer's voice over the R/T, fainter, less strident than before above the hissing of the static.

'Hey, man – can you hear me?' Packer sounded dangerously happy, as if the storm fed him, like some laboratory creation in a Gothic novel.

Latymer motioned Seaborne to his side and answered him, 'Yes, Mr Packer, I can hear you. What can I do for you?'

'It's party-time, Latymer – we gonna get you to give us a new engine for this bird!'

'Just what was in my mind, Mr Packer – this is something we shall have to negotiate.'

There was a silence and then Packer's voice, in a break in the interference, sounded preternaturally loud.

'Man – you never give up, do you? You want these good people here to go down the toilet, baby? 'Cause that's what you're asking me to do to them – the big flush!' Then he laughed and Latymer, grimacing as if with physical pain, knew that Packer was high. The man was flying, not merely on the wings of storm like some avenging angel, but on his own storm, the storm in a needle. *That* was factor X, the one he

84

had refused to think about, which hit him now like a wave of nausea. Packer the heroin addict – Packer the superman.

He shook his head, as if to clear it, and said levelly, 'No, Mr Packer, that is not what I want. But you must realise that we have cards in this game as well as you. You need a new engine and a fuel load. We need those people on the aircraft.'

'No, baby!' Packer's voice was venomous, hate-filled. 'You'll get them through the hatches, one at a time, if you try bargaining!'

'We have to talk, Packer – I mean that.'

'We're talking, Latymer – haven't you noticed?'

'Face-to-face – out on the tarmac.'

Packer giggled. 'It's raining, baby – hadn't you noticed?'

'I had noticed. I still want that talk.'

Packer considered the statement, then he said, 'I'll call you. Maybe I will grant you an audience with the President of the World!'

Latymer flicked the intercom switch savagely. His eyes were screwed tight. He banged his hand down on the console. With Packer high on drugs, there was no game left to play. He was beaten. He knew he was beaten.

4: A Confrontation

The voice of the stubby, sandy-haired young Special Branch man whose name was McCarthy rang across the 'Greenhouse'.

'The information from the FBI on Packer is coming over the wireprint now, sir!'

There was a hush, as at the downstroke of a conductor's hand – typewriters stilled, men spoke more softly and with half their attention into telephone mouthpieces. They had studiously ignored Latymer's mood, the sudden noise of despair indicated by his striking his hand on the R/T console. Now, however, they responded to anything that promised a swing of the emotional pendulum.

Latymer looked up, focused on McCarthy, then, as if snapped into a role he had momentarily forgotten, he straightened himself, and said, 'When it's complete, let me have it.' He smiled at Seaborne. 'Let's hope we learn something to our advantage, as the anonymous correspondents have it.' Then he listened, as did Seaborne, to the chatter of men and instruments around them increasing in volume and tempo, absorbed in the rising tension like mariners picking up signals from a failing radio.

'Let's get that list of passengers over here, McCarthy – and the snaps from Kennedy!' Seaborne shouted, and the young man, shirt-sleeved like something from a sub-editors' room, trundled across the room, a sheaf of papers and prints in his hands. Seaborne took them with a nod and McCarthy returned to his vigil at the wireprint. Seaborne scanned the sheets swiftly, while Latymer selected and laid out the photographs of those still unidentified by police on both sides of the Atlantic.

There were more than a dozen photographs, all taken from the same angle by the hidden camera at Kennedy customs, all showing faces whitened and strained by artificial lighting. Latymer pushed the photograph he guessed was of Joanne Fender to one side. Then he selected the photograph of a negro, Clay, who had, according to the N.Y.P.D., a record of violence. Then he studied photographs of three Arabs, selected one, and pushed it to one side – Asif, identified by the Mossad and confirmed by the Dutch Special Branch as a known terrorist. As for the others, they were as yet only suspects – he looked closely at a photograph of a young man with hard eyes and long fair hair. His long forefinger tapped the print. He was prepared to wager that he was staring into Packer's eyes, even though there was no one of that name on the passenger manifest.

Seaborne ended his scrutiny of the passenger list and picked up the photograph of the girl. He smiled without humour and shook his head. 'She didn't used to look this scruffy and underfed at one time,' he observed.

'Quite. Unless I'm mistaken, we have the company of Miss Joanne Fender, daughter of plastics millionaire and Senator Hubert Fender . . . another Patti Hearst, I'm afraid, Clarence.'

'She's wanted by the police all over America – no wonder she travelled under another name.'

'When was it she dropped out of sight?'

'Unsuccessful bank-raid, though she managed to wound two employees of the bank. She was identified from TV pictures taken inside the bank.'

'Mm. You know, I wonder whether her presence might not have influenced our transatlantic cousins to play their part. Eh? After all, we send back her photograph, and they send us, all at once, the delayed information on Packer . . . ?' Latymer was smiling ironically.

Seaborne nodded, and said, 'Does this mean the rest of that gang out there are her new soul-mates, sir?'

'It could be, Clarence – it could be.' He looked across at McCarthy and added, 'Interesting read, McCarthy?' The young man looked up from the sheets he had pulled from the wire-print, flushed and brought them to Latymer.

'Nice sort of chap, by all accounts, sir,' he offered by way of apology. Latymer studied the sheets he had been handed, ignoring the young man.

It seemed a very long time to Seaborne before Latymer looked up again. 'There's a great deal of useful stuff here, Clarence. I think we can echo that wartime motto, "Know your Enemy", now!' Seaborne took the proferred sheets and perused them. He read aloud, in a soft monotone. The activity in the 'Greenhouse' died away again. Seaborne had acquired an audience.

'Packer, Lee Arnold: born 1944, San Diego, California; student of politics at Berkeley, 1963–66; first offences, possession of marijuana, two counts, and anti-war demonstrations on the college campus – the latter involving extensive damage to property; 1966, convicted of felony, breaking into a pharmaceutical warehouse, San Diego County; political associations unknown at this time; 1967, on release from penitentiary, joined religious commune known as "People of the Lord", arrested on suspicion of robbery in 1968, released for lack of evidence; 1969, moved from California to New York, with other members of commune, which by 1971 became known as "Splinters of Light"; two charges of possessing heroin, 1971, 1973; suspicion of armed robbery, 1972; Packer and others of the group disappeared, early 1974; suspect in kidnapping of Joanne Fender, daughter of Senator Hubert Fender, 1974, as part of political extremist group known as the "Army of the Night" – possibly comprising members of the original religious commune; suspicion of armed robbery and narcotics offences, 1974–75; identified as member of gang involved in raid (unsuccessful) on Queen's Branch of the Second National Bank, December 1974 – suspect Fender also identified in same raid; heroin addict.'

Seaborne looked up from the sheets in his hand, and added, 'Busy little bee, isn't he?'

'Quite.' Latymer held out a limp, poor photograph that had been transmitted together with the dossier. He held it alongside the photograph from Kennedy. Both of them were of the same man. 'It was him,' he said, as if to himself, then: 'The "Army of the Night", eh, Clarence? I wonder if that's them out there?'

'Could be, sir.'

'You note the accompanying file on Joanne Fender, which seems to suggest our friends in the FBI have suddenly become a little more interested in the case. Also, you will note that the negro, Clay, is identified as a known associate of Packer, and the man, Rice, who is also among the passengers . . .'

Seaborne held up his hand, as if to stem the flood of information. 'Christ – fancy this little lot calmly boarding a plane at Kennedy International!'

'Quite so, Clarence. Very remiss. It really makes you wonder whether we ought not just to lie down and let ourselves be steamrollered, doesn't it?' He rubbed his chin. 'Hm. The "Army of the Night", is it? I don't suppose Mr packer has read T. E. Lawrence, or he might have echoed his thoughts . . .' He closed his eyes, as if recalling a lesson, and then said, his voice growing stronger as he recalled the quotation: ' "All men dream, but not equally. Those who dream by night in the dusty recesses of their minds wake in the day to find that it was vanity: but the dreamers of the day are dangerous men, for they may act their dream with open eyes, to make it possible . . ." '

He looked clearly into Seaborne's face, and said, 'Find out what you can about this so-called army, would you, Clarence – as quickly as possible? I think we may assume, for the present, that they are precisely who we have squatting on our doorstep at the moment!'

'Sir.'

'And Barbara – get me the Home Secretary on the line, would you? I shall want the classified file on Nasoud.'

'Yes, Mr Latymer.'

Latymer went on staring out of the window, apparently unconcerned, until his secretary tapped him on the elbow and handed him the telephone receiver she was balancing on the palm of one hand.

'Thank you, Barbara.' He took the receiver and sat down on the bench running beneath the observation windows of the 'Greenhouse'. There was no necessity for confidentiality now. Latymer felt that the men working with him in the tower, though they might be unaware of the fact, were his allies in a contest he was waging on two fronts – against the hijackers, and against Whitehall and Downing Street.

'Home Secretary?' he said.

'Latymer – what can I do for you?'

The Home Secretary's first remark, he noted, had not been an enquiry after the progress of the negotiations. Something had been settled. He wondered whether the Lebanese were prepared to take part in the deadly game. A thought struck him, and he said, 'Excuse me, Home Secretary. . . .' He cupped his hand over the mouthpiece and raised his voice: 'Mr Seaborne – ask the FBI whether they have access to any psychiatric reports on Packer and the girl, will you? She must have been to an expensive analyst about something – I want to know whether her trouble goes deeper than depression and hyper-tension!' He smiled in reply to Seaborne's nod and then said, 'Sorry about that, Minister – a matter of detail.'

'Very well. How are things proceeding?'

'We're trying to buy you your time, Home Secretary. I'm afraid it's rather difficult, working in the dark as we are. However, the information we need is slowly becoming available to us. However, what I would like is the confidential report on Nasoud.'

'You already have the report, Latymer.'

'Minister – both you and I know very well that there must be at least one other report, in the hands of the security services – a fuller transcript, shall we say, of the interrogations? I need to see that report.'

'Why?'

'If I'm to buy time, Minister, I need to understand who I'm dealing with – I need to know how much they want Nasoud . . . especially since we don't have him, at the moment.' He added, with an assumed blandness, 'Are the Lebanese prepared to receive their unexpected guests?'

There was a silence at the other end of the line, and then the Home Secretary said, 'We will need as much time as you can gain for us. I'll be honest with you, Latymer. At the moment, they're not prepared to play ball. They do not recognise that the hijackers have any connection with any Arab cause to which they might normally respond favourably.'

'So – the answer is no.'

'At the moment, yes. It would seem that pressure will need to be applied from – a more unofficial source.'

'The P.L.O., you mean?'

'That is in hand.'

'In that case, I need that file. The deadline is midnight. If we don't have Nasoud here then, I want to know whether they're likely to go away without him.'

'Very well. I accept that. The P.M. wants to take a strong line on television this evening. He wishes it to be impressed upon the public that we are standing firm.'

'Even though we may be up to our ears in quicksand?' Latymer replied with a forced lightness.

'What are your chances of gaining more time to allow for the recapture of Nasoud, and for our more – delicate negotiations?'

'I don't know – to be honest. On the surface, poor. We're dealing with a fanatical fringe group here, unless I'm mistaken. On the other hand, it is possible that they may settle for something less than the full price. Might I suggest you decide upon a large sum of money, to be available if all else fails?'

'I'll put it to the Cabinet,' the Home Secretary said after a silence. 'You think that might be the only way?'

'Possibly.'

'Very well. The P.M. would like pictures of the army on duty at Heathrow to be included in the nine-o'clock edition of the news. Just before his broadcast. Would you arrange that?'

Latymer's face was grim as he listened. In Whitehall and Downing Street they were playing politics. As he had already surmised, only for him was the safety of the passengers a real issue. And even for him, he conceded, there was the issue of the capture or death of the hijackers complicating the matter. The international lesson and precedent of Heathrow It was a very great pity.

'I see,' he replied. 'Very well, Minister. I'll call up our special detachment to deploy themselves for the cameras as soon as I have the file.'

'You'll have that file,' the Home Secretary snapped. 'Goodbye, Latymer.'

Latymer put down the telephone and rubbed his hands up and down his cheeks, as if tired. Yes, he would be swimming against the tide if he tried to reverse the tendency evident in the Home Secretary's remarks; the tendency that was becoming universal, with the sole exception of Israel – the placation of terrorists, the surrender to their demands to avoid bloodshed. And was he not assuming the mantle of the divine, in presuming to decide the lives and deaths of seventy-two passengers and a flight crew? It was not a good situation in which to face the challenge of one's life – yet Latymer knew that indeed his challenge lay here. He knew he would attempt the impossible – the rescue of the passengers, the capture of the hijackers. Yet he was afraid of the vigour of his conscience if anything went wrong. And he also suspected that the appointment of the Executive Officer had, indeed, been the appointment of a scapegoat. If anything went wrong – anything – then it would be laid at his door, and he would be dismissed; a commission of enquiry would follow, and there would be no more officials like himself appointed, with the same sweeping powers. So . . . ?

Latymer sighed audibly. He had begun to understand whom and what he had to deal with. He did not think Packer would surrender, or even that he would settle for something less than the price he had asked. Latymer felt himself being forced, inexorably, into a confrontation with the hijackers. It was to be the challenge of his life – and not a challenge he had chosen.

Nasoud had lit a fire in the tunnel, masked from view by the arch of one of the inspection shelters. The tunnel was damp and cold. He had found pieces of coal and broken splinters of old sleepers, and had brought in dry grass and wood from outside. His wet clothing was causing him to shiver, and the only thing that seemed to matter to him, following the realisation that the Harriers overhead had not reduced him to oblivious dust, was his physical comfort. The gas lighter had sputtered in his shaking grasp, the grass had caught with a weak yellow flame, the smoke had stung his throat, raw with the laboured breathing of his flight – then the small heap of combustible material had become a fire. He was that primitive creature, animal-man, in the shelter of his cave, with his precious gift of fire. Slowly, his sodden clothes had dried.

He had cowered instinctively as another aircraft had passed overhead at zero feet, yet, after that, there had been no further sound, except the distant murmur of a helicopter reaching him down the dark whispering tunnel. He had not moved on, yet he understood that the tunnel might well become a trap for him. It was likely that it would be searched more than once. He had no idea whether it had already been searched. Yet it was a womb, a safe dark place, clinking with drops of water from the roof, silent otherwise, except as it magnified his breathing and the little noises of the fire.

His watch, which had survived its baptism in the stream, told him that it was seven-thirty. Darkness, and the comparative safety of the night, lay only a few hours ahead of him. Yet those few hours could not be spent in the tunnel, whatever its illusion of safety. To stay, as he was doing, became every minute less and less like safety, more like stupidity, whereas to go out into the evening light, paradoxically, seemed the safer premise.

His mind had wandered, he realised, idling like the blood in his body after its extremes of release and terror. He was unable to think constructively, despite the need to do so. His brain refused to render things logically in sequence, and he cursed its incapacity. The sense that he did not know where he was – what had they said that town was, away to his left before the crash – Cheltenham, was it? Where was Cheltenham? Between the prison and London. He had no compass, no weapon, no food. He was beginning to feel hungry and food would become an absorbing necessity in the coming hours. He did not want to be hungry.

He thrust the thought aside. It had interrupted his attempt to think logically. This was farming country, there would be isolated buildings in the area, perhaps a source of food and shelter for the night. Further than that, unless he could obtain a compass and a map – even a disguise – from such a source, he could plan only hours, perhaps as little as minutes, ahead.

Yes, he needed to find an isolated farm of some description.

Nasoud did not understand the deepest of his motives here, the unconscious desire for the proximity of other persons, the chance to disguise from himself his isolation, his utter aloneness.

Yes, he thought once again, he would soon have to move on. At that same instant he heard the voice, carried down the tunnel wall as it might have been in some whispering-gallery. It was speaking English. He could hear, in his frozen, hunted attention, each word clearly.

'Take it easy, lads. We don't want a mess all over the floor, so no shooting!'

They had smelt the smoke, heard a cough, found his footprints, his mind screamed. They talked as if they *knew* he was there! The limp, blackened bundle of the fire, its ashes glowing faintly, filled his vision. They would know!

The voices were coming, he decided, from the far end of the tunnel, round a dark corner, coming from the direction in which he had been heading. He could run, back out of the tunnel . . . He realised, almost with surprise, that he was on his feet, crouching, as if to spring or flee. The glow of the fire was very bright. The ashes would still be hot, declaiming his proximity. He sensed, rather than saw, the flash of torchlight flicker across the roof of the tunnel, and heard a throaty voice call out:

'Hey, sarge – don't forget to look in these little archways!'

'You tellin' me my job, Bolton?' the first voice replied.

'No, sarge.'

He could hear, in the strained silence that followed, the clinking of heavy boots on the ground, a whispering echo-wave preceding the soldiers. They were armed soldiers, certainly. He looked down at the fire and did the only thing he could to destroy its heat-evidence. He urinated over the embers. They hissed like a call, a signal.

Pressing his back against the angle of the inspection shelter he saw above him, like a chimney behind a fireplace, a ventilation shaft. With his feet against the far side, he began to hoist himself as if he were climbing a vertical tunnel, using his back and feet to pressure him up and away from the ground.

The pain in his ribs caused him to grind his teeth to prevent himself from crying out. He winced when his head struck the roof of the arch, his breath seeming to explode. He felt the draught of cold air coming from above him and could not believe his fortune. He wriggled and pushed himself into the shaft, out of sight he hoped, and hung there, pressing his face against the grimy, smoke-tainted wall and trying not to breathe. The footsteps were loud now – they were almost upon him and they must have heard his exertions!

There were four soldiers, a sergeant and three privates, all armed with slim, deadly SLRs. Their boots struck sharp echoes from the walls of the tunnel, and the flashlights they carried bounced their weak beams against the roof and walls. Suddenly, as the various footsteps and their echoes came together in a mutter of sound, a voice directly below Nasoud cried:

'Here, sarge! Over here with the light!'

Nasoud choked at the bile in his throat and grabbed back the breath that threatened to explode from his lips.

'What's up, Fraser?'

'Signs of a fire, sarge.'

'What?' The boot-noises flurried across the tunnel, scruffling into silence directly beneath him. He pressed his eyes shut, stilling the capacities of movement, of breathing. The seconds stretched out, interminably.

'Christ – old Hawkeye himself!' the sergeant said. 'What do you make of it, Tonto?'

'He must have been here, sarge,' the voice of Fraser said.

'Jesus – what an effin' deduction!' the voice identified as that of Bolton commented.

'Cut out the funnies – look around. This stuff's still wet ... Does that mean he's long gone, or has he just put it out ... ?'

'Think he heard us, sarge?' Bolton asked.

'He could effin' well hear you lot if you was still at Aldershot, Bolton!'

'Yes, sarge,' Bolton replied without rancour.

'You lot found any other signs of occupation?'

'No, sarge.'

A torch flickered over the ground and ceiling while Nasoud, feeling horribly vulnerable and exposed, like an insect on a pin, an aircraft caught in a searchlight, clung rigidly above the soldiers' heads.

'See anything?'

'No, sarge – nothing here except the makings he used for the fire.'

'Nor here -- no signs of him.'

'Right, you lot. At the double -- keep your eyes peeled and get moving! He must have heard us, or moved on some time ago. Either way, he's gone up the line away from Chedworth. And as soon as we're out of the tunnel, Fraser, call up HQ and make a report!'

'Right-oh, sarge!'

The footsteps clattered away, moving swiftly, the torchlight danced against the walls and roof. Before the sounds died away and while the soldiers were still close, Nasoud, his body beginning to tremble violently in reaction to the pressure on his muscles needed to hold him aloft, dropped noiselessly to the ground.

He lay there for more than a minute, allowing his breathing to become louder, deeper. The noises of the soldiers died away, faded as they left the tunnel. There was a sudden cessation in the whispering evidence of their departure -- they were out in daylight once more. He did not hear Fraser reporting their find in the tunnel.

He got slowly and shakily to his feet, brushing down his filthy clothes, an instinctive movement. The action kept his hands from shaking so much. Then, without warning, he doubled over and was sick, in great rasping, sobbing heaves. The silence when he had finished spitting the bile from the back of his throat was horribly evident. He listened, but heard nothing, no further sound. Then, praying that he was doing the right thing, he began to run down the tunnel, away from the soldiers, in the direction from which they had come.

Philip Bracken chewed on a ham sandwich as he stood before the wall map, its thickening circle of blue cold and stark. In his right hand he held a bottle of beer from which he swigged occasionally. Spencer-Handley had disappeared for a breath of fresh air and the caravan seemed suddenly deserted. The sergeant with the box of pins was an immobile figure to Bracken's left, part of the furniture.

Bracken swallowed noisily, cocked an ear to listen to a mutter of response behind him, detected the negative tone in the corporal's voice and returned his attention to the map. There was nothing to be done. Frustration had lost its edge. Now it was really a job for someone like Seaborne, a plodding, unrewarding, waiting task. Then he heard another voice from the receiver behind him, abnormally loud, he thought, and whirled in anticipation.

'He was here, all right, not long ago . . .'

'Reference 127 054,' the corporal sang out. 'Abandoned railway tunnel, west of Chedworth.'

The spot bulged in Bracken's vision as he turned back to the map. The sergeant was already placing a bulbous-headed pin in the appropriate reference. Less than a mile away!

'Get a couple of choppers over there – at once!' Bracken snapped.

'Sir.' A second corporal snapped a transmit switch and spoke softly, without seeming to hurry, to the neighbouring communications caravan. The 'Wasp' helicopters nearest to the reference were directed to overfly the tunnel, one to the north of it, one to the south. Even before the corporal finished issuing Bracken's instruction, and made his own additions instructing the nearest foot-patrols to proceed to the spot, the door of the caravan opened and the brigadier entered, a sheaf of photographs in his hand. He was followed by a young, dark-haired R.A.F. officer, a Flight Lieutenant.

'Bracken!' he said excitedly, his words overlapping with Bracken's.

'They've picked up a trace, Brigadier . . . ?'

'Better than that, my boy. We've got him on film – the railway tunnel west of here – less than a mile away!'

Spencer-Handley saw the disappointment on the policeman's face and listened to Bracken's explanation, an explanation that was drowned by the noise of a descending Harrier.

The R.A.F. man at his side said, 'Photo-recce Harrier – overflying the target area. Bringing in supposed confirmation of a hit . . .'

'Well, let's have the film as soon as possible!' the brigadier snapped.

'It'll be infra-red film, I'm afraid.'

'Damn! Get it over here, anyway.'

The Flight Lieutenant left. Spencer-Handley pushed the sheaf of prints into Bracken's hands and Bracken rifled through them. Each one of them showed the prone figure of a man at the entrance of the tunnel, his white face staring at the camera, terror frozen on the features.

'What are these?' Bracken asked. 'Why haven't we had photo-surveys of the rest of the area?'

Spencer-Handley looked as if he were about to lose his temper, then said levelly, 'These photographs are from the simulated attack on the tunnel.'

Bracken nodded. 'When were they taken?'

Spencer-Handley looked at the topmost picture and turned it over. The precise time of the attack was scribbled in green felt pen on the reverse.

'Half an hour ago, thereabouts,' he said.

'Half a bloody hour!' Bracken breathed. 'We've just had a patrol report in that they found the tunnel abandoned – he's flown, Brigadier – flown!' He banged a fist on the table between them.

'What have we got in that area, sergeant?' Spencer-Handley asked.

The phlegmatic man beside the map said, 'Apart from the foot-patrols and the choppers already on their way – not very much, sir. It's too close to home to be in range of our closing circle, and we've got most of our criss-crossing stuff further out.'

'Right. Get me Major Anderson on the line, corporal. He's with Captain Cowley in the supply caravan.' He looked at Bracken. 'We'll put a large patrol down at either end of that tunnel and let them fan out from there – suit?'

Bracken nodded.

'Major Anderson on the line, sir.'

Spencer-Handley crossed to the transmitter and issued his orders. He was precise, calm, urgent. When he had finished, it was obvious that he felt relieved. The chase was, for him, drawing to a close. He could scent the man Nasoud and was confident that he could not escape.

'Do you want to hurry the closing circle now?' he said to Bracken.

Bracken shook his head. He could not share the soldier's confidence. Somehow for him, the hunt had become a thing confined to paper. He suspected it was the result of his being confined to the caravan, staring at the map on the wall. Nasoud had lost his reality for Bracken. He was a phantom figure, leaving faint traces of where he had once been – a quarry Bracken would never overtake. Nasoud was doing the impossible, lying low while the complex, multifarious units of the pursuit overlooked him.

The door of the caravan opened and the Flt. Lieutenant returned, a set of prints in his hand, accompanied by Mayhew, the brigadier's ADC.

'Well?' Bracken asked.

'A good job it was infra-red!' the airman exclaimed. 'We've got him – he's still in the tunnel!'

'What?'

Bracken and the brigadier crowded round the sheaf of prints as the Flt. Lieutenant preeningly spilled them on the table, spreading them like a winning hand of cards.

'Look here,' he said. 'This is an infra-red shot of the tunnel – we use infra-red to detect heat emission from any target. It tells us, among other things, what's on fire and what isn't, without having to peer through smoke and dust . . .' He jabbed his finger on a smudge of red near the centre of the picture. 'Railway tunnels are cold except when they've got trains running through them. This one hasn't. Now, that smudge is a heat emission from a ventilation shaft in the tunnel. My guess is your boy lit himself a fire to warm him while he was hiding.'

'Well done, Royston-Jones!' the brigadier exclaimed.

'When – when was this?' Bracken asked in a small voice.

Royston-Jones looked at his watch.

'Ten – eleven minutes ago,' he said.

Bracken turned to the corporal at the receiver, as if to accuse him. Then he exclaimed, 'He was there – he *must* have

99

been there – when that patrol passed through the tunnel!'

'Oh my God,' the brigadier breathed in the sudden silence. Then, while the others stared unbelievingly at each other, he snapped out an order. 'Corporal – get the foot patrol on the blower and turn them around. I want that tunnel searched from end to end!'

'What – what happened?' Bracken asked. He could imagine the wrathful figure of A.C.C. Maxon, smiling in a superior manner. If they had used dogs ... if *only* they had used dogs!

'You mentioned ventilation shafts, Royston-Jones?' the brigadier said quietly.

'Sir?'

'Then that's it! He shinnied up one of them ... could he do it?'

Mayhew filled the silence with his assertion. 'There are shafts built into the sides of the tunnel – they go up from the inspection arches ...'

'Then he's still there!' Bracken cried. 'Christ – he's still there, waiting for the all-clear!'

'Are those choppers down yet, corporal?'

'Yes, sir.'

'Block that tunnel off!' Spencer-Handley snapped. 'I want it sealed up tight – now!'

'Sir.'

The brigadier looked at Bracken and smiled.

'All aboard,' Mayhew said softly. 'We're going for a ride.'

Bracken knelt by the small, sodden heap of twigs and grass that had been Nasoud's pitiful fire. The smell of vomit was strong in his nostrils. He looked up and saw the immobile figure of Sergeant Mills standing close to him.

'I take it this puke wasn't here when you examined these – remains?' he said in an icy tone.

'No, sir,' the sergeant agreed woodenly.

'Then he was here when you said he wasn't?' Bracken's voice was a breathy, cold whisper.

'Yes, sir.'

'And now he isn't here?'

'No, sir.'

They had searched the tunnel, called and threatened at each of the ventilation shafts, without result. From end to end of the cold, curving, disused tunnel, they had drawn a blank. Nasoud had flown. It was no more than a temporary set-back, the brigadier had assured him. Bracken knew that was the case. Yet, in the moment of having the prize snatched from him, reason was insufficient. It failed to pacify the furious cold anger he felt. Mills, as the nearest object in any way culpable, was bearing the brunt of his rage. Bracken stood up, staring at the sergeant, whose features registered a complicity of disappointment, yet more stoically presented.

The anger drained away. It was a stupid, tiring display which drained him of logic.

'I'm sorry, Mills,' he said haltingly.

'So am I, sir. We – didn't know about the air-shafts – thought these little arches were sealed at the top . . . just shelters.' Bracken nodded, and dismissed Mills. He went trotting off down the tunnel to collect his patrol, now designated to board a chopper and be dropped a couple of miles away to the south to work their way back along the disused line.

Spencer-Handley, who had diplomatically allowed Bracken to consort with Mills in private, crossed to his side, and said, 'Hope you weren't too rough on poor old Mills – he's likely to feel it as much as we do.'

'No, brigadier. It wasn't his fault.'

'Look, my boy, it's a matter of minutes, that's all. Judging by the fact that he's just got rid of breakfast and lunch, he can't be in any great shape. Let's get back to the chopper and have a look at the map. I left Mayhew and Anderson sorting the details – let's see what they've come up with, shall we?'

Bracken nodded and they walked side by side down the echoing tunnel, leaving experts to examine the signs of Nasoud's small sojourn. Bracken had already informed Maxon that dogs might now be required and suffered the withering contempt of the A.C.C. Those dogs were now on their way, pulled in from the limits of the second circle whose nearest point was more than eight miles away. Maxon himself, Bracken had allowed, could supervise the tracker search. The roadblocks remained in operation, but house-to-house calls in Cirencester and Cheltenham had been further postponed. Instead, Chedworth would be searched thoroughly.

As they emerged from the tunnel into the soft evening light, the threatened storm having swiftly dispersed, Bracken glanced at the short, confident, almost strutting figure at his side. He envied the brigadier his absolute faith in routines and systems. Now that another stage of the search had been mounted, the brigadier no longer looked as if he had been winded, as he had done when they first drew a blank in the tunnel. He could still retain a confidence in the eventual outcome of the proceedings. Bracken, on the other hand, could not rid himself of a sense of failure. Unlike the brigadier, the multiplicity of arms surrounding him unnerved him. It required only one well-aimed, instinctive shot – and Alison was dead.

He thought about his wife only in the lapses of tension, between rounds. Yet the thoughts insidiously bore the same pattern, ending in her death in an exploding airliner, and they sapped his will, his confidence. He had to make a violent effort to shake them off, as he did as they approached the brigadier's command helicopter.

Mayhew the ADC, and Anderson the Executive Officer, were leaning close to one another over an OS map, a radio-corporal at their side transmitting the complex of instructions they issued. They saluted as the brigadier and Bracken joined them.

'Well, my lads – what have you been doing?' Spencer-Handley asked.

Mayhew, despite his junior rank, answered, a presumption that Anderson did not seem to resent.

'This is the area, sir,' Mayhew said, as Anderson moved to one side to let the brigadier and the policeman close to the folding picnic table on which the map rested. 'Here we are, and here's the airfield, just to the west.' His finger tapped the points on the map. 'Major Anderson and I reckon our boy's been in the water, on the north side of the tunnel, which means the Coln, here . . . that's why he lit the fire.'

'That's possible,' Bracken observed.

'Thanks,' Mayhew said, smiling. 'Now, the track runs south, then south-east about half a mile away, but it runs through Chedworth itself. With all our activity and the police roaring up and down the roads, he'll want to turn away, either back this way, which is unlikely, or to east or west. West it's flat and open, with few trees, let alone a wood, and only one road – while east we've got these two parallel roads, this small wood, Listercombe Bottom, and . . .' Mayhew's voice was light with pleasure . . . 'this little waterway here, which joins the Coln at Fossebridge, on the old A429, about two miles away. That waterway runs out of this cutting we're in now – it's what makes the tunnel so damp!'

'Anthony, my boy – and you, Richard – you're bloody marvellous!' the brigadier exclaimed in genuine pleasure. 'What have you done about it?'

'Ah – we've got the villages staked out and as many of the outlying farms and cottages as possible. Just in case chummy tries to steal a car. We've put men down there, at this end of the stream, and at Fossebridge. There's another group dropping in on Listercombe Bottom, and more working their way up the railway line from south of Chedworth.'

'Choppers?' Bracken asked urgently.

'Overflying these areas, and to the west and south of Chedworth.' Mayhew looked at his C.O., and added with a smile, 'I think we've got him this time, sir – I really think we've got him!'

'So you are Mr Packer?'

Latymer stared consciously at the figure before him, slightly shorter than himself. Packer's face was mobile, bearing at that moment a confidence that was nervous at the edges. His lank fair hair was being lifted by the gusty wind. The storm had died away to a rumbling accompaniment and the flashes of lightning were miles off. Latymer noticed the curiously dilated pupils of Packer's pale eyes, and recognised the signature of his addiction.

They stood under the lee of the wing of the 707, one huge engine-pod looming over them. At the top of the steps where he could keep them in sight, was the negro Clay, apparently oblivious, but watchful and silent. He had a machine-pistol cradled at his hip. Its barrel pointed nonchalantly down at the pair beneath the wing. Latymer's car stood more than a hundred yards away, its driver linked to the tower by radio.

'That's me, man,' Packer replied, smiling. 'And you – you must be the Latymer-man?'

Latymer nodded. He hunched his shoulders slightly in his dark overcoat. The breeze ebbing behind the storm seemed cold. The sky was still a sullen grey and, unless the cloud cover dissipated, darkness would come early. That was something else he had to consider. He realised he was out of condition for this encounter, like an under-trained fighter. There was too much running through his mind, too much clogging the machinery of analysis and deduction. Out there on the tarmac, under the wing of the 707, he felt the urgent demands for safe deliverance of the seventy-two passengers. His resolve that he would engineer a stand-off, breaking the hijackers mentally and morally, no longer possessed any reality.

'Packer – you want an engine and you want fuel – I want lives for those commodities.'

Packer laughed, an obscene braying sound. 'Man – what do you have to offer? I could fade these people, waste them, baby! You got no position from which to bargain.'

'I think I have, Mr Packer. You don't *want* to kill if you don't have to . . . therein lies my bargaining position.' Latymer wondered whether Packer would believe the statement about his reservations. Perhaps Packer did want to kill, to appall . . .

'Don't you bet on it, man!' Packer snarled. He waved the pistol he had been holding at his side. 'This is no candy-bay, Latymer!'

'I am aware of that,' Latymer observed acidly. 'However, whatever *final* arrangement is worked out, you do not want to throw away the advantage of suspense. I don't *know* whether you would kill, or not – at the moment. If you killed, indiscriminately, then you would decide my course of action for me. I would have no alternative but to order the army here and to open fire on the aircraft.'

'Bullshit!'

'You don't believe me? You see, you can't be sure. While

104

the passengers are safe, I am inhibited because I dare not put them at ultimate risk. While you *keep* them safe, you yourselves are safe.' Latymer watched the reactions of Packer in fascination. He willed the man to believe him, willed into his voice sincerity, determination – neither of which he felt. It was as if he were a ventriloquist, wanting Packer to say things he put in his mouth, while he saw himself in the same instant as a ventriloquist's dummy, mouthing the atmosphere of capitulation strengthening in the Home Office and the Cabinet.

'You tryin' to hypnotise me, Latymer-man?' Packer said, frowning, as if suspicious that he was in some way being cheated.

'Not at all, Mr Packer. I merely believe in putting my cards on the table. You are creating something of an historical precedent here – the first armed hijacking at Heathrow. A great deal is at stake for my government, as for you.' He paused, and then said levelly, 'Are you absolute for death, Mr Packer?'

'What?'

'I merely ask whether you are firmly resolved to die?' The gun flickered in Packer's hands, as if he were immediately threatened. 'No – not at this moment. That is what is in the minds of my principals in this affair. They do not necessarily believe that you would carry out your threat against the passengers, and thereby seal your own fate.'

'Jesus!' Packer breathed. 'They don't believe . . .'

'Some of them do not. Others are as certain that you will do as you have threatened.'

'And you, Latymer-man – what do you believe?' Packer sneered.

'I – am not sure. I shall not be the one to decide. I merely tell you as plainly as I can that you have no way out unless this aircraft is refuelled and the engine replaced – whatever you do to the passengers.'

'Where's Nasoud? Why isn't he here?'

'He is here,' Latymer said. 'You will have to take my word for that, however. At the moment, we are not discussing the final trade – merely opening the haggling – lives for paraffin!'

Packer was silent for a time – Latymer relied on the man's

drugged condition, his blurred logicality; he was gambling, playing with the unstable explosive of Packer's heroin-awareness. Going over his words in the silence, Latymer wondered whether he had said too much, whether the tone of his voice had been calculated to a sufficient nicety.

Packer said, 'You reckon we're over a barrel, Latymer-man – but *you* are! Your cupboard's bare, man – the white of your backside is showing through the rags on your ass!'

'I don't think that's quite fair,' Latymer said. 'You are a merchant of oblivion, Mr Packer – but do you wish to buy oblivion for yourself, when the price of petrol is going down?'

Packer grinned savagely. 'Man, I gotta hand it to you – this is the reallest put-on I ever seen!' He laughed again, that harsh braying sound. Latymer's gaze never left his eyes. 'Show me Nasoud!' he snapped.

'I can't,' Latymer said, spreading his arms.

'Why?'

'Your friend has been on hunger-strike – he is being attended by medical experts – he's very weak . . .'

'He's dead!' Packer blurted out.

'He is not dead, Mr Packer, merely very weak!' Latymer snapped.

So far in the conversation he had contented himself with establishing a superiority of words, a baffling complexity of statement and counter-statement to test Packer's intellectual reflexes, to probe his heroin mood. Now he realised he had to take command of the situation, that part, at least, of Packer's mind was undecided, had registered something of his arguments. He had to bear down on the weakening part.

'Listen to me, Packer! You're on a one-way trip to deadsville, unless I see some sign from you that you intend to keep your side of the bargain! By the very nature of this situation, there must be compromises on both sides, if not trust . . . I have no guarantee that you will release the passengers if you are given Nasoud, and you have no idea how far I am prepared to go to checkmate you. Unless you are prepared to trade lives for fuel and a new engine, *and* guarantee the safety of the repair team, I can only recommend that the passengers are as good as dead, and that you and your associates must be captured or eliminated as quickly as possible!'

Latymer's hands trembled at his sides, his face worked with the fury he was simulating. He was at the point of no return – if Packer's sluggish unfocusing mind now jumped the wrong way, then he had opened Pandora's box and the flesh and blood and bone it contained would spill all over the tarmac. He was gambling with seventy-two lives – gambling that Packer was not a lunatic, a psychopath.

The silence seemed to go on for ever. Thunder rumbled distantly, hardly impinging on the awareness of either man. It was as if they inhabited a cone of strained silence, a narrow, whispering cell.

Then Packer said, 'O.K., Latymer-man. I give you a dozen – for a new engine. And another dozen for the paraffin – *and* the guarantee that we can land at Beirut and be allowed to run free from there.' Latymer nodded stiffly, as if he had not intended giving in quite so easily. 'Twelve apostles,' Packer added. 'Each time, twelve apostles . . .'

'Women and children,' Latymer stipulated but Packer shook his head.

'I decide, baby – not you. And don't think this is a home-run, Latymer. No more bargains – no more deals! Understand?'

'I understand only too well, Mr Packer. I am glad we could come to this – settlement.'

'That leaves me with four dozen passengers, the flight crew and the fire officers,' Packer observed.

'I know that,' Latymer said softly.

'If you try anything – *anything* – a passenger comes through that hatch, minus his head – then another and another . . .'

Latymer sensed the returning madness in Packer who possibly felt somehow defeated by the exchange, as if he had backed down. Latymer was aware that two dozen passengers might be all that would walk free from the 707. He glanced up at Clay – the guardian of a tomb.

'I'll get my end of things organised, Mr Packer. Shall we say ten minutes?' Packer nodded. 'Good.'

He turned away and began to walk towards the hunched black shape of his car. He felt no sense of victory, or elation.

The weight of his responsibilities almost crushed him, pressed on his chest like a stone, so that he had to catch at his breath. He knew he had played his last high card. Nausea suddenly gripped at his stomach, twisting like a knife. At midnight he would have to produce Nasoud. And Nasoud was running, still running. . . .

5: Trade

Joanne Fender's face worked with the fury she felt. Her anger was manic, uncontrolled, and she spat and threatened her contempt for Packer and the trade to which he had agreed.

'You stupid bastard!' she railed. 'You should have taken a couple of these pigs outside and blown air through them! Proven to him we mean what we say!'

Packer was angry himself, wanted to quarrel, to vent his anger on someone. Clay and Asif had accepted the trade with calculated foresight. Rice and McGruder didn't count. But the girl, the daughter of Senator Hubert Fender, plastics millionaire, was different. She was everything that Packer had been taught to despise, everything that he loathed and envied and feared. Money, assurance, arrogance. Until the aftermath of her kidnapping, which had been in part designed to establish the identity of the 'Army of the Night' and its finances; after that, she was suddenly no longer the girl they had intended to exchange for a million dollars. Big money had been needed and quickly. Robbery was insufficient – Mr J., into whose sphere of influence the commune had gravitated, had suggested the kidnapping. Kidnap Fender's spoiled brat – ask a million. With a million they could buy guns, or they could buy Horse from Mr J. which would earn them more than their gun money. Mr J., as Packer knew, had intended from the day when he had sent the black sedan to take him to his interview, that the 'Army of the Night' should be a self-sufficient organisation, even though it worked for him.

And then, Packer thought, staring at the dilated pupils, the strained, white face of the girl – then Asif and Clay had converted the spoilt, rich daughter of a corrupt man to become one of the brotherhood. It was the classic conversion, the recent convert providing the catalyst, the booster-shot, for the whole group. Packer resented her taking over – more than that, he resented the body she had given him and which she now refused. He hated Joanne Fender – now more than ever.

'Shut up – shut up!' he yelled, his voice ragged. 'You loud-mouthed bitch! I'm running this picture-show!'

'You couldn't run the town john!' she snapped back. A grin crossed Clay's features while Asif looked merely bored by the temperaments on display; his face betraying, perhaps, the contempt of the professional for the untidy, illogical amateur.

They were in the galley of the first class, a tiny space, while Rice and McGruder covered the two passenger compartments. It was hot, sweaty, and their faces and bodies were pressed together. Joanne Fender, six inches shorter than Packer, confronted him like a dangerous animal, her eyes glaring into his. Packer raised his arm to strike her, and then appeared to think better of it.

'Don't cross me, soul-sister,' he whispered. 'We do this my way – my way, understand?'

'Packer,' the girl said, 'you couldn't terrorise your grand-mother! This whole lousy operation stinks! What in hell's name are we doing here, hour after hour? We should be clear by now. You gave them till midnight, you shit. They *want* time – don't you understand that? They could blow us off the runway any time they like!'

'The army ain't here,' Clay observed.

'Of course it ain't!' Packer added, welcoming Clay's support. He was, though he would never admit it to himself, more than a little afraid of Joanne Fender. It had been her idea, the bank raid, to replace the money they would not get from her father – and she had shot and wounded two bank employees when there was no need. He sometimes wondered at the muddy depths they might have stirred in her nature.

'Hell – just because you don't *see* them!' she snapped. 'You've been taken for a ride, Packer. They get two dozen lives for a lousy engine that doesn't need replacing, and a tank full of gas. What in hell kind of trade is that?'

Packer sensed that he had carried his point, that the girl was now merely venting spite. The support of Clay, and the silent impatience of Asif, had registered upon her. She was too clever, he realised, to go against the majority opinion.

'Just get a dozen people lined up ready to leave!' he said. 'Do it!' He spoke in Clay's direction but the words were for the girl.

'Just you get us out of here, Captain Marvel,' she said, 'or I'll sure as hell blow your head off before they kill me!'

'Can it!' he snarled.

Clay and Asif moved out of the galley. 'Who do you suggest?' Asif called back over the girl's head.

'Second class,' said Packer with a grin. 'Let's give them second class stuff.' Then, as if to placate the furious girl, he added, 'And check around among the first class – find out if we got ourselves any big fish, anyone we can use to make a noise.' He looked at Joanne.

'Now you're beginning to use your substitute for brains,' was all she said.

Packer glanced scornfully at her and then pushed her aside with unnecessary force and joined Clay and Asif in the corridor. He passed through the first class, brushed aside the curtain and stood behind McGruder, looking at the second class passengers. There was an almost palpable atmosphere of weary defeat emanating from the rows of tired, strained faces. They looked as if they had not seen sunlight for a long time; undernourished, sick plants. One or two raised their eyes as he came in. There was no hum of conversation, no mutter of expectancy. There was nothing to expect – except the unthinkable.

Packer was suddenly filled with a loathing for the white, dead faces. These were the people he really hated, this section sliced by circumstances from the body of the system he despised. With a savage glee, he registered, recognised and fed upon their helplessness. He wanted to frighten them. Suddenly their stunned apathy was itself irritating. He wanted to shake them out of their collective stupor, to terrify, to see in their faces a true image of himself.

He bent over a middle-aged, well-upholstered female in one of the front seats, and jabbed the gun painfully into the stiff ribs of her foundation garment, below the over-ample breasts.

The woman's face registered terror – pure, unadulterated. She thought she was going to die and was watching the gun with the whole of her consciousness. Packer pulled back the hammer with this thumb, and the click of the chamber was audible in the silence. He could sense the others, spectators of a distant drama, leaning forward in their seats. There was a small, frightened gasp from the grey-haired, fat woman. He jabbed the gun harder, to make her repeat the sound. Then he allowed his finger to tighten on the trigger, slowly, holding the gun so that she could see the movement. The eye behind the butterfly spectacles widened, stupefied with horror.

Packer did not know whether or not he intended killing the woman. He had never considered the idea. It was the terror of her awareness of death that pleased him – and which probably saved her life. As if unable to sustain the pitch of horror at which she now existed, the woman slumped in her seat in a faint. He watched her face for a moment, then removed the gun from her ribs, as if the game had ended and he would derive no more pleasure from it. Standing up, he addressed the remainder of the passengers, alive to the almost obscene relief he saw on their faces.

'One dozen,' he said. 'The Latymer-man, your personal saviour! I give him a dozen of you and I get a new engine for this bird!' He laughed, luxuriating in the changing, mobile features presented to him. It was like watching a dirty tide sweep across white sand. He saw the selfishness of each look, saw the side-glances, the obscenity of sudden hope on each face. One or two glanced at wives or husbands or children, as if willing that their partners or families be spared. Packer waited, knowing that the tide had a voice. The silence was mounting to a pitch of audibility. It was this he wanted.

Packer had never explained himself in terms of his horrific upbringing in middle America – in terms of the rigid, hypocritical selfishness that had pervaded his home, the distorted self-righteousness of his parents. His father had been a small-time, small-town politician, a corrupt pillar of a corrupt community. He had been a church-goer and a lecher, a philanthropist and a drunk. His mother was a cold stick of a woman, a firebrand of stifling rectitude and good works, and adoration of her husband. His sister, in the small cataclysm that finally opened his eyes, had become pregnant and been exiled, and had dosed herself into oblivion after an horrific abortion. Her lover had been black. As he had made no conscious decision then to ruin himself in order to spite his parents, who had killed his sister, so he made no conscious analysis of his feelings now. Yet he saw, with terrible clarity, the faces of his parents occupying every seat in the compartment.

A man spoke, obscene with grooming and money. He obviously travelled second class to save money. 'A thousand dollars, feller, if you count me in!'

There was a surprised disgusted murmur, the last reaction of communal identity. Packer knew what would follow, and called out, 'You heard the man – I'm bid one thousand dollars for his fat hide! How much are the rest of you worth?' He laughed the braying, cruel laugh.

'Five hundred.' a young man called in a west coast accent.

'I gotta hundred, that's all!' an old man called. 'What about American Express . . . ?' The offer was desperate, ludicrous.

Then the flood-gates burst. The cries came from all corners of the second class, strident, furious, defeated. The reality of their situation had been lost to them; they were in an insane auction, and the only reality was to call out impossible sums of money.

Packer heard one voice in the babble call out. 'Everything, if you'll take my wife . . . !'

Packer turned his gaze and saw an old, grey-haired man with a wispy, shrivelled woman clinging to his arm, shaking her head. The vision seemed unreal, or more real than anything else that was happening. As if the two shrunken figures were an unpalatable truth, Packer ignored them.

'You make me puke!' he roared at the top of his voice. Like beaten animals, they subsided into silence. 'You are the shit of the world, people, you know that? You make me sick to my stomach!' He was standing forward on the balls of his feet, the muscles on his neck standing out like cords. His hands were trembling. 'You wanna buy your way off this bird? You can't – you hear me? You can't – no way! We could strip you down to the bone, people, and you wouldn't say a word, and still keep you here. You'd offer me your wives, your life insurance, anything . . . to walk down that gangway!'

He realised he was patrolling the gangway, berating them, his gun waving. He was feeling what he said, and he was acting at the same time. He was enjoying himself. Some deep need was being satisfied, a need which had nothing to do with his evident power over them. Rather, it had something to do with what he had always felt, always wanted to say – something that had emerged in dropping out of college, emerged in the scheme to kidnap Joanne Fender, emerged in the bank raid, emerged in every occasion when he had helped hook one kid from a good home on H. Every time there was that fierce pleasure, as though his fist had sunk deep into a soft, complacent belly.

'I decide!' he shouted. He looked round him, at the pleading, the desperate, the defeated, the stoical – the old, the middle-aged, the young. He saw a woman who was pregnant and waved his gun at her. 'You!' he snapped, as if ashamed of the motives guiding his choice. 'And you – both of you!' he said to the old man who had tried to bribe him for his wife's sake. 'You,' he said to a negro, and passed down the gangway.

In this way, he assembled a dozen passengers, who tugged their hand luggage from the racks above their seats as if every second that passed might bring a change of mind. His motives in selecting those he had done were not clear to him. He had gazed at the faces with olympian detachment and with true olympian pique what he had seen there had persuaded him. The fat, the well-to-do, the pleading, the angry, were dismissed from his choice.

'What about me, feller?' the fat man with the original offer asked, aggrieved, angry. Packer moved swiftly and struck him across the face with the barrel of the gun. The mutter that was growing in those unselected for life died down as at a command. Packer heard the satisfying crunch as the man's teeth shattered, saw the bubbled blood come from between the full, sagging lips, and knew that he had broken the man's jaw. Flushed, he turned to address the rest of the passengers.

'Any more questions?' he screamed in an unearthly voice, as if crying out at the climax of some bloody ritual. 'Any more of you want the same?' He waved his gun, almost hopping from foot to foot in his orgasmic excitement. There was no reply. The mood of exultation suddenly deserted him. 'Get them out to the steps,' he said to Clay, observing him as a mute witness behind McGruder. Clay nodded and stepped aside to let the first of the dozen passengers move past him into the first class, towards the hatch and the passenger gangway.

Latymer lowered the glasses from his eyes which he rubbed wearily. The trade was complete. He had watched the small troop of passengers straggle across the tarmac to where ambulances and uniformed police waited for them. All the way they had been under the watchful stare of the hijackers' guns. The cameras in the 'Greenhouse' had chattered to a climax since four of the hijackers were visible during the operations of the trade, but it was the impotent chatter of bystanders. They had sufficient pictures of the hijackers to paper the walls of the Home Office.

Now out on the tarmac there was a bright glow beneath the port wing, light splashing garishly against the side of the aircraft from a circle of mounted spotlights. Leads snaked to a humming generator parked near the aircraft. Latymer had watched until the drivers of the generator and the cradle on to which the engine was to be lowered for removal had pulled back from the 707, leaving only the four volunteers, the engineers who would dismantle and replace the giant engine. Guarding them, sitting comfortably on a seat torn from one of the passenger compartments, was the Arab, armed and impassive.

It had been decided that no police officer should be inserted into the repair team. Anyone unqualified would be instantly noticeable. Latymer was not prepared to hand Packer an extra high card, just for the sake of appearing to be doing something.

He had hoped, irrationally, that one of the released passengers would be Alison Bracken. It was as if she had

115

become a separate and noticeable part of the weight he carried on his shoulders. But she had not been among the released dozen. As he shook his head, he realised that Seaborne was at his elbow.

'Report from Disneyland, sir,' he said, holding a sheaf of flimsies towards Latymer. Latymer looked at him quizzically. 'The FBI,' Seaborne explained, allowing himself a small smile. 'Seems that they want to be helpful now – they want us to be helpful, too!'

'Anything we can use?'

'Like to read the revolutionary manifesto of the "Army of the Night", sir?' He held out a photocopied document.

'Manifesto?'

'Yes – full of good stuff. You get points for recognising the sources of the material – Marx and Lenin naturally, Ché, Mao – Debré, I think, Angela Davis, and a little Marcuse . . .'

'A very learned document, then?' Latymer said, relaxing slightly. There was a pressure in him to respond to the temporary lightness of Seaborne's mood as if, as Eliot said, human beings cannot bear very much reality. Humour was an avoidance, but it was also a sedative, which he needed.

'Not very well spelt – or very practical,' Seaborne commented.

Latymer glanced through the sheets, folding them one over the other without removing the paper-clip binding them. It was true, he thought. The document was abominably printed and incredibly illogical. But it was all there; if he needed to depress himself further, he had only to read it carefully. Angrily, he thrust it back into Seaborne's huge hand.

'Mad,' he breathed.

'As hatters. Easy to say, easy to make all those threats.'

'God, Clarence – if they acted out only half of those fantasies . . . !'

'Yes, sir – kaput, the whole bloody show!'

'Mm. However, get one of your department's tame trick-cyclists to look it over. He might be able to tell us something.'

'Right you are.'

'What do the FBI want from us, Clarence?' he asked, sitting

down, carefully adjusting the knife-edged creases in his trousers. He motioned Seaborne to the bench alongside him and the big man lowered himself to a sitting position.

'Well – they want pictures, tapes, analysis – everything we've got.'

'Why the sudden interest?'

Seaborne smiled, and rubbed his chin.

'I think the Narcotics Bureau is applying the pressure, sir.' Latymer raised his eyebrows. 'Yes, sir. They want the supplier back home in the States.'

'The supplier?'

'Yes, sir. Some word must have reached the Bureau that this little gang had appeared en masse in London. They're wanted on umpteen drug counts. At home, they double as pushers as well as revolutionaries. At least, that's the theory.'

'And how might that help us, Clarence?' Latymer rubbed his eyes and yawned. Looking across at Barbara Martindale, he called: 'Rustle us up some coffee, would you, Barbara – one for myself and one for Mr Seaborne.'

'Tea for me, sir – if you don't mind.'

'Sorry, Clarence – my mind's getting as clogged as my throat. Please to continue.'

'They're suspects in the heroin business – at least that. Whether anything the Bureau turns up will be helpful, I have my doubts. They might pull in the Charlie responsible for this little effort, if there is a Mr Big at the back of it . . .'

'There usually is, Clarence. And he is usually discovered far too late to be of help to people like us.' He nodded, and added, 'Give them all the help we can. We might prevent it happening again – we might not. Anything else?'

'The Lebanese are still playing up, sir – according to one of my contacts. Don't want anything to do with this lot.'

'We mustn't blame them for that. However, I suspect that diplomatic pressure will win the day. The ambassador, or one of his senior staff, will be here before midnight, ready to board the plane. What about the Mossad?'

'Ah. They're as keen as mustard to get their hands on Asif – and anything concerning the American end of the operation. I think we might find the Mossad having a very good go at

117

getting their hands on at least one of our chums, should they ever set foot in the Lebanon . . .'

'I trust they won't jump the gun and endanger the flight crew,' Latymer observed. Seaborne stared into his face for a long moment, and then Latymer nodded and added in a low voice, 'I'm afraid there's little doubt about the eventual outcome, Clarence – you understand me, I take it?'

'Sir. Not much choice left is there, sir . . . as long as they can find that slippery little bastard Nasoud before midnight!'

Latymer nodded. Then he straightened his body and said, 'Your marksmen have the Arab in their sights, Clarence?' It was an attempt to convince himself that there were courses still open to him, paths he could take.

'Yes, sir. If he makes a move, any move against the repair team – they'll blow him to bits!'

'Let's hope it doesn't come to that – let's just hope we can be sufficiently cowardly to do what our friends ask of us.' Suddenly, as if possessed by purpose, he stood up. 'Let's have a progress report on our manhunt, shall we?'

He reflected that they had travelled a long road since four that afternoon. Now all that mattered, it seemed, was to have Nasoud at Heathrow by midnight, in fulfilment of the bargain thrust upon them. He sighed, and with some deep instinct, opened his wallet. For a long time, he stared at the ticket he had removed – a ticket for that evening's Promenade Concert at the Albert Hall. Beethoven . . .

As he lay in the shadow of the low hedge, crushing his body to the grass, with the police car on the road guarding the crossroads, Nasoud remembered a moment of the past. The smell of burning flesh was rank in his nostrils and he heard the cries of agony and the roar of the Israeli jets diminishing in the distance, out over the hard blue sea. He was standing, his arms pinned to his sides by restraining friends, his mouth screaming obscenities at them as the girl and the child burned to death in the wooden shack that had caught alight. Halima, with whom he had been living for months, and the child he had come to regard as his own son – they had burned to death. There were tears now, squeezed through the clamped eyelids,

118

and the hands that gripped at the grass shook with recollected impotence and despair.

His watch had shattered when he had tumbled from the ventilation shaft and he had no idea of the time. The evening sun was warm on his back and he guessed that there were, perhaps, two more hours of daylight left. He was hungry and tired, but determined.

He knew now that he had to steal a car if he was to out-distance the pursuit. There was no other way of breaking clear of the landscape of soldiers that surrounded him. He had pressed downstream from the railway cutting for more than a mile before he had been forced to leave the water – there had been soldiers guarding the bridge at the last hamlet, Pancake-hill, and he had heard the barking of dogs. He had seen the soldiers deposited from the helicopter on the edge of the smudge of woodland that was Listercombe Bottom, less than a mile away. He had decided that he had to go north because to the south the downland was bare and treeless and he would be a fly crawling across a map of white paper. There was a road, lined by a low hedge, running north-east from the hamlet whose bridge was closed against him. He would parallel that for as long as he dare.

He had begun to want a weapon of some description. His mood had changed again as he had laboured downstream. It was impossible for his mind to remain in the suspended animation of the flight, to go on behaving instinctively. He was a stranger in a strange landscape, hunted by other men, and he could not help beginning to function again as a human being. Already a perspective of intentions began to unfold in his mind. He would need safety and shelter for the night, and he was prepared to obtain them by any means possible. A farm was what he needed to find, and close to hand – and a weapon, so that he could enforce help, and food, and shelter. . . . A farm would possess at least one vehicle.

Staying in the fields he kept parallel to the road, and when it reached a T-junction, he continued north. Within ten minutes of the junction, he reached a crossroads – and the police car. He had been about to raise his head above the level of the hedge, now thicker so that it masked his crouching run, when he had heard the voice, a voice that chilled him, made him bury his face in the grass and lie there, shivering with the proximity of the hunt. His ears strained to catch the words.

'Seen any sign of him, mate?' he caught as the crimping stutter of nailed boots subsided.

'Nothing doing here, sergeant,' a second voice replied.

'Same with us – bloody chopper dumped us in Listercombe Bottom, and the officer tells us to spread out and cover every bleedin' point of the compass, and keep our eyes skinned!' The soldier sounded disgruntled, tired. 'I tell you, son, you've got it nice and easy here, smoking your way through a packet of fags in your little panda car! We been on "Exercise Stroller" for four days already, without this caper of chasing a bloody wog all over Gloucestershire!'

'He must be important . . .' the policeman offered.

'Too bloody true! You know the army's got nearly a thousand men looking for the little bleeder?'

'Christ!'

Nasoud's left leg was trembling uncontrollably. Had he attempted to run at that moment, he would have fallen. A thousand men! The idea, by its very magnitude, took his breath away and, for a long moment, his will to continue.

'You might well call Him to witness, son,' the soldier observed. 'Bleedin' wog! I'd like to stuff this bayonet right up his jacksee – little bleeder!' The policeman appeared to regard the comment as self-sufficient, and a moment later the soldier added, 'See you, mate. Come on, you lot – and keep your eyes open!'

The noise of army boots scuffling on the gravel road diminished. The sound had, for Nasoud, a strange, distant echo of retreating aircraft engines. He bit his lip in the anguish of the memory. The loneliness that had overwhelmed him at the thought of the dead Halima had been strengthened by the thoughts of the number of his enemies. He was utterly alone.

It was a long time before he could summon up the energy to move, to move along the hedge in a crouching run, heading west for some hundreds of yards before a bend in the road obscured him from the police car. He crossed the road then, and headed north once more. Ahead of him, through eyes rubbed clean of tears, he could see the woods jogging down to meet him, clear of soldiers.

He reached the outlying trees of Chedworth Woods at eight-fifteen.

The Home Secretary was angry. Latymer had taken the call on the private telephone one floor below the 'Greenhouse', in a cramped, windowless office, as his sense of his superior's understanding of diplomatic decencies dictated. Down the wire to Latymer came the whiff of defeat, the subtle pressure to surrender, to agree to the price demanded for the lives of the passengers. The Home Secretary, Latymer realised, was more worried than he cared to admit about the recapture of Nasoud.

'We've cleared the matter of the Lebanese, Latymer,' he said. 'The Foreign Secretary is engaged in talks with Beirut and landing permission should soon be given, together with a guarantee of safe-conduct. His Excellency the Lebanese Ambassador should be with you himself before midnight, when it has been agreed that he should travel on the aircraft.'

'I see,' Latymer said drily. 'You feel this is the course we must adopt, in the circumstances.'

'This is a Cabinet decision, Latymer – one you are not, I presume, going to question . . . ?'

'Of course not, Minister.'

'Good.' The little man seemed placated. The Cabinet, it was obvious, had been unable to swallow the bitter pill of the sacrifice of a number of passengers in order to defy the hijackers. They were prepared to surrender to Packer. There was, after all, an election in the offing, and an election had had the effect of over-developing the humanity of the political attitude.

'What will the P.M. be saying in his speech tonight?' Latymer asked wearily. Now that the decision was no longer his, he resented the surrender of the Cabinet, even though it was based on his own analysis of the people with whom they had to deal.

'He will emphasise the humane considerations, Latymer –

the very real threat to life in this case. He will explain the Cabinet's decision by drawing a vivid parallel with Munich, the fiasco of the rescue-attempt there. . . . We cannot allow the same thing to happen again!' The minister ended with an angry little note in his voice, as if he were anticipating a reaction by Latymer.

However, in a level tone, Latymer said, 'I understand, Minister. It is the easier way out of the dilemma – also, perhaps, the only way short of slaughter!'

'You agree, then? There's nothing else to be done?'

'No, Home Secretary, I don't think there's anything else to be done. I – think we might have saved a number of lives if we had rushed the aircraft, but we would have undoubtedly lost some, if not a great many. And, of course, there is the question of the bomb . . .'

'Indeed. Were it not for the bomb . . .'

'Yes, of course, Minister. I think the bomb is too powerful an argument for us to counter.'

'At least you have absolutely guaranteed the safety of two dozen passengers, and the P.M. wishes me to congratulate you there . . . he will, of course, mention that fact in the broadcast.'

'Thank you, Minister.'

'It was a hard bargain – perhaps the best we could hope for?'

'Perhaps, Minister.'

'Very well, Latymer. All that remains is to get those people off that aircraft – it must not leave with a single passenger on board!'

'Naturally, Minister. As soon as Nasoud has been recaptured, I shall request another meeting with the man Packer.'

'Yes, indeed – *when* he is recaptured. You have less than four hours, Latymer, and only one of those with reasonable daylight. We shall, of course, have a sum of money standing by, in the event that . . .'

'Goodbye, Minister,' Latymer said abruptly and put down the receiver.

As he stretched and yawned, he cursorily examined his own feelings. He had been right, though self-critical, to recommend that the bargain be struck, the placing of Nasoud into the terrorists' hands go ahead. The sight of Packer's mad eyes, the reports of the released passengers about their treatment, and Packer's manic behaviour towards the man whose jaw was broken. . . . The evidence had crowded his awareness, demanded his attention. He could not take the monumental risk with four dozen lives that an attack would create.

As he left the room, shoulders bowed, he wondered whether he would be able to secure the release of the remaining passengers, even if the man Nasoud were available for trade. He decided not to think about it at all, for the present.

The sun was low in the west, streaming across a green and golden landscape. Nasoud lay on his stomach on the edge of Compton Grove, more than three miles due north of the village of Chedworth, the nerve-centre of the search. He was on the eastern border of the wedge-shaped belt of trees; the stream had narrowed until it threatened to peter out directly below him in the narrow neck of the valley. He had made good time. It was considerably less than an hour, he reckoned, since he had crouched at the crossroads. He had jog-trotted along a footpath which bordered Chedworth Woods, following the River Coln until it branched away due north of the woods and then he had descended the narrow bottleneck of the valley to follow it towards its source. The sight of Compton Grove above him had seemed to emphasise the weariness of his limbs, and the emptiness of his stomach. He sensed rather than knew that he had circled back upon himself in a great loop, and at one point had been within half a mile of the old railway track as it turned south.

There had been relatively little ground activity. Once he had spotted a foot patrol, climbing up the railway towards Chedworth Woods, but an increase of pace had carried him across their path before they spotted him. The helicopter activity had been more pronounced, as though they were disturbed insects, frightened and angry with woodsmoke. The trees had sheltered him, the gloom just within the out-liers of the woods providing a screen, a mask for his movements.

He had begun to feel a curious elation, a sense of superiority over his pursuers – the idea of a thousand men engaged in the hunt for him had worked subtly upon him, so that each successive moment he remained free was some kind of victory for him. He ought to stand no chance whatsoever of escape – yet here he was, well to the north of his last reported position, and still free. He had begun to be lulled into hope.

As his breathing calmed and the grin of exertion on his face settled into a smile of satisfaction, he saw them. Black spots against darkening green or rich gold, moving across the fields in a great looping semicircle. Frantically, the adrenalin pumping through his system under the sledge-hammer impact of the shock, he began to count them. A dozen, two dozen, three . . . perhaps more that he could not see. A cold part of his mind described the pattern of search they were obeying – a closing circle. Soldiers, each one armed, he did not doubt. One section of the arc had passed through the hamlet of Compton Abdale that Nasoud could see a mile away to the north-east, dropping a search party that even now struggled to catch up with the snake-like, sidewinding approach of the main body of men.

He knew that he was beaten – his whole outraged system told him he was beaten. He could not move, the paralysis of the rabbit watching the serpentine approach of the enemy flooded his limbs. Already men were crossing the stream, splashing through the shallow water and mounting the side of the shallow valley towards the wood.

Most of the huge arc was now out of sight, but his mind concentrated on the half-dozen men who would pass closest to him. They were less than twenty yards apart. The hugeness of the search now gave him no satisfaction.

Swiftly, as if stung into movement or as if his paralysed limbs had discovered the power of movement for the first time, he crawled backwards through the long grass beneath the trees, into the gloom of the wood. The men were less than a couple of hundred yards away, but now the slope obscured them. He searched frantically round for a hiding-place, some earth to which he might run – anywhere.

He spotted a decaying hollow oak and his first impulse was to run towards it. Then he realised his stupidity – it was too obvious to be overlooked by a professional hunter. Despair trembled at the edge of his mind, poised to hammer its way in. He looked at the ground around him – he had left no tracks. Should he try to outdistance his pursuers, keep ahead of them? His body revolted against the idea, reminding him of its weariness. No. He could only hope for cover. . . .

He heard the chatter of a radio device, the calm order of the search. That, more than anything, caused him to panic. It maddened him, caused him to feel anger, impotent fury. He was unarmed. In a last moment before despair froze his limbs completely, he wriggled headlong under a canopy of low bushes, thick, hard to penetrate. He tugged and heaved himself into the centre of the small thicket, every crack and grumble of wood and leaf loud in his ears. Then, not daring to breathe, his cotton jacket caught in half-a-dozen places, he waited.

He heard the crunch of boots growing louder, the whisper of a walkie-talkie, the snapped orders, the halts and progressions of the search. Noises buzzed round him like flies, as if the whole arc he had seen at first were concentrated on the thicket in which he lay. He was an animal again. His emergence into humanity had been crushed out of him by the proximity of his danger. There was nothing he could do but wait, lying with heaving flanks, head crushed against damp, dank-smelling earth, a twig scratching at his cheek. He waited.

He heard the soldiers search the tree, heard footsteps, regular, unhurried, come towards the thicket. Then a voice spoke, almost in his ear.

'Shall I wade through this lot, corp?'

Nasoud stilled the heaving body, froze in his prone position.

'And get your battledress torn to pieces, Furlong? Don't be so bloody soft! It's what you've got that knife on the end of your gun for – poke it around in there a bit!'

Nasoud, unable to prevent himself, looked up through the tangle of branches. He heard something slither through the thicket, stab down again and again, an unseen horror. As if by some sympathetic magic, the pain in his ribs stabbed through him, a pain he had forgotten, so much a part of him had it become. For a moment, the knife was grey and sharp, inches from his face, and he bit his lip; then it was gone, withdrawn. It stabbed again, near his side, then beside his leg – and was gone.

'Nothing here, corp!' he heard the voice call, preternaturally loud.

'Right you are – move on, you lot!'

Nasoud counted the steps of the retreating soldier. He imagined he could hear his footsteps clearly above the general mutter of retreating boots. Then, for a long time, there was silence, and the evening cries of birds spilled back into the great bowl of silence. He noticed the salt taste of blood in his mouth where he had bitten his lip. He grinned at his fear – it had gone away, walking beside the soldiers, his gift to them. He began to struggle back through the thicket, found that he could turn himself with an effort, and picked his cotton jacket away from the restraining twigs and thorns.

He emerged on hands and knees – and a pair of highly-polished boots filled his vision. There were legs clad in combat dress above them, and then the rest of the body. But this was obscured, thrown into an impossible background by the slim barrel of the SLR, the bayonet fixed, glinting. He quashed a grotesque desire to giggle, and his mood transformed instantly into swelling despair.

'Right-oh, sunshine – on your feet. Nice and easy now. Softly, softly, that's the ticket,' the voice of the soldier called Furlong said.

6: The Runner Pauses

Nasoud looked up into the shadowy face of the soldier called Furlong, and saw in the gloom the glint of his eyes, the fierce smile of the white teeth. Furlong was a short, stocky man with wide shoulders and a composed, balanced stance. Nasoud knew that he was beaten. With the SLR cradled in the crook of his arm, the finger of the right hand touching the trigger, Furlong reached for the pocket R/T clipped to his tunic.

Furlong had sensed rather than seen the presence of Nasoud in the thicket. He had called his all clear to the N.C.O. in charge of the unit, and then silently signalled his intention of staying behind. The others, unbelieving but cooperative, had moved off as noisily as was realistic and he had remained, eyes strained in the gloom. He felt that he had probably made an error and that his only reward would be laughter of the N.C.O. until he had seen the bushes move. He had waited until the struggling form of the Arab had emerged at his feet. The rest was simple. All he had to do now was summon his unit and they would take over the scared form on the ground in front of him. He looked a push-over, as if Furlong's presence had knocked the breath from him. Even as Furlong's eyes moved to the R/T to which he bent his head, Nasoud's head hit him in the groin with an agonising pain. He doubled over, falling backwards with the impact of the bow. He held limply on to the SLR, felt it tugged from his hand.

Nasoud had done the only thing possible, the instinctive, animal thing. Furlong's groin. He had driven his head in under the guard of the rifle, lifting it, neck muscles tight, bunched, in a desperate attempt to disable the armed soldier. It had worked. The rifle had not discharged. Furlong fell away from him and he grabbed for the barrel of the gun, avoiding the bayonet, tugging it out and away from the soldier's right hand with a vicious twist. Furlong rolled on his side, his hands grasping at his groin, his face twisted in agony.

Nasoud stood over the limp, rocking form, and realized what he had to do. Suddenly, all the emotions of the past minutes, perhaps all the emotions of the hours since the crash, welled up in him and, ignoring the bayonet and still holding the rifle by its slim barrel and by the stock, he drove it against the face that whitely turned up to him in the gloom. There was a sickening cracking noise, like the breaking of dry twigs, and then the gun butt came down again and again, until there was no sound but a dull, feeble squashing as of ripe fruit being trodden.

He turned away from what he had done, without looking at the mess that had once been Furlong's face, and carefully wiped the stock in the long grass. Then he removed the bayonet and put it in his pocket, but it bulged, ripped the cloth and he threw it down. He did not need it, he thought. He felt the comfort of the stock against his hip, the neatness and fit of the finger that curled inside the trigger-guard. He would not need the bayonet. He purposely avoided looking at the motionless shape in the ground. The man must have been winded from the initial attack. He had moaned through split teeth just once, and then had died mute.

The wood was silent, the trees losing their sharp outlines with the approach of night and becoming a comforting world of huge shadows. There was no sound. Then he heard a tinny, distant voice.

'Furlong – come on, son. It's no go. Catch up with the platoon, will you.'

Wildly, Nasoud looked down at the form on the ground. The voice was coming from the tiny R/T still clipped to the camouflage blouse.

'Furlong – Furlong! Where the hell are you, Furlong?' Nasoud turned the gun again and brought it down on the blouse. There was a cracking of metal, and then silence again. Nasoud knew he had to move, to run. Now the patrol would know that something was wrong.

He stooped to the still form, and fumbled in the combat

dress pockets until he found the spare clips of ammunition. He inspected them, then, with a satisfied nod, he slipped them into his own pockets. His actions were neat, economical, unfussy. It was an action he had performed many times before, taking spare ammunition from dead comrades, dead enemies. In the moments since his violent death, Furlong had lost all the human reality he ever possessed. Methodically and still without hurry, Nasoud checked the SLR, discovered the live round up the spout and nodded again.

Then, the gun level at his hip, he turned to the spot in the trees from whence the patrol would emerge. They had been moving south. He knew that, for the moment, he was outside the vast circle of the search – that, to the north, there would be no one. And now he possessed a gun and this cut him off from the small regrets he had had in not surrendering at the cross-roads. Now, there could be no surrender. With the gun nestled to him, he was a soldier again; simply that. In a war that remained undeclared, in foreign terrain, but nevertheless, a soldier.

Bending low, he began to run. The pain in his ribs surfaced again, nagging at him, making breathing a painful act. The exertion of bringing the rifle-butt down with that force, so many times, had caused that. With his left hand clutching at his ribs, he entered the thicker growth of trees.

Within ten minutes, he was on the northern edge of the woods and the ground sloped away beneath him into a darkened hollow. He reckoned that the land flattened out to the north and west. Then he saw what he wanted to see: lights, blooming yellow below him, the lights of a single building. He guessed they must belong to a farmhouse, and saw in the light a promise of food and shelter. He could go to earth. With the gun he could enforce aid, where before he would have needed to steal. A farm also meant vehicles, a car that would enable him to put distance between himself and the now-enraged pursuit, the greatest possible distance in the shortest possible time.

He had heard no sounds of the pursuit behind him. The great circle that had been closing in on him would now have to reorganize, change its shape. The pursuit had once more become slow-moving, unwieldy. No doubt they had found the body of Furlong and realised that his rifle was missing. That, in itself, would inspire caution and, consequently, stealth and slowness in any pursuit.

He debated the prospect of the farm coolly. Without doubt, it would attract professional searchers. It could be the one blind-alley in this whole stretch of open country. In which case, he decided, he need not stay. The car the farmer undoubtedly possessed would take him far away, as far as ... where was that town, Cheltenham, that had been just below the port wing, just before the crash? West? North-west? The farm might possess a map ...

He accepted the risks involved. The farm was too tempting to ignore. The lights seemed to glow with an additional warmth, and he shrugged his shoulders and began to pick his way carefully down the tussocky slope towards the warm yellow smudge.

'Brigadier – I realise what the death of this man must mean to you, but I must stress that it now becomes a matter of the utmost priority that the "No shooting" order be reiterated!'

Brigadier Spencer-Handley was a very angry man. His face was suffused with rage though his voice, when he had spoken to Bracken, had been little more than an intense whisper. He stood face-to-face with him in the garish lighting of the caravan, before the huge map on the wall where a black-headed pin marked the spot of Furlong's extinction. The only sign, apart from his colour, that the brigadier was engaged in a struggle to control his feelings came from the knotted, clenched hands at his sides. Bracken, too, was angry – almost as angry as he would have been had a policeman been killed. Yet he sensed a new mood among the staff officers in the caravan. This had been an exercise, a war-game. It had been the civilian, the outsider, who had introduced the reality of death. For that, Bracken realised, Anderson, Stanton, Mayhew and the others would not forgive him.

Bracken was also angry with the dead man, even as he felt a deep pity for the manner of his death. The man had been, in the words of the advertisement, a professional, and yet he had let himself be taken by a weary, unarmed, desperate man. It should never have happened.

After a long silence, the brigadier said, 'Very well, Bracken, I'll reinforce that order!'

'Thank you, sir,' Bracken said. The relief in his voice was evident to the company. None of them knew about Alison, and they thought that his decision that Nasoud must be taken alive was an unselfish one. It was only when her image appeared in his mind, in the aftermath of relief, did he wonder how much special pleading there had been. The last conversation he had held with Latymer, over an hour before, had encouraged the growth of hope. It had appeared that Latymer was coming gradually to the view that the exchange should take place. Alison might, after all, be safe. If only Nasoud had not killed that soldier; he must not get himself shot in turn by another soldier too eager for revenge.

Bracken was suddenly assailed by nerves. He realised that the next hours would allow him no moment of confidence or rest, not until the man was taken. And that taking now presented distinct problems. It seemed the most difficult task he had ever had to face in his whole career – the capture of an armed man one dare not hit. It was, he saw, the situation at Heathrow in microcosm. All it lacked was . . . hostages. If Nasoud obtained hostages, then it was a stand-off and everything could be poised to slide down the drain.

He crossed to the map.

'These farms,' he said, his finger stabbing the map to the north and west of Compton Grove. 'I want them guarded!'

'Why so?' The brigadier wandered over to the map, his colour back to normal, his professional detachment reasserting itself.

'He must be running this way – outside the circle.'

'Agreed.'

'Then these farms have lights showing now. They offer him warmth, shelter, food and hostages. . . .'

'God – you're right, my boy! I'll get choppers and patrols over there as quick as I can.'

'Put a call through to the A.C.C., would you, and warn him to keep his road-patrols on the move, and to intensify . . .'

Bracken's words were sufficiently loud to carry to the radio-man, who acknowledged the order. Maxon had established his own H.Q. in the village hall in Chedworth itself, his only link with Bracken being via the radio. However, Bracken knew he would not disobey a direct request.

Bracken listened to the chatter flowing from the operators, and then said: 'This farm here – Stonefield, is it?' He strained forward to read the fine print of the map. 'Yes. It's the nearest to where ... The road from Withington runs less than a mile from it. Maxon should have patrols on that road.' He raised his voice. 'Request the A.C.C. to send a couple of cars to that farm and to get dogs on it, spreading out to the south-east of the farm ... And tell him the men must be armed!'

'Sir.'

Bracken knew that Maxon had armed a member of each car patrol as an extra precaution, and because Bracken had asked him specifically not to do so. Now, however, he was glad of the man's bloody-minded foresight.

'No shooting. Just warn the farmer, and leave a couple of men at the farm.'

'Sir.'

The brigadier finished his calculations.

'Four farms within half-an-hour of Compton Grove, on foot,' he observed. 'I'll get men set down at each of them and place a guard overnight.'

'We've got less than three hours.' Bracken muttered. 'All drivers in the area – I want them warned not to stop for any-thing – anything! Let Maxon do that.'

'Luckily the traffic's fairly light after dark,' the brigadier remarked.

'Luckily.'

'You'll need to report to Latymer, I presume?'

Bracken nodded. 'He may have to stall for time,' he said. 'Worse luck.'

'Damnable luck. How dangerous do you consider this fellow is, now that he's armed?'

'Very. An extreme danger to anyone in the area of those farms – your troops, the farmers and their families, motorists – anyone. He's got a gun now, he'll be feeling ten feet tall, invincible, by comparison with his earlier state of mind. Besides which, he is a soldier in an underground army.' He shook his head and looked down at the brigadier. 'I'm very sorry, sir. It could be very bloody for some of your men.'

'Quite. Look, I'll get some mobile searchlights into the area. Anything to give him an impression of the size and resources of the enemy – eh?'

'Yes. He's got to be frightened again – badly, and soon!'

'He's a lucky bastard,' Spencer-Handley muttered. 'I must confess to believing in luck, my boy. I wonder just how lucky he's going to be?'

'God only knows,' Bracken replied. 'I just hope we come in for a share of it – and the luck we need right now is to get to that farm' – he stabbed at the map with his forefinger – 'before he does!'

Nasoud had, in fact, reached Stonefield Farm as Bracken's first order was being transmitted to A.C.C. Maxon. Even as his finger pressed against the wall map and his thoughts reached out towards the name on the map, Nasoud was standing in the huge, low-ceilinged, beamed kitchen of the seventeenth-century farmhouse. The gun was cradled at his hip and his back was against the wall as he watched the family grouped around the wooden table in the centre of the room.

The door swung open, obscuring him from the person entering, and the cowman, reeking of the byre and the warm sweet smell of the evening milking, paused on the threshold, struck by the anxious, stupefied faces of the farmer, his wife and daughter.

'Come in, George,' the farmer said levelly. The cowman moved into the room. The door slammed violently behind him and he turned to find the barrel of the SLR levelled at his stomach. Slowly, as he registered the scene before him and examined the swarthy face, his mouth dropped open.

The farmer said: 'Don't do anything silly, George. Just come and sit down. Where's Ian?'

'He – he's gone 'ome for his supper, boss,' the cowman replied, his eyes gaping at the gun.

'Good, then he won't come back up here tonight. Sit down,

George!' He barked out the last words as he saw the cowman's fists bunch against his sides, saw the body straighten and become rigid with tension. 'Sit yourself down, George.'

The cowman nodded and lumped his way to the table, his head turned so that he never lost sight of the gun in Nasoud's hands.

'That's an army gun, ain't it?' he said, tugging a chair away from the table and collapsing heavily into it.

'Yes,' the farmer replied. 'God knows what happened to the poor beggar carryin' it!' He paused, then said, 'This is the chap Marge heard about on the radio, the cause of all them helicopters and soldiers . . . escaped from Dartmoor. Crashed in that plane over in Withington Woods this afternoon.' To each part of his explanation, the cowman slowly nodded. He was a big, burly man, in his thirties.

'What does 'e want?' he asked.

'Food!' Nasoud snapped, his foreign accent thick to the ears of his captives. 'You have a car?'

The farmer nodded.

'If we give you food, and the car . . . you'll leave us?'

'Perhaps. You . . . !' The gun waggled towards the farmer's wife, steadied, and Nasoud added, 'You have food – get it!'

She looked at her husband.

'Bill . . . ?'

'Do what he says, Marge.'

She stood up, irresolute, frightened. Nasoud said, 'The child – send her over here to stand by me – now!'

Orrell, fear in his eyes for the first time since the initial shock of Nasoud's entry, after the howl of the dog had become a piercing whine dying into silence, looked at his daughter.

'No!' he said through gritted teeth.

'You will do so!' Nasoud cried. The gun was pointing at Orrell's chest. 'I will not harm you, any of you – this is a precaution for your good behaviour.'

'The child's terrified, man – can't you see that?' Orrell barked. 'For God's sake, leave her alone!'

'You, girl – stand up!' He waved the gun at the shrinking form of the girl, a wispy blonde of twelve or thirteen. The

134

girl stood up, her whole body trembling visibly. Orrell made as if to rise from his chair. 'Stay where you are!' Then Nasoud spoke to the girl. 'Come here, or I shall shoot your father.'

There was a gasp from the immobile figure of Marjorie Orrell, and then the girl sidled across to Nasoud and cowered trembling against the wall at his side. 'Good! That is better. Now, woman, get me food.'

'You do as he says, Marge,' Orrell said. Then, to his daughter: 'Betty. Don't you be frightened, girl. Just stand still and don't do anything silly.'

The girl looked at him with large, saucer-like eyes, wide with terror and said, 'Patch . . . ?' in a choked voice.

'Patch is dead, my love,' Orrell said very gently, calmly, a simple statement of fact. When he transferred his gaze to Nasoud, the Arab clearly saw the hatred in his eyes. There was the same fierce, impotent smouldering in the slow cowman's eyes.

Marjorie Orrell moved like a plump, nervous animal about the kitchen, slicing a great white loaf, gathering cheese and pickles on a huge plate. When she had finished, Nasoud ordered her to place it on the table. Then he motioned the woman, Orrell and the cowman away from the table, so that they sat lined against the wall in the upright chairs. Then Betty, silent and tearful, and he sat at the table. Carefully, his eyes never wavering from the farmer's stony gaze, he laid the SLR on the table and blindly picked up a lump of bread and a hunk of cheese, and began to eat like a starved animal.

Marjorie had told Orrell when he had come in from the forty-acre field about the news of the plane crash, but he had taken little notice. Withington Woods was a good three miles or more away. Even as the evening wore on and he had seen from the seat of the tractor the great line of black dots crossing his land, and had realised that they were soldiers and therefore engaged in some kind of search of the area, apart from anger at troops moving through his unharvested fields, he had not felt that those events had anything to do with him. It had looked very much like a storm was brewing and he had the remainder of the harvesting, with only Ian to help him.

Now, however, he sat under the naked bulb in his own kitchen and stared at the man, the Arab terrorist, as he devoured the bread and cheese. Marjorie, unsolicited, had drawn him a mug of beer from the small barrel in the outhouse and placed it on the table. She was frightened, but acted as if, given time and a great deal of concentration, the vision before her would go away. She would be worried about Betty, he thought, but she would be incapable of believing that anything fatal could happen to any of them. George – George would do as he was told, despite the death of the dog.

It was that that marked the incident for Orrell. The dog had barked suddenly, furiously, while they were at supper and he had cocked an ear, expecting to hear the approach of some vehicle. Then the barking had turned into a hostile howl, then a broken-backed whine dying into silence. The dog had been despatched by the Arab as if he had no right to life. Orrell suspected that he alone realised that all their lives were in terrible danger.

Nasoud watched the three adults carefully. The woman, making small, fussing movements in her chair, he discounted. The cowman's hate was evident on his face, but Nasoud possessed the superiority of the armed man and he didn't take the countryman seriously. The farmer, however, was an altogether different matter. His hatred was slow, like a burning fuse, and calculating. He was the father of the whimpering child and Nasoud recollected his own hysterical attempts to rescue the woman and child from the burning shanty in the refugee camp. He realised he might well have to kill the farmer.

He did not wish to harm these people. The food in his belly and the warm glow induced by the alcohol made him feel, however desperate his situation, a certain sense of well-being. It would be difficult to kill any of them in cold blood, so totally unlike the despatching of Furlong when the soldier had had the gun and he had been unarmed.

As he swallowed the last of the beer and wiped his lips, he heard the sounds of a helicopter approaching. Swiftly, he lifted the gun from the table, forestalling any movements on the part of the three people opposite him, all of whom had turned their eyes to the ceiling.

'You better get out, mister...' Orrell said, a note of infuriating triumph in his voice.

Nasoud glowered at him. 'Shut up!' he snapped.

'They're looking for you.' Orrell said, driving home his point, seizing the only weapon to hand, that of fear.

Nasoud got to his feet, the chair crashing over behind him. He roughly caught hold of the girl's arm and grinned at the hunching of the farmer's body, the little gasp and the hand in front of the mouth of the woman, as if she had indigestion. George watched him stolidly, and Nasoud saw the strong hands that only the sight of the gun stilled.

'It's landing,' Orrell said. 'You better run, mister!'

'Shut up! Take me – you, take me upstairs!' he ordered. He pointed the gun at Marjorie and tugged the girl to his left side, the gun against his right hip. 'I will kill the girl if you betray me,' he warned. 'Now, take me – tell them you have not seen me, to go away – or the girl dies!'

George towered to his feet and loomed over the Arab. The gun pointed at the bottom button of his old, stained waistcoat.

'No, George,' Orrell said, holding his arm. 'Leave it. Marjorie, take him upstairs.' He nodded. 'All right, mister – I'll do what you ask!'

Latymer was talking over a transatlantic telephone link with the Californian psychiatrist who had treated Joanne Fender. He had already had an unsuccessful conversation with Senator Hubert Fender, the plastics millionaire, which had led to threats and cajolings, a whimpering self-pity, and a bludgeoning refusal to be responsible for the sort of human being his daughter had become. Latymer had put down the receiver with a heavy hand at the end of the conversation.

Now the cool, detached voice of the analyst was confirming his worst fears. Listening, Latymer heard sentence of execution being passed upon the passengers.

'You can blame her father for most of it,' the analyst was saying. 'When she was kidnapped, she was on the verge of a

137

nervous breakdown. I was spending a great deal of my time seeing her, trying to persuade her into a sanatorium. . . . She had spent years of her growing life watching him build his empire, and destroy his own wife . . .'

'In what way, destroy, might I ask, doctor?' Latymer interrupted sharply.

'His wife was a weak woman, a gentle woman. She was chosen because she would be an ornament to Fender. She came from an old eastern family, and he was a nobody with money from the mid-west . . .'

'Good God – does that sort of thing still go on in the United States?' Latymer exclaimed.

'I'm afraid it does, Mr Latymer – a lot. Fender is the classic self-made man – a bully, a cheat and a liar. His wife just disappeared into an alcoholic haze under the weight of his personality. Joanne was like her mother, and yet also like her father. She despised him for what he was and what he did, yet she couldn't help despising her mother for being weak, for not fighting back, or leaving him. Result, tensions which she could not overcome, and which she could not resolve, without psychiatric help.'

'I see. And now – what is she like now?'

'Hard to say, Mr Latymer. I haven't examined her since she – she went over the hill and joined the fun people.'

'But – your educated guess, doctor?'

'My guess would be – dangerous. She's polarised everything, I should say. Life has become simple – what was so complex before it was making her ill, has now become simple. To hate is simple. She hates everyone, and everything. Most of all, the wilful streak – if I can call it that – has assumed paranoid proportions. Say no to her, and you sign your life away . . . or the lives of your passengers.'

There was a short silence and then the analyst added, 'That's only my guess, of course, based on what you've told me, and what the FBI has shown me in her dossier. I could be wrong.'

'Would you advise me to play with the lives of four dozen passengers on the basis of your being wrong, doctor?'

There was a silence, and then the man at the other end of the line said, 'No, I wouldn't advise that, Mr Latymer.'

Latymer rubbed his forehead. 'Thank you, doctor,' and he put down the receiver without another word. He seemed fascinated by the thin film of perspiration on his finger-tips and rubbed at his forehead again. Then he looked up at Barbara Martindale who was putting down one of the extensions. Seaborne had already replaced the other.

'Well?' he said, trying to smile. 'Rather a dismal catalogue, I'm afraid – wouldn't you say?'

Seaborne sniffed and nodded. He had returned from interviewing the released passengers in time to hear the psychiatrist. First-hand accounts of the atmosphere inside the 707 had darkened his mood – the psychiatrist's words had increased his sense of foreboding. His heavy brows were contracted with concern.

Barbara patted his hand gently. 'There's really nothing else you can do, is there?' she said.

Suddenly her tone angered him, or perhaps only released the anger and impotence he already felt. It was as if she had closed the door of the cell. He shook her hand away and said, his face suffused with anger, 'For God's sake, Barbara! This isn't some noble tragic situation in which our hero is discovered at the beginning of act five suffering from a poignant indecision!'

He turned towards the window, looking out into the darkness, at the bright, splashed spot of light round the aircraft. The repair-crew, it had been reported, were close to finishing their job. The old engine had been rushed away for expert examination, and the second dolley had trundled out under the wing with the replacement.

'It's about six lunatics who are holding guns on innocent people and who hold all the cards in this game, damn them! It's about dirt, and violence, and death – a real and tawdry tragedy of our times, as contemporary as communal fornication!' He turned back to the girl and saw the hurt expression on her face. His mood softened. 'I'm sorry, Barbara – turn the radio up, would you, there's a good girl.'

She nodded, sniffed, and got up from her seat. The activity in the tower had died down, so that only a skeleton crew remained at the teleprinters, the radios and the telephone lines. They had collected, sifted, collated, until the brute matter had stared them factually, unavoidably, in the face. There was nowhere to go, no answer available.

The joyous climax of Beethoven's seventh symphony swelled in the room. The music caught his attention instantly, as music always did. Seaborne scowled, as though he felt Latymer were being somehow irreverent. Latymer clasped his hands behind his head and leaned back on the bench, his head touching the cool glass.

There was a music-filled silence for a long time, and then Latymer said, 'Do you have any hopes of a successful conclusion to our voyage, Clarence? Do you think our day will end like the music – in joy?' His voice sounded distant, bitter and dry, like something speaking from a sepulchre.

'Beg pardon?' said Seaborne, bemused by the figurative phrasing.

'Sorry, Clarence,' Latymer said, a thin smile on his lips. 'I was merely enquiring as to whether you had a miracle up your sleeve.'

'I don't think so, sir,' the policeman replied, his irritation at the futility of Latymer's question evident.

Latymer smiled and said, as the symphony ended and the applause thundered through the 'Greenhouse', 'Will they applaud us as fervently, Clarence, when those people walk off the aircraft, and we allow the hijackers to run free?'

'Probably, sir. For a day or so – then they'll get more critical, asking why we didn't adopt a firmer line. Then, by the end of the week, they'll all have forgotten it!'

Latymer's eyes widened.

'Clarence – you're a cynic,' he said.

'No, sir – just being realistic,' he replied. Latymer looked at the dogged form of the policeman as he rubbed a hand through the sandy, greying hair that would not lie flat on his head. The Chief Superintendent was a hard man, he realised. Unlike himself, Seaborne was a natural rat-catcher. He was a man to whom the political niceties of any given situation would matter little. If he could save the passengers on the 707 by any means in his power, he would seize the opportunity with both hands.

140

'What does Directive 316 tell us to do now, Clarence?' he asked.

Seaborne wrinkled his nose, rubbed his chin and said, 'It's a metaphysical half-hour you'd be looking for, is it, sir?'

'I disappoint you, Clarence?'

'Not really, sir. You've done all you can . . .'

'But it isn't sufficient, you privately consider?' Latymer realised that he was looking at Seaborne intently, as if prompting him to utter some leading statement.

'Well, sir – they're going to get away with it, aren't they?' he burst out. 'Then every bugger with a grievance is going to be able to knock us over with a bladder on a stick! Hands up, England!' He snorted loudly, expressing his contempt for the whole situation.

'I didn't realise you were a hawk, Clarence,' Latymer said softly.

'I'm not, sir. It's just that – in a time of hawks, how does the dove get a look-in?'

There was a long silence, and then Latymer said, 'We have extracted the maximum from our bargain, Clarence. Unfortunately, the safety of the passengers is our first consideration – and must be so.'

'I accept that, sir. That's what makes it such a bloody cock-up from the very beginning! We're in the fight with our hands tied from the moment the bell rings!'

There was another silence. Latymer steepled his long fingers and placed them under his chin. He seemed to be looking at a spot on the ceiling, just above Seaborne's head. Then, softly, he said, 'Have we saved those passengers, Clarence – really saved them, I mean?'

'Beg pardon, sir?'

'If we recapture Nasoud and hand him over – can we be sure that we will recover our four dozen souls, not to mention the flight-crew and the other personnel. Will we?'

'Christ! You don't think there's a chance that they won't hand them over when we give them the Sheik of Araby, do you?' Seaborne's huge jaw jutted out and his eyes glared at Latymer.

'What do *you* make the odds in our favour?'

Seaborne thought, and then said, 'In most hijacking cases, the hostages have walked out free, as long as the demands have been met in full. In some cases, like that banana republic job last year, all the hijackers ended up with was wanting to be let go free – leaving the demanded political prisoners and the million dollars behind!' He spread his hands. 'It's in the nature of the game – they have to fulfil their side of their bargains, or the next hijacking doesn't work – their credibility's gone down the drain.' He looked up at Latymer, and his eyes were suddenly bleak. 'In this case, I don't know, sir,' he ended.

Latymer motioned Seaborne to sit beside him. He wrapped his hands round his knees and leaned over, as if he were going to be ill. He stared at his highly-polished shoes for a moment, then said:

'We've broken down each and every hijacking over the past five years, Clarence – wherever it's happened. We've looked for patterns, for methods of prevention and limitation. We've looked for psychological types. Most of all, we've looked for a bargain, a method of getting lives on the cheap.' Seaborne nodded in agreement. 'This one is different – you must know it, as I know it. There is too much – too much *violence* involved already. The treatment of the passengers and the crew has differed from the classic pattern. Even the Israeli athletes at Munich were not physically ill-treated prior to their murder. No – hijackers tend to be like collectors. They keep their valuables in mint condition, up to the moment of their release . . .' He looked sideways at Seaborne. 'You agree?'

'It would seem to be the case, sir.'

'It *is* the case, man!' Latymer snapped, an excitement beginning in his eyes, as if he were infatuated with his own argument. 'Now, all hijackers have a disregard for human life, often for their own lives – especially the kamikaze units the Arabs have hired on occasion. But to them, hostages are not *lives*, they're *property*, valuable property. That makes them special – it protects them. Now, you heard the passengers you spoke to – they were horrified!'

'True.' Seaborne seemed reluctant to follow Latymer's line of reasoning.

'So – in this case, the lives of the passengers do not appear to be especially valuable to our hijackers. A man had his jaw broken because he wanted to live. Packer selected the passengers to be released on no rational grounds whatsoever, especially not those of cupidity. Purely random – it did not matter who lives, who dies.' He paused, then added, 'Do you see where I'm leading, Clarence?'

'Yes – and no, sir. What do you think is going to happen? As soon as they get Nasoud, then the passengers will become an encumbrance. They'll want to get rid of them, won't they?'

'Perhaps. But what if they retain them, as an extra insurance? If they fly them to the Lebanon, what happens then?'

'They release them in Beirut – surely?'

'And how many of them will there be by that time? How many? Three dozen, two – twelve . . .?'

'No!' Seaborne shouted. 'I can't agree with you, Mr Latymer! It couldn't happen like that.'

There was a silence, and then Latymer said, 'I hope not, Clarence. I hope to God it couldn't. But do you really believe that we're going to watch those people walk away from there, free and unharmed? Do you?'

'Y – yes, sir – I do!'

'Nevertheless, Clarence – I want you to draw up a plan of action to be put into operation in conjunction with the refuelling of the aircraft. You will assume, for the moment, that we are going to rush the aircraft!'

Latymer looked round the room. Every face registered signs of weariness still, but he had removed the routine and boredom from each one. There was a new, humming tension in the 'Greenhouse', a poised nervousness and suspicion. Latymer saw Barbara Martindale's face as her eyes swivelled to the window. There was a look of appalled horror on it. With an effort, he avoided looking out of the windows, and crossed the room to turn off the radio.

Nasoud was crouched at the bedroom window, looking down into the farmyard, the shivering form of Betty crushed against him, his hand over her mouth. The scene below him was like something from a garish nightmare. The helicopter stood in

143

the middle of the yard, illuminated brightly, starkly, by the headlights of the police cars parked in a semicircle along the walls of the yard. He could feel the form of the girl, skinny, breastless, shuddering against him, and knew that his own body was suffering an ague of fear. The SLR, held upright, butt against the floor, seemed as ineffectual as a stick against the numbers below him. There were four police cars, and the helicopter. Some of the policemen were armed with rifles, he saw, though as yet they wore them over their shoulders, and clutched the straps in their fists. They were, he guessed, ordered not to open fire except in the utmost emergency. That was on his side, at least, though he did not doubt that his life was in the most extreme danger from the moment he showed himself.

They had discovered the dead dog within moments. They had grouped loosely around it, and then knocked on the door of the farmhouse. Nasoud was angry that Orrell, the farmer, had not opened the door as soon as the chopper had landed, which would have been natural, innocent.

Nasoud cocked his head on one side, pressing his ear against the bottom of the glass. Though he could not catch the drift of the questions, except in snatches, he realised that the farmer was speaking loudly, as if to assure him that his answers were innocent, were not betraying him.

Orrell explained away the death of the dog – yes, he had heard the news, and the noises the dog had made – he had ordered his wife not to go outside, and they had sat, frightened, silent, until they had heard the noise of the helicopter.

Bracken studied the face of the farmer in the white lights of the cars. He had felt an initial thankfulness that these people had not been harmed; that, though frightened, they seemed to have been ignored by Nasoud. The dog had been killed very recently, he knew. Nasoud had been there, that was certain. Perhaps it had been the noise of the approaching helicopter that had frightened him off. In which case the impulse that had made him commandeer a chopper, drag Spencer-Handley with him into the night, had been a right one. Had they waited for Maxon's patrol cars to arrive, it might have been too late. Nasoud would have, undoubtedly, forced his way in and would now have had Orrell, his wife, and the cowman as his hostages.

'And you are sure the man could not have entered the house without your knowing it?' he said.

The man seemed reluctant to allow them inside, but Bracken assumed that it was the effect of the death of the dog, and the sudden arrival of the army and the police in his backyard.

'No way,' Orrell said eagerly. 'No, he's not inside here – he could be in the barn, though.'

'It's being searched at the moment,' Bracken said. 'Along with the byres, and the outbuildings.' He saw that the man was pale-faced, plainly frightened, and added, 'There's no need to worry, Mr Orrell – we'll be leaving a guard here overnight.'

'No! I mean – we don't need one. I got my gun . . .' Orrell realised that he had sounded too eager to have the police and the army gone from the farm. He lowered his gaze as Bracken spoke.

'I'm sorry, Mr Orrell – it's your welfare we're interested in, not your ability with a shotgun.' Bracken's voice was stiff with anger – this farmer seemed to object to his presence. He assumed the man was incapable of appreciating the danger he had so narrowly avoided. 'This man is a known terrorist, Mr Orrell. He is armed, and very dangerous. I must leave at least two men here overnight!'

'I see – all right, then,' Orrell said, with what Bracken considered to be very poor grace. Uppermost in Orrell's mind was the thought that Nasoud was trapped and lurid images of his attempt to break out, using Betty or Marge as a shield, terrified him.

The brigadier crossed the farmyard from the direction of the barn and, as he joined them, said, 'No sign of him, Bracken. The bird has flown, I'm afraid.'

Bracken turned to him, obviously disappointed. 'In that case, we'll leave your corporal and two other men here overnight. He could be out there somewhere, just waiting for us to disappear.'

'Agreed. Look, I'll get as many men into the area as I can, and have them spread out. Meanwhile, you get these dogs casting around for a scent. Reports are coming in that the other farms are clear for the moment, and are now guarded. He's in open country now, which won't help him.'

'What about lights?'

'They're on their way, my boy. Not too much use, I'm afraid, except as frighteners.'

'Still, we must use what we've got.' He looked thoughtfully back to Orrell. 'Stay inside tonight, Mr Orrell, you and your wife – whatever happens. Your cowman lives in?'

'He eats with us – got a cottage . . .'

'Can you put him up for tonight?'

'Yes.'

'Do so, then. And if you could feed and water the brigadier's men, we'd be obliged.'

'Yes, of course,' Orrell said dully.

'No need to worry, Mr Orrell,' Bracken said encouragingly. 'You'll be quite safe now. Good night to you, then.' He nodded and turned away with the brigadier.

Nasoud heard the detective calling his orders, watched the withdrawal of the cars and the lift-off of the chopper, with profound relief. He had not been betrayed by Orrell. There would be no false heroics and no reason to kill – for the moment. As his eyes adjusted to the renewed darkness of the farmyard, he picked out the figures below him – tall, straight figures, armed, patrolling the open space, the boundary wall. Soldiers! They had left a guard behind, a guard that cut him off from the car in the barn. Three armed men stood between him and freedom. He was trapped in the farmhouse.

7: *Past and* Present

Nasoud waited for twenty minutes, crouched motionless against the wall, his face lifted to peer out of the window, until cramp was biting at his thighs and calves, and he groaned when he first moved. Betty, held in the crook of his arm all that time, seemed to have subsided into a stillness, silent and watchful. The moon was not yet up and the sky, though clear and star-filled, shed no light in the room and little on the yard below.

He released his grip on the girl and she sat herself on the bed, a hunched shape, rubbing her arms and legs to rid herself of cramp and cold. Nasoud watched her, then turned away again to the window. He had analysed the movements and positions of the soldiers. None of them expected danger from the house; their faces were constantly turned towards the silent, black countryside beyond the farmyard. If he moved against them, he would have the terrible advantage of surprise.

Cradling the SLR, he stretched his legs across the floor and pondered his situation. He needed the car. He had heard the noises of helicopters passing low over the house and he could see, in the bright arena of his mind, the silent, cork-faced figures dropping from the open doors of the machines, into the pasture and the unharvested corn. The fields would be filled with troops, all of whom would be driven by the memory that he had killed one of their number, that he was armed and dangerous. Once more, the thought crossed his mind that a stray shot, whatever the orders to the contrary, might well signal his sudden demise.

For the moment he was safe. He had been fed, even though the cheese and pickles were now giving him indigestion pains, and he had rested. The pain in his ribs had subsided. In the safe dark, he felt a certain confidence, even though he knew

147

it was the confidence of ignorance, of inaction. It would not be very long before at least one of the soldiers took advantage of the warmth and comfort of the farmhouse, and when that happened he did not have any illusions as to the farmer's ability to act as if nothing was wrong. And unless he kept the child with him, then he was as good as dead.

He shrugged the cramp from his shoulders and turned his gaze into the room. In the dark, he could see the form of Betty, still motionless on the edge of the bed, a statue. He had no real desire to hurt the child and he wondered, indeed, whether he possessed the capacity.

This meant, he realised, that he would have to move soon. Before moonrise. He did not know when that was but he assumed it could not be more than a couple of hours away. In the dark, he might choose one of two ways of escape – he could steal across country, as he had been doing since the crash, or he could take the farmer's car and try to outrun the troops and the road-patrols that would be waiting for him. It would be a suicidal attempt, but his hours in the open, the isolated, slow movement of the day now past, tempted him to snatch at the speed and the cover of the car. The car, at least, would be an unexpected means of escape. He could ask the farmer for a map. . . .

Nasoud no longer thought directly and solely in terms of London. A town, any town – Cheltenham, perhaps – would suffice. He could dump the car, if he got that far with it, steal another and then find a motorway that would take him swiftly well away from the area of the search.

The thought of the dark fields, the crouching run, the frequent halts and hiding, were unpleasant to him. That and the constant danger of the stray shot, and the wearing, destructive sense of always being within a ring of hunters sapped the will. No, he would not go on foot, he would use the car. Which meant, he thought – yes, it meant taking the girl. He looked at Betty, whose face was still turned from him, as if she were engaged in pretending that he wasn't there at all. He sighed audibly but the noise brought no reaction from the child. It was a pity, he thought. Yet he was a soldier in a war without civilians. The Israelis, with American weapons

148

and British support, killed women and children indiscriminately in their punitive raids in the Lebanon. Thus he reasoned himself into a state of mind in which he could kill, and kill again – his mind ascended to a high place, where it looked down dispassionately on the ant-like dots of other people far below.

Yet he needed a disguise if he were to reach the garage without revealing his presence to the soldiers outside. He would need the farmer's assistance for the journey across the yard. Then would come the starting of the car and the attempt to drive out. How would he accomplish that? What excuse might there be for anyone to leave the farm? If he acted swiftly, he realised, he could manage it. He would have to assume the identity of the slow-witted cowman, that stupid oaf with the burning hate in his eyes. George – that was the name. He could be returning to his cottage, even though it was not supposed to be permitted, according to the detective who had spoken to Orrell. Yes, it was a desperate move, but it might work.

He heard footsteps on the stairs and then on the landing outside the bedroom door. When Orrell entered, he found the SLR levelled at his stomach. Swiftly he assessed his daughter's situation and then turned to Nasoud.

'When you leaving?' he said, his voice acknowledging his impotence.

'There are soldiers outside,' Nasoud replied flatly. 'You made that detective suspicious?'

'No – he's done it for our safety!' Orrell's cynical snort was audible in the room. 'Worse luck!'

'Then I am trapped . . .' Nasoud said, playing on the desperate anxiety of the farmer.

'You can't stay 'ere!' Orrell was at his wit's end. Nasoud seemed to plan on remaining. Nasoud felt no pity for the farmer's terror. He despised those he could frighten.

'Why not? You will tell the soldiers, perhaps?' Nasoud laughed softly, an unpleasant, exulting sound.

'For God's sake, man – get out of here and leave us alone!' Orrell begged, moving closer to Nasoud, seeming oblivious of the SLR. Nasoud, leaning forward even as he sat on the floor,

149

prodded the farmer in the pit of the stomach with the barrel.

'You are eager for death, my friend?' he asked softly. He almost wished that the man before him had been George, stupid, big George, who would have taken no notice of the gun until it had blown a scorching, tearing hole through his guts. Nasoud prodded Orrell again, harder, and the man stepped backwards and tumbled into a sitting position on the edge of the bed. Betty stirred and silently wrapped her arms around her father. He pressed her close to him and sat regarding Nasoud. Nasoud could feel the hatred emanating from him, crackling like static electricity in the room.

'Get out – please.' Orrell breathed.

'I shall go soon,' Nasoud replied, 'but only with your help.'

'Anything . . .'

'How many soldiers are there?'

'Three.'

'No more?'

'I can check.'

'Your car is in the barn?'

'Yes.'

Orrell's answers were dull, mechanical, his voice as level as he could make it. Yet hope flared unreasonably in him, as if he could already see the tail-lights of the car winking their way down the rutted track towards the road.

'What car is it – is it new?'

'Rover – powerful. One year old.'

'Good.'

'You – you'll leave us be? All you want is the car?'

'You must do more than that to earn your freedom!'

'What?' Orrell's voice was lifeless.

'I must have a disguise, to fool the soldiers. You must explain that I am George, the stupid one . . . I am going to my cottage. You can do that?'

'Yes.' Orrell was relieved. He had feared . . .

'I must take the girl . . .'

'No!' Orrell came up off the bed, made one step across the gap of floorboard between them, and came face to face with Nasoud's grin and the tiny, visible hole in the end of the barrel. He stopped. 'No . . .' he repeated pleadingly.

'I must have a guarantee . . .' Nasoud began, as if trying to temper the shock, explain. Then he added, 'The girl goes with me – she will be safe!'

Orrell sank back on to the bed, cradling the child in his arms again, as if daring Nasoud to take her. He said, 'You bastard! You sodding bastard! Doesn't *any* life mean anything to you?'

Nasoud wanted to say yes, to explain to him about the girl and the child in the camp, tell him that there was a human being inside him, that everything else was a mask. All he said was, '*My* life – that is what matters to me.' He thought for a moment about taking the girl openly. It might have advantages – then he realised that it was less safe than a disguise, a secret departure, if such were possible. The girl would be a burden, he realised, as the hunt closed in.

He did not admit his doubts to Orrell. The girl would be useful in securing the farmer's help, at least.

'Have they seen the stupid George?' he said.

'No.'

'Lucky for you – and for them. We will go downstairs now, and you will find me an old coat and hat, and then we shall walk calmly across the yard to your car. You will explain to the soldiers that I have some domestic animals to attend to, or some such story as that. Then you will drive the car out of the yard – when we are well away from the farm, you will get out . . .'

'You're taking me – leavin' Betty?' Orrell said, incredulous. He could not believe what the Arab was saying. He experienced a moment of utter selflessness. He did not care about his own safety, not at that moment.

Nasoud realised that the child was the more potent weapon as a hostage, and also the person least likely to make any attempt against him. Yet the child's presence would arouse the suspicions of the soldiers. What should he do? Orrell would consider it possible to overpower him, even with the rifle – Orrell would demand so much of his attention during the drive. Orrell could drive the car, he had that advantage . . .

His mind full of conflicting decisions, Nasoud followed Betty and her father down the narrow, steep staircase and passed behind them into the kitchen. The wife got to her feet and Betty left the shelter of her father's arms for those of her mother. George the cowman appeared not to have left his seat, rooted to it since Nasoud had gone upstairs. His head lifted balefully as Nasoud entered the kitchen, but his hands remained dangling limply from his lap. His eyes watched the gun, as if still not comprehending the threat it posed, and then his gaze returned to the stone floor.

'Get me a coat and hat,' Nasoud demanded.

'What's going on, Bill?' the wife asked.

'Nothin' to worry about, Marge. He's going now. I have to drive him down to George's cottage, then I'll be back. Now, don't fret yourself, old woman, I shan't be long.' He opened a closet in the wall and rummaged among garments Nasoud could see hanging from pegs. Then he brought out a stained, weather-beaten mackintosh and a crumpled, shapeless felt hat. 'Here you are,' he said, handing them to the Arab.

Nasoud motioned him against the wall, and then struggled into the coat without loosening his hold on the gun. The four people watched him, the strange presence disturbing the familiar calm of their kitchen. Then he put on the hat, which was too big for him.

'Very well, open the door.' He looked round him. 'You understand that if anything happens to alert the soldiers, I shall kill this man?' He saw by their faces that they believed him, and nodded in satisfaction. 'You will remain here until he returns!'

He held the SLR rigidly at his side and motioned Orrell through the open door. Yellow light spilled on the stones of the yard and a breath of cool air entered the kitchen. He straightened himself, checked that the gun was invisible at his side, and then followed Orrell outside.

He blinked and tried to adjust to night-vision so he could pick out the three soldiers. He heard one of them call, saw the form black against the stars.

'Halt!' the soldier called. There was the scraping of nailed boots and the steps of two men towards them. 'Who is it?'

'Me,' Orrell said.

'Please remain indoors, Mr Orrell,' the corporal said, reaching them. He was a tall man and seemed to Nasoud to tower over him.

Orrell said, 'It's my cowman, George.' He waved his hand at his side. 'He's got to get down to feed his dogs, let them out for a breather . . .'

'Sorry, Mr Orrell, can't be done. My orders are to make sure you all stay indoors. Sorry, George,' he added with a smile. 'The dogs'll have to wet the floor tonight!' He laughed good-naturedly, without really looking in Nasoud's direction.

Nasoud could see all three soldiers clearly now, outlined against the stars. One of them was less than ten yards away behind the corporal, and the third one was over by the low wall, thirty yards away. He remained still, sensing Orrell's determination to persuade the soldier.

'Come on, corporal – turn a blind eye. That chap's probably a couple of miles away by now!' Orrell tried unconvincingly to laugh.

'No can do,' the corporal replied, his voice firm. 'Now, please go inside, Mr Orrell, and take George with you. And perhaps you could ask your good lady to rustle up three cups of tea for us?'

The corporal was still smiling when Nasoud stepped from behind Orrell and pointed the SLR in his direction. Slowly the smile disappeared from his face. The whiteness of his teeth vanished as his mouth closed to a grim line. He stared into Nasoud's face, his own gun at his side angled down to the ground.

'O.K., corp?' the soldier behind him called, breaking the thin cord of tension that represented the N.C.O.'s life. Nasoud's gun roared and the corporal was flung away from him, as if by a giant wind. Nasoud dropped to one knee and fired across the sprawled, untidy body in the dirt, and the soldier who had caused the corporal's death by his call seemed to duck to one side, then stagger and collapse very slowly, groaning and clutching his stomach.

When Nasoud turned in the direction of the third soldier, he could no longer see him. He guessed that the man had dropped to one knee, so that he was no longer skylined. He, on the other hand, would be visible as a dark stain against the whitewashed wall of the farmhouse. Bending double, he dashed across the white backcloth of the wall, a hunched, speeding shape. Three shots puckered at the wall, whined away into the darkness, but he kept running to where Orrell, regardless of violent death occurring before his eyes, was tugging open the doors of the barn. At any cost, Nasoud had to be aided in his escape, had to be got away from the vicinity of his family.

A splinter of wood lifted from the door with the plashing impact of a fourth bullet and Nasoud could clearly hear, above the storm of his breathing, the soldier, still invisible to him, calling on his R/T for assistance. Orrell stood beside the car like a grotesque and helpless imitation of a salesman, holding the door open. Nasoud, threatening with the gun, shoved him into the driving-seat. Orrell did not pause to argue the point, fished in his pocket for the key and, at the same time, tugged out the choke.

The engine fired at the second attempt and there was a squeal of tyres as the saloon backed out of the barn and into the night. One bullet, the shot silent because of the roar of the three-and-a-half litre engine, screamed off the bonnet, and another shattered a portion of the windscreen, digging into the fabric of the back seat. Then Nasoud saw the soldier in the headlights, standing up, drawing a bead. Orrell, as if a willing accomplice, dragged the steering-wheel over and the car slewed towards the shocked soldier. He dived out of its path and Orrell changed direction again and was out through the gates, and the car was heaving down the track, headlights ablaze. Two more bullets sang overhead, unheard by the men in the car, and then the soldier turned his full attention to the task of reporting the escape.

'You were very sensible,' Nasoud choked out, as the car bucked its way down the track at more than forty.

'Fuck you!' Orrell spat, his hands gripping the wheel, sweat and fear paling his features. 'I got to get you away from my wife and kiddy – you bloody murdering bastard!'

Nasoud, feeling free, at least for the moment, felt the return of an emotion not unlike that first elation, when he had run from the wood to the stream. He laughed aloud.

'You almost killed the third one by yourself!' he said.

'I'd like to kill you, you bastard!' Orrell replied through clenched teeth.

'Drive the car – that will require all your attention for the moment,' Nasoud ordered.

He turned in his seat and saw nothing from the direction of the farm, and then rolled down the window. He stuck his head into the rushing gulf of air, listening for the note of helicopter engines. He could hear nothing, but the silence beyond the wind and roar of their passage did not comfort him. He quartered as much of the night sky as he could see and then realised that anything trailing him would be flying without navigation lights.

'Lights!' he snapped, pulling his head in. 'Put the lights out!' He wound up the window.

Orrell obeyed him and they drove on in a new darkness, the farmer straining to pick up the faint whiteness of the track.

'They'll be waiting for you where the track meets the road,' Orrell said, confirming Nasoud's worst fear. He had been unable to silence all three soldiers. He had had to kill again, but he had not done it successfully. One of the three had lived to report his escape, giving him no advantage of time in which to stretch and widen the ring of the hunt until it began to reveal gaps, one of which he could slip through. He felt no remorse for what he had done, nothing except that disappointment in a task left uncompleted. His mood was now established and he had moved into the final stage of his transmutation. Now he was the hunted human, and vicious as only a human being could be.

'How far is it?'

'A few hundred yards now.'

'Slow down – stop!'

Orrell pulled the car to a slewing halt. Then he leaned heavily on the wheel, his face blank of all expression. He expected Nasoud to kill him there and then. Nasoud wound down the window again and listened. Silence. He opened the door cautiously and got out, motioning Orrell to switch off the engine. He looked ahead of him into the darkness. He could see what was the boundary hedge of Orrell's land, which also marked the line of the road. Yet there was no sign of any lights, no movement along the narrow country road. He found that hard to believe. It had to be a trap. Yet the road was there, just beyond the hedge, and it tempted him. Should he walk to the gates, which hung invitingly open – he could see the faint whiteness of one of the posts – should he take the risk? Or should they drive straight through them, taking perhaps a larger risk?

He heard the chatter of a helicopter away behind him and saw the landing-lights flicker down as it came into the farm-yard. He saw Orrell looking back.

'Get in the car!' he said. 'We shall take the risk. Go through the gates as fast as you can – and then head in the direction of the nearest large town – understand?'

Orrell nodded and climbed wearily back into the car. The relief at being alive had already waned and he accepted once more that the time of death had merely been postponed. Still, Betty and Marge . . . he thought, but the reflection was little comfort to him.

He started the car and let out the clutch. The Rover surged forward and Nasoud steeled himself to watch the gates. The headlights, directly in front of them, dazzled him as they came on, glaring at full beam into his eyes, into Orrell's eyes.

'Pull away – pull away!' Nasoud screamed, seeing the bulked shape of the police car filling the drive, blocking the gate. Orrell swung the wheel only yards from the other car and the Rover pulled away, off the road and down the dip beside it, bumping and lifting across the pasture. Nasoud saw, at the very last second, the hedge, dark and looming, coming to meet them. He flung open his door, and rolled out of his seat. The ground came up to strike him, releasing his breath and then, like an automaton, as light spilled from beyond the hedge and men shouted and the Rover ploughed with a crunch of twisting metal and breaking glass into the hedge, he was on his feet and running – in which direction he had no idea, the SLR cradled in a hand still numb from its jarring contact with the ground. Shots rang out, but the bullets passed well over him. He was ordered to stop – but he kept on, bending low, until the noises behind him were confused and distant, the roar of engines like the buzzing of flies.

In the rear compartment, noisy and crowded, of the Wessex helicopter that was the brigadier's airborne HQ, Bracken and Spencer-Handley had listened grim-faced and silent to the reports from Stonefield Farm. When he had learned of the deaths of two more of his men, the soldier had retreated into a shell, as if he had a personal grief within him, as if the two dead men had been friends of his. The behaviour of the farmer, Orrell, had now become luridly clear to Bracken and he silently cursed himself for not having been more suspicious. Yet he was able to shake off the stupor of guilt long before the soldier beside him, who had seen more death and violence than Bracken ever expected to have to witness. Bracken realised the need for urgent action and had leaned forward in the helicopter until he could speak into the radio-operator's ear to request a radio link with A.C.C. Maxon. He silently fumed through Maxon's preliminaries, even though the man's tone of voice, which hovered on the contrite, surprised him.

Then Maxon said, 'The dogs have picked up a scent, but they're minutes behind – I couldn't get dogs to the road-block at Stonefield Farm before the car arrived. I'm sorry about that.'

'I understand, sir. Where was that scent picked up – exactly?'

'Hang on – I'll get a fix.' Maxon disappeared from the radio link for some seconds, while the helicopter continued in its orbit of the village of Withington, strangely unlit below them except for the rushing beams of police cars moving along the north-south ribbon of the road. The moon had risen, Bracken noted gratefully, and the land was bathed below him in pale light.

Maxon came back. 'The old railway,' he said.

'Is he using it again?'

'No. He crossed it half a mile outside Withington, to the north, and seems to be moving in the direction of Bubb's Farm, which is about a mile north-west of the village. Do you want my men in the area?'

'No – there's a patrol there. Keep your men active on the road he'll have to cross ...' Bracken looked at the map in his hand. 'And the road running west out of the village. Can we put dogs along the north-south road, to support ...?'

'Can do,' Maxon said, almost eagerly. Then he added, 'We – we will get him, Bracken, will we not?'

'I hope so, sir. I hope so. Stay tuned.'

'Of course – my boy.'

Bracken smiled at the unexpected familiarity. He said to the sergeant from the caravan, the man with the box of pins, 'What have we got down there?' His finger tapped at the sergeant's map on the table bolted to the fuselage.

The sergeant leaned across his view and screwed his forehead into lines of concentration. 'He's moving west towards the Brig's old field HQ in Hilcot Wood. That's here, sir,' he added, pointing to the map. 'We pulled most of our stuff away from there when the balloon went up. However,' he added as Bracken showed obvious signs of impatience, 'we've got an APC at the foot of Shill Hill – here ... there's a foot-patrol moving north and east along this line to the copse of trees near Bubb's Farm, and – and we can get a couple of scout cars into that area in a few minutes, if they'd help ...?'

Bracken looked at the sergeant in blank amazement for a moment, then said, 'Where are the mobile searchlights?'

'Three of them – south-east of Bubb's Farm, coming up that road moving north. Where do you want them, sir?'

'Around Bubb's Farm, as quick as you can.'

'Right, sir. O.K. Corporal Hiskins, you heard the officer – let's be having it!'

'Choppers, as many as you can – flying low over the farm area, all lights on.'

'Sir, I'll have to relay all this through the communications caravan at Chedworth – but it shouldn't take a minute.'

'Good. We're going to have a look for ourselves.'

Bracken stumbled forward and heaved his way into the cramped cockpit of the helicopter. He tapped the pilot on the shoulder and yelled in his ear.

'Bubb's Farm! I want you to do a recce job in that area – our man must be near there now!'

158

The pilot's eye wandered over the illuminated map on the folding table at his side. Then he looked up and raised his thumb to Bracken with a smile.

'Hang on!' he shouted and the chopper tugged away to the right, turning in a north-westerly direction. Bracken grabbed a strap hanging from the fuselage above him, and watched through the cockpit as the ground rushed to meet them. Then, with a speed that loosened Bracken's stomach, the pilot levelled out and they were rushing at little more than a hundred feet across the washed, silver pastureland that surrounded Bubb's Farm.

'What lights have you got?' he asked.

'One big landing light – angled down. Not much use unless we pass right above him. Look – I'll show you.'

The pilot reached over and flipped a switch. A pool of light beneath them flicked across the silent folds and humps of the meadows passing below. Bracken stared at the racing ground, as if he expected to spot the white, upturned face of Nasoud. He was aware that the Arab could bring down the helicopter using the SLR, but he could not consider that risk. The hunt, he sensed, was reaching some kind of climax and he, the hunter, had to be there, not stuck in the headquarters caravan miles away.

There was another overpowering reason. He was dreadfully aware, and his fear mounted as the minutes passed, that it would be he, if anyone, who would prevent Nasoud from being shot and killed by the soldiers seeking him. The news of the deaths at Stonefield Farm would spread like a plague of hatred among the searchers. If Nasoud failed to respond to a challenge, or fired on troops, then they would kill him out of hand.

A hand fell on his shoulder and he turned to see the face of the brigadier smiling sheepishly at him. The soldier was strap-hanging, like himself, and they were two passengers on the same tube train for a brief instant, jogging home from work – except for the noise of the jet helicopter beating across the landscape.

'Sorry, my boy,' Spencer-Handley said. 'Haven't been too much use to you in the last few minutes. Got over it now–

couldn't help but blame you personally for what happened at the farm . . . not true, of course.'

'I'm sorry, sir. I was to blame.'

'Nonsense. Fortunes of war. What are we doing now, by the way? I see you've got my mobile searchlights on the move down there.' The pilot pulled the chopper into a wide orbit around the darkened spot of Bubb's Farm and, below them, two swathes of light emanating from invisible sources cut across the fields. The pattern of movement of the searchlight beams seemed random but they were, to a trained observer, quartering the expanse of land between them, creating the impression that there was nowhere to hide, that the night had lost its safety. Bracken considered that, were he Nasoud, the psychological effect of those lights would be profound.

Beyond the cutting beams of the searchlights as they circled above the area, they could see the pattern of car headlights as police and army vehicles closed upon the vicinity of the farm. Bubb's Farm lay in a slight hollow of the land, with one north-south road and one running east to west forming two of its boundaries. The outskirts of Cheltenham lay four miles to the north-west, at Charlton Kings.

Bracken was relatively certain that Nasoud could not gain any of the roads and thereby commandeer transport. He was isolated and on foot, and would remain so. He had been forced to throw away his only hostage and he had little chance now, unless he gained a hamlet or village, of acquiring another. The only chance he had, Bracken realised, would be to gain the woodland a couple of miles to the south-west, and lie up for as long as he could. As a protracted manhunt, it placed all the cards before Bracken; but time pressed at his back like something palpable. It was after ten now and it would take three-quarters of an hour to get the Arab to Heathrow – which gave the police and army an effective time of eighty minutes in which to recapture the desperate, running man.

Bracken unfolded the OS map he had fished from his pocket and attempted to read it in the light of the map table, drawing the brigadier's attention with his pointed finger.

'We have to cut him off from this woodland here,' he said.

'A ring of men spread out in front of the woods, running that far . . .'

Spencer-Handley nodded and called the orders back to the radio-operator. He surprised Bracken, who marvelled at the gazetteer that was the brigadier's mind. It took him little more than a minute and then he returned his attention to Bracken, who grinned with almost childlike awe.

'It's nothing, my boy,' Spencer-Handley said with a smile. 'After all, we've been doing the same sort of thing for the last four days!'

Bracken returned his attention to the pilot, and yelled, 'See anything?'

'Lots of bodies, moving around rather aimlessly!' the pilot replied with a grin. 'All good stuff, but no Arabs – sorry!'

'So am I. What's the chopper activity like?'

'D-Day, and then some! They're dropping men like flies! Should make you feel very confident.'

'It doesn't!'

Bracken looked forward again, out into the gleaming night at the pattern of headlights below him. He saw racing lights converging to the west of them, beyond Bubb's Farm and towards Shill Hill. The slower beams of the mobile searchlights lumbered in the same general direction. It was suddenly as if a hole had opened in the night beneath them, a hole towards which the lights were rushing, to fill it.

Bracken said, a note of excitement in his voice, 'What's going on down there?'

'Someone heard a fiver falling to the ground!' the pilot said. He tugged the helicopter over and they raced towards the place where the lights were converging. Even as they neared it, Bracken saw the diminishing circle falter, then stretch out like the tail of a comet, lose its shape, so that vehicles and lights were racing in two parallel lines towards the base of Shill Hill, whose wooded clump he could see massed ahead of the helicopter. Nasoud was there, he thought – he had to be there!

'Take her down, man – take her down!' he yelled in the pilot's ear.

*   *   *

'Well, Clarence – I take it you are with me. In principle, at least? Unfortunately for us, spurred on by their raw nerves, that repair team has been working much too fast!' There was no humour in Latymer's smile.

The silence in the 'Greenhouse' was oppressive, a tense stillness in which the tiny sounds of men shifting their bodies to be more comfortable, the tapping of pencils, the sucking of cheeks, even the noises of regular breathing, became exaggerated and caused others to look up from their work. The silence had lasted for minutes, ever since the flurry of preparation, the babble of suggestion, discussion, moderation, had died down and the plan of attack on the 707 had been finalised. It was then that Latymer had asked for Seaborne's support.

The big policeman paced up and down the room, knowing that the eyes of every one of his men were deliberately averted. The development of the plan was simple – it consisted of using the refuelling tankers, of which there needed to be two for an aircraft of the capacity and range of the 707, and manning them with Special Branch men. Two men to each driving cab. Other men to be concealed by the simple expedient of clinging to the tail of each tanker – making eight men in all. They could risk no more – Packer had already given his orders concerning the numbers of men the tankers should contain.

The lights had been switched on throughout Heathrow. Packer, his voice angry, abusive, more strained and desperate than formerly, had demanded that they light the airport like a Christmas tree. Latymer, with some reluctance, had ordered this to be done. The main terminal buildings blazed with light, the runway lights were on, the perimeter lights could be picked out ringing the airport – all of which made the silence of Heathrow the more uncanny.

It was now impossible for the 707 to be approached under cover of darkness. There was no darkness; it had ceased to exist. Only by using the cover of the tankers could they approach the aircraft without detection. The pool of white light round the aircraft had diminished in brightness, but was still clearly visible to Seaborne as he looked out of the windows and debated with himself. Latymer alone could give the order for the attack to be mounted, but Seaborne knew he would never do it without his spoken approval. It would be Branch men, his men, out there at risk on the tarmac. The repair crew had called in only minutes before. They were ready to pack up and withdraw. When they did, Packer would call for the tankers and the moment that would not again present itself would have arrived.

In theory, Seaborne agreed with Latymer's analysis of the situation. The passengers were in the most extreme danger. As their common analysis had revealed, there would be a power-struggle aboard the 707 when Nasoud was handed over. Asif, the other Arab, would in all probability release the passengers, according to the unwritten rules of international hijacking. However, Packer and the girl Fender were amateurs, and of the very worst kind. For them there were no rules. They would want safety, and the way of safety to them would lie in keeping hold of their high cards – the four dozen passengers . . . five dozen, unless Packer held to his agreement over the exchange for fuel. And once the attack started, if it started, there would be no guarantee of their safety.

What should he do? They had no ace, no one on board and undiscovered who could act as an advance fire controller, who could call out to his men over a radio link the positions of those hijackers they could not see. Worse than that, they had no idea of the exact position of the bomb aboard the 707.

As if the thought prompted his muscles, he turned his head to the large scale cutaway diagram of the interior of a 707 that Latymer had used for his briefing. They had decided, with dubious accuracy, the dispositions of the hijackers and had worked out their fire-angles. They had estimated, like ghouls, the probable death count and produced a time-scale for the attack. The result was a terrifying, cold chart of slaughter. It was likely that at least two of the hijackers would be outside the aircraft to meet the fuel tankers and perhaps two more in the first class; the remaining two being posted in the second class. The hatch to the first class would have to be gained, via the ladder, within five seconds of the first shot being fired, and by at least two Special Branch men. Clay, with the machine-pistol on automatic, could wreak havoc if the first shots triggered him to that response. Judging from the psychological reports that Latymer had seen some time ago in connection with the episode of the prison hostages at Scheveningen in Holland in 1974, there might be as much as five or six seconds before the hijackers, alert as they were, reacted to a surprise attack. In those seconds, the first class had to be gained, and the hijackers eliminated. And the bomb defused . . .

At a conservative estimate, allowing for evasive action on the part of many of the passengers, they could not hope to avoid a death toll in double figures – perhaps as high as half the passengers. Unless, he admitted, the hijackers attempted to resist the boarding party instead of destroying the captives. He knew that Latymer was banking on this latter reaction – in which case, still assuming his men to be successful, they might hope to rescue the majority of the passengers unharmed.

Nothing about the reasoning, the plan of attack, and the prognostications quelled Seaborne's darkest forebodings.

Seaborne wished devoutly that Latymer had not placed him in his present position. He suspected Latymer almost of wishing to ruin his political future in some strange act of ritual defiance. For himself, his concern was for his men. The results of failure, or success, could be equally damaging to his career and neither weighed with him. If he knew for certain that those passengers would walk away unharmed from the 707, or even that only a handful of them would meet their deaths and that the majority of his men would survive, then he would agree to the attack. But he could not be sure. There was still a chance, and pe rhaps a good one, that the passengers would be released in exchange for Nasoud.

At the sound of the man's voice he turned to Latymer and said, 'I – frankly, sir – I don't *know*!'

'I'm sorry you're still undecided,' Latymer said, disappointed.

'There's too much at stake, sir,' Seaborne argued. 'For example – you ask my men here – what chances they would have of knocking over *all* the hijackers, even with clear, unhurried shots, at close-range, in the sort of time limit you've set on the operation. It's only in the films that hand-guns knock out the enemy with single shots . . . and rifles are too unwieldy for single-shooting at close quarters!'

164

'You have marksmen, Clarence! You've given me a list of names – your best men.'

'Yes, sir. But it's not the men, it's the guns themselves. It doesn't matter how good a shot a man is, on the range – or whether he uses a Walther, a Browning, or a Smith & Wesson . . . the guns just aren't good enough!'

Latymer nodded, accepting the advice being proferred by an expert. He looked at Seaborne intently, and said, 'Can you give those poor devils out there *any* hope, any *real* hope, that they will walk off that aircraft at midnight, or whenever? Answer that, Clarence.'

There was a long silence, and then Seaborne said, 'This attempt could trigger off the very thing you fear – the sacrificial exit, the bomb going off . . .'

'I know that, Clarence.' Latymer's voice sounded cold and remote. 'Yes, I know that. Yet – the element of surprise, Clarence, the fact that the girl will not be screwed up for her – *liebestöd* – her love-death, when we choose to attack . . . it might stall her for long enough . . .' His words seemed to lack conviction.

'It's – possible, sir. I grant you that. But why should she do it at all? How can you be sure that she will?'

Latymer stared at the ground for a long time and then said, 'It was a long time ago, Clarence . . .' His voice was soft, his eyes still regarding the ground, as if he were addressing himself. Yet every man of the skeleton duty-team in the room looked up and became drawn by the storyteller's voice. He went on, after a pause in which he allowed the past to flicker in his mind, an old, grainy newsreel.

'During the last war, when I was in army intelligence, I had an agent, a young French girl, who was so good at killing, it just wasn't true. Her parents had died at the hands of the Gestapo in Bordeaux. That, I always assumed, was her motive. Her hatred of the Germans was terrible, comprehensive, unremitting. I used her again and again, on the most difficult missions. She survived every one. Then, towards the end of forty-four, when the Allies were bogged down in northern France, we planned a spectacular piece of terror warfare. We would blow up the Gestapo headquarters in Bordeaux, blow it to the moon. This would be followed by further terror-strikes against military, SS, and Gestapo targets. It would signal to the Germans the existence, we hoped, of a huge network of agents behind their own lines. . . .' He paused and Seaborne saw his hands rubbing together, as if he were engaged in the act of washing them.

He continued, his voice small and distant, and level: 'Naturally, it was Marie who was selected – she volunteered. She was flown to London, where I met her for only the second time and instructed her in the use of the explosive. Then she was parachuted back into France. The operation was timed for the evening of the sixteenth. She was to visit Gestapo head-quarters, on the pretext of wishing to lay information before the local Kommandant concerning agents known to her. She would plant the bomb in the toilet, or wherever seemed best and most secret to her; and the bomb, by the way, she would be wearing, like a life-jacket, her clothes being specially designed to accommodate the extra bulk. Then she would leave.'

He looked up, as if meeting an old objection. 'She knew it might well be suicidal, as we did – but she had volunteered. She was to set the bomb to go off after she left the building with Gestapo officers, to lead them to the supposed agents. Those who would rescue her from ambush. Or – if she found that she was not believed and could not escape, she would trigger the bomb for instantaneous explosion.'

He paused again for a while, and then said: 'On the night of the sixteenth, there was a ball at the Hôtel de Ville. The place was packed with wealthy French – not collaborators, merely those who gave the Germans no trouble, went on with their lives as ordinarily as they could. Marie, the bomb strapped round her body, walked into the hotel, and triggered . . .' His voice faltered and then, clearing his throat, he said, 'triggered the bomb in the middle of the dance floor, during a fox-trot – the death toll amounted to sixty-four, and there were over a hundred injured. Three SS officers were among the dead, just three.'

Latymer continued looking at the floor. The silence was long and tense, and empty like some huge vacuum.

Finally Seaborne said, 'Why?'

Latymer looked up at him and the policeman almost winced at the naked pain in his eyes.

'Why, Clarence? Why? That's what I asked myself, over and over again. I went to France, early in forty-five, as soon as I could, and I asked that question. I asked it of each of my agents, of her relatives, of her friends, of half the town. And do you know – I never found the answer.' He looked up with a thin, bitter smile on his lips and then deliberately looked out of the window.

'I found the answer today, in Joanne Fender, and her case-history. Marie's father and mother were replicas, prototypes if you like, of Senator and Mrs Hubert Fender. When I listened to the analyst over the telephone, I wasn't thinking about her. I was thinking of Marie. Her parents had not been killed by the Gestapo – that was a polite fiction Marie had invented to hide the truth. They were killed by the Resistance, because they were collaborators. M. Foucard was a magistrate, a wealthy, important man – and he was a pig to his wife. He was hated by his daughter, who pitied the mother – and who despised that same mother for being weak. An old aunt of hers told me that much of her domestic life – to which I listened, but the significance of which eluded me . . . until now. The wife was not a collaborator at all, but Foucard was.'

He looked up at Seaborne and added, 'You know why she killed her own countrymen and countrywomen, don't you, Clarence?'

'Revenge? But for what?' Seaborne said after a pause.

'Revenge – because, for her, they were like her father and mother – she joined the people who had killed her father and mother, and murdered those who had been their friends, or belonged to the same class as they.' Latymer stood up stiffly. 'Joanne Fender is out there now, with a bomb, and with an aircraft full of people like Daddy and Mommy – she wants to kill them, Clarence – she wants to!'

Latymer's final words, with little more emphasis than was usual in his expression, dropped like pebbles into the silence of the room. Every eye regarded him with a mixture of surprise and conviction. Like a superb actor, he had held his audience within the spell of a spotlit soliloquy, enacted a raw

167

piece of the past, made them look into another soul. More than anything else, he had convinced them. He saw, as his eyes refocused on the room, eyes stray from his face to the window as attention began to rivet on the 707. Someone coughed, close at hand. Latymer realised it was Seaborne.

'You can't know,' he said unconvincingly.

Latymer compressed his features into a shrug. 'I know, Clarence – I know,' he said softly.

Seaborne nodded.

'Then – she will kill them all?' Barbara asked, her voice a hoarse appalled whisper. 'She really will?'

'I'm afraid so, Barbara – at least, that is my contention.' He smiled with bleak encouragement. 'I never realised till now in what dark cause Marie had performed her act of ritual slaughter. It was her father and her mother she was killing. The Germans were substitutes that failed, eventually, to satisfy her desire for revenge. When we – when I gave her the bomb, I gave her not only the means of self-immolation, but the means of destroying the whole class she hated and despised!'

Barbara's face mirrored his pain, briefly, then filled with pity. The strength of the expression disconcerted him and he looked away.

To Seaborne he said, 'Well, Clarence, will you come with me on this part of our journey?'

There was a silence, shorter than he had anticipated, and then the big policeman said gruffly, 'Yes, Mr Latymer, if by that means we can save some of those poor beggars.'

There was a communal sigh emanating from the skeleton team in the room. Seaborne had bowed to the unvoiced pressure of his subordinates, acquiesced in their mood.

'Thank you, Clarence.'

'One thing, sir. Are you going to request permission from the Home Office for this attack?'

Latymer sighed. 'Do you think I could convince the Home Secretary and the Cabinet by mere reference to an incident that happened more than thirty years ago?' he asked, a sardonic smile, despite his sombre mood, pinching his lips. Seaborne shook his head. 'No, quite so. I would have just about as much chance of convincing them that they ought, out of decency, to lose the general election in order to give the other chaps a chance. Do you think they would listen? You heard the P.M.'s broadcast, Clarence – did he sound as if he were blowing the whistle for your men to go in mob-handed? Indeed, no. I'm afraid, Clarence, that we have moved into the grey area of Directive 316 – the power vested, by implication only, by the ambiguity of words. The directive hints, but it does no more than that, that the Executive Officer may decide, pragmatically, that an attack against the hijackers should be made, if the safety of the passengers is thereby guaranteed. This, I believe, is a situation where there is no other way of ensuring the safety of any of the passengers.'

He was silent while his emphasis reached to each man in the room. Then he said, 'The Cabinet are convinced, because they are sensible men in a sensible world, that if we give the hijackers Nasoud, then we are bound, by the laws of common sense, to receive in exchange the captive passengers. Cabinets and governments do not admit the existence of people like Joanne Fender.' He shrugged his shoulders, and added, 'Time for us to get down to work, Clarence. That repair team has finished and Mr Packer will very likely be asking for his fuel in a matter of moments. We musn't keep him waiting – eh?'

Latymer smiled, but without warmth. Seaborne's face remained grim and expressionless. He felt himself beginning a very long journey – more accurately, he felt his moral feet slipping from under him, and his mind begin to tumble into darkness.

8: Extreme Occurrence

For a moment, a moment of paralysing terror, the lights seemed to be all around Nasoud. His lungs were straining, his legs were becoming leaden and the gun banged painfully against his thigh. He was struggling uphill, to the left of the armoured truck that had fixed him in its headlights, and from the direction of which came the cries and orders – but no shooting. Car engines raced across the grassy slope and filed in behind him, and he was caught in a spotlit glare, transfixed, an insect on a pin, a pin of white light. He almost stopped for an instant and then he was away again, head bowed, breath ragged and loud above the shouting behind him, the roar of engines, the blood thundering in his ears. He was in a private world, as if surrounded by some shield from the sounds around him, and from which his own sounds bounced back at him, amplified.

He had no time to wonder whether there were troops on the crest of the hill ahead of him, in the trees. If he was being driven into a corral of men, then it must be so. All his desire was to reach the shelter of the trees, to escape the crucifix of light upon which he was nailed.

The lights, all of a sudden, seemed all behind him or to either side. There were no lights burning ahead, no vehicle on the slopes or the crest, just the wash of light throwing forward a multiple shadow of himself. He heaved his unwilling limbs into a longer stride, battling the slope. The trees, as he looked briefly up, seemed nearer. He was light-headed, filled with an ecstasy of fear and elation. This was the battle ground, the scene of the contest, this sloping mass of hill. He knew he was still moving to the west, but the way in which his movements had been anticipated made him realise that he would have to change direction. He had no idea of the shape of the woodland, but he knew that he would have to emerge from it at some unexpected point.

Huge shadows cut off the beams of light, leaving a flickering, dancing haze crossed by filtered streaks. He was inside the trees and, perhaps in only an illusion of safety, the sounds of the pursuit seemed to dwindle. Still there had been no shooting and he thanked his luck that he was still considered a valuable prize. It was a chase in which the fox had prior warning that he was not to be harmed.

He had no time to look back, no time to take stock of the pursuit. He had to assume that it was still advancing on a broad front, a sweeping crescent nearing the crest of the hill. Instinctively he dived to the left, ducking low, and the concentration of diffused and interrupted light seemed to be left behind. He ran on, into darkness.

The desperate hysteria of the hunted remained with him. It elated him, even as it reported, coldly and factually, the condition of his body. He would have to halt soon, yet he knew that to stop would mean the collapse of the mood that drove him on. While he ran, the branches of trees stinging him and the blood roaring in his ears, he was free; to stop running was equivalent to surrender.

He was now heading roughly southwards, realising as he did so that the safety of the trees could become an advantage to the pursuers. If the wood was small, then they could close it off with a ring of men and he would not escape. He feared being wounded. There would be marksmen with night-sights among the hunters, and they could cripple him, slow him, so that he would lie panting on the grass, his face working, chest heaving, while they closed in on him and looked down at him.

He changed direction again, but making only a small deviation from his general southward movement. A copse of silver birches glistened coldly in the filtered moonlight of the wood and he passed through them into the deeper darkness of trees which were more closely planted. Then he stopped. His chest felt that it was outside him, blown open by his exertions, by the bursting of the heart. He rested, his shaking back pressed and heaving against the bas-relief of the trunk of a tree, the gun pressed cold against his cheek, his hearing strained to catch a level of sound above the roar of his blood.

Looking back the way he had come, he thought he could see lights. There was a diffused glow climbing the hill like a mist from, he assumed, the headlights of the vehicles that had followed him and those that had attempted to cut him off. But there were also other lights – small, weak, dancing lights, as of marsh-gas or candles. Men with torches, moving slowly and carefully through the wood. The general movement of the lights was ponderous, exact. Nothing was missed. The lights increased in number and brightness, hovering – and there were voices now, calls and orders across clearings, through copses. The pattern was logical, a wide net of lights. Most of them were moving in the direction he would have taken had he kept straight on after entering the trees, but a filigree-work of dancing beams flowed off that wedge of men fanning out, assuming that he would have deviated from his course once out of sight.

The lights began to hypnotise him. Something scurrying through the undergrowth at his feet hardly disturbed him. Only slowly, as the dancing lights, or a section of them, detached like spinning satellites, came nearer and nearer, did he shake off the lethargy that had softly gripped him and look about for a safe direction in which to move. He began to realise that the longer he stayed within the cover of the wood, the more assistance he gave his enemies.

Away to his left, roughly in the direction in which he wished to go there were, as yet, no lights. Only the blobs detached from the haze of light that crept towards him from the right. He eased his body away from the tree trunk and moved off, soft-footed. The ground snagged at his ankles and his trouser-legs, low bushes and thick grass. He felt that the noises he was making would betray him, but pressed on, pausing only for brief moments every couple of hundred yards to check on the waving lights. He seemed to be leaving them behind, to be outstripping them despite his weariness. Fear and desperation drove him – nothing so powerful spurred on the pursuit.

The wood appeared to be getting thicker, the gaps between

the trees fewer and less obvious. Before long, there were no lights to be seen, no shouts and orders trailing in his wake. The silence of the wood assailed him.

Light, jumping at him as if from a bush, flickered across his face, passed on, and then began to return across the dark boles of the trees. He pressed against a trunk, his face hidden by the curve of his arm, flung up as if to ward off a blow. He listened. He heard the rustle of grass, the snapping of a twig, and his pulse-rate leapt and loudened as if triggered by the tiny, sharp noise. He stood motionless, not crouching at the foot of the trunk since that action seemed to him craven, submissive. This was a small patrol, two, three, maybe four men, moving into the wood from its southern flank. Already, he realised, a ring of searchers had been thrown round the wood. As he analysed the information, he recognised that if he could pass these men, then his best hope of escape would come from tracking back along the path they had taken, since their presence might well have left a hole in the ring. He stopped breathing.

Two figures passed the tree, less than ten yards away, keeping close together, their torches splaying out light to right and left, quartering the spaces between the trees.

They passed him. One of them spoke. 'See anything, Charlie?'

'Nothing, Taffy. Christ – I'm still knackered from that sprint around the hill!'

'Stop talking, boy – don't want to let 'im know we're here, do we?'

'Why not? Might start him running, if he's hiding anywhere here. Anyway, how the hell do they expect us to find him in this place with a couple of flashlights?'

'Shut up, man.'

The soldier addressed as Charlie sniffed loudly in disdain and the two of them moved on. Nasoud waited until they were out of sight and only the dimmest radiance from their flashlights remained, then he ducked round the tree and headed back down the way they had come. He had not taken ten paces when he collided with something soft and yielding that let out a grunt of air as Nasoud cannoned into it.

Even as he stared down at the man, he realised what had happened. The soldiers with the torches were an advance-guard not really expected to find him, so long as he hid himself. But the third soldier was coming up behind them, in complete darkness, in order to net any bird they might startle. The soldier was on his back, on the ground, fumbling with his rifle. The barrel swung towards Nasoud, who could barely make out the form of the man, when the soldier felt a blinding pain across his temple from the butt of the SLR and collapsed into oblivion.

Nasoud, breathing hoarsely with reaction, went down on his knees and rapidly went through the soldier's pockets. He extracted the clips of ammunition and stuffed them into the pockets of his jacket. Then he groped for the water-bottle that had clinked as the man went down and, still on his knees, tilted it to his lips and swallowed greedily. Wiping his mouth, he screwed the cap back into place and slung the bottle over his shoulder.

He listened to the man's breathing. It was irregular, but strong. He had not killed him. He debated for a moment, and then decided that it would be an unnecessary death, and got to his feet. Undoubtedly the patrol would come back looking for him before very long, and whether the man were alive or dead he would betray his presence. He looked about him and saw a holly bush, thick, dark, tangled, away to his right. He slung the SLR over his shoulder and placed his hands beneath the soldier's armpits. Then, with a huge effort of his exhausted form, he dragged the man into the cover of the bush. The dark leaves pricked at his face and hands and when the man was hidden, at least from casual inspection, he paused to take stock of his situation.

He was sweating freely, breathing heavily and his heart was pumping in a laboured manner. He was tired, very tired. Shaking off a creeping lethargy that was already beginning to take possession of his legs, he moved away from the bush, following the unmarked track that the three soldiers had taken, keeping a careful eye to right and left for signs of similar patrols.

He saw no more lights, and within ten minutes he came to

a halt on the edge of the wood on Shill Hill. He was looking southwards towards the road running westwards from the village of Withington. As he watched, a car, moving fast, headlights glowing above the bordering hedge, passed along the road. Turning west, he could see the lights of what must have been a farm, less than a mile away across open country. There were no other lights visible and, deciding that he ought to stay away from the road, which lay to the south, he turned west, heading towards the lights of the farm. He did not assume for a moment that the place offered him either shelter or hostages. Yet it was a marker, something in the moonlit night that was of human origin. Away to the west, further than the lights, he could discern that faint radiance of a town which he assumed, correctly, was Cheltenham.

His human capacity to plan and predict had narrowed to the lights of the town. He knew he must be heading further away from London with every step that he took, but he had to continue towards some local target, something more immediate than the capital to prompt his tired limbs to keep moving. Cheltenham had given him that. He had no idea what he might do when he reached the outskirts of the town, except that he might steal a car. Nevertheless Cheltenham assumed in his mind an inordinate power, a symbol of some kind of rest and security.

It was his memory that betrayed him. As he jogged across the fields, he had begun to slide back into the past. Images of his own childhood in a refugee camp and of his later training, came unwilled into his consciousness. He had been thinking of an escape he had made across the desert from an Israeli ambush, more than three years before, when he froze to the sound of a challenge from ahead of him.

'Halt! Who goes there?'

It was so patently ridiculous, after all he had been through, to have run so blindly into the noose, that he wanted to laugh. He stopped and stared ahead of him into the darkness. To his left, the ground rose steadily to a strip of woodland on a hill's crest. Before him, less than a hundred yards away, were the lights of the farm. But no human form was darkly outlined against them and the moonlight, which must have revealed him to the soldier, showed him nothing of the number and whereabouts of the enemy. Slowly, not knowing how much of what he did was visible, he unslung the SLR at his side, then lowered the barrel and gripped the trigger with his forefinger. If he were plainly visible, and more than one man had drawn a bead on him, then he knew he would be a dead man within the next few seconds. He breathed deeply and loosed off four shots in rapid succession before ducking away, bending low so that the pain in his ribs came suddenly back to frighten him.

Two shots followed him and then he heard the voice that had challenged him call out: 'Stop firing, you stupid buggers! Cut him off! There he goes, away to the right there!'

He had been plainly visible, he realised, toiling up the slope, as if repeating the action of his flight up the slope of Shill Hill once again. Men were shouting now behind him and a whistle was blowing. Then the world sprang into red flame as a flare burst over his head.

'There he is – a couple of hundred yards up the hill!' the same voice called out, like a huntsman in view. 'For Chrissake, cut him off before he gets into the trees!'

The light of the flare fizzled down into darkness again, but when he lifted his head, the trees ahead of him were tinged with the infra-red vision the light had given him. He stumbled, felt his ankle go over but righted himself before his whole weight could press upon it, and almost hopped into the outlying trees. This time he made no change of direction, but plunged through the thin cover of the trees. Another flare burst redly over the slope of the hill, and two more shots were loosed off, in frustration. But now the hunters had a sight of him and they were close on his trail. Already he could see the cold stars winking through the cover of the trees ahead. He would be out in open country again, and he could hear the tramping, careless rush of the soldiers behind him.

A voice close to him, closer than he expected, cried: 'Halt, or I fire!'

He checked instinctively, then plunged on, a stinging, thin branch whipping across his face. Bullets tore at the trunk just above his head. Whatever the orders, the game had changed.

These men were determined not to let him go. They were detached from their central command and the force of the order not to kill him had been blunted by the hours of waiting, the thoughts of the dead soldiers already to his credit.

He broke out into open country, into a wash of moonlight. He felt suddenly exposed, as if the night were full of eyes. Yet the sense of being observed was illusory. He knew that there were pursuers behind him but whether or not there were others ahead of him, he didn't know. There were more trees ahead and he made for them, blindly, as swiftly as his weary legs would carry him.

The first of the pursuers, the soldier who had summoned him to halt, who had fired on him, broke from the cover of the trees and saw his crouching, running form moving heavily down the gentle slope towards the trees. He raised his rifle to his shoulder and squinted through the night-sight. Slowly the cross-hairs settled on the lighter patch of the fugitive's cotton jacket. He steadied himself and his finger, curled round the trigger, squeezed gently. Then the gun was knocked into the air and the shot discharged itself harmlessly.

'What the bloody hell do you think you're doing?' the sergeant demanded, his face dark with anger. 'You heard the officer's order – no bloody shooting! Even if it is a bastard wog you're aiming at!'

Figures flowed past the two men, heading on down the slope. But they had lost the advantage they might have gained had the foremost pursuer continued running, instead of pausing to aim. The light patch of the cotton jacket disappeared into the trees further down the slope, even as the sergeant was hauling the recalcitrant private over the metaphorical coals.

Nasoud had made the trees and he could hear, sharp and tinkling like something softly striking iron, the noise of water ahead of him. By instinct, he headed for the source of the noise. The slope increased but the trees were thicker as he headed toward, though he did not know it, Hilcot Brook, running almost due south from where he now was.

The brook ran in a shallow, narrow cutting in the wood with great trees hanging over it, almost touching the water in some places. There was a pleasant, soothing quality in the noise of the water and, without considering the noise he would make, he slithered down the grassy bank. The water was cold and it refreshed his aching, sapped body. It swilled whitely round his thighs, chattering, almost comforting, such had been the loneliness of his past hours. His consciousness passed into his thighs and his ears. Then he heard, above the sound of the rushing water, the breaking of twigs, the rustle of grass. Turning south, he headed away down the brook.

Behind him, he heard voices calling again as he splashed noisily through the water, aware that he was tiring himself, but elated by the surge of the current that was flowing with him, and unwilling to leave the water, as if it were a natural environment. For almost a mile he ploughed through the gleaming, dark water, knowing that his pursuers would take the same route if they wished to keep in contact with him. The banks, tree-lined and narrow, would allow them no easy passage. Eventually, with a great effort, he forced himself to the bank and dragged himself with difficulty out of the brook. Stumbling over tree roots, he clambered away from the twisted root-mass at the stream's edge, and entered the wood proper, heading still in a south-westerly direction. The wood seemed to roll on before him for miles.

He stopped and listened. There were no sounds, but he knew that assistance must have been summoned, that they understood the general direction in which he had been heading. He cocked his head, like a listening animal. Yes, there it was – the noise of a helicopter beating over the wood, becoming louder. Only one, at that moment, but he knew there would be more. The thousand men he knew to be engaged in the hunt must have been on some kind of military exercise which meant that they would possess a great range of equipment, including numerous transport helicopters. There was no time to rest now. Rest would come later – at some indefinable time far in the future. He refused to think about it, slowed his pace to an energy-conserving jog and passed through the wood like a phantom.

There was no point in anger. Bracken was beyond the expression of frustration by means of that emotion. As he stood

178

beside Spencer-Handley alongside their helicopter, perched as it was on the southern edge of Shill Hill, looking across towards Taylor's Hill and beyond that to Lyde Bank, he existed in an almost hallucinatory state. He had come to believe that the man he was pursuing existed in a dream, that he was a ghost, one who flowed through the landscape, but never close enough to touch, to pull down. He no longer regarded Nasoud as an animal, with no real chance. The man held the key to Alison's safety in his hands and they were hands Bracken felt he was destined never to grasp, to restrain, to shake until Alison's life came tumbling out of them like freed water.

He had reported to Latymer, who had been non-committal, perfunctory. Bracken had a suspicion that his superior was contemplating some desperate measure against the hijackers, but his brain refused to consider the matter. All it would do was to forge a short-circuit in his thinking. The key to his wife's safety lay with the man Nasoud.

'He's got the devil's own luck, my boy,' the brigadier said at his side.

'Mm?' Bracken replied abstractedly.

'I said he's got the luck of Old Nick,' Spencer-Handley said softly.

The brigadier was inspecting the landscape before him through night-glasses. After he seemed satisfied, he lowered them and shone a torch on the OS map on a tiny, rickety table that had been erected for his use by the map-sergeant, who now hovered behind it, looking like a uniformed shop-keeper, poised in readiness for an order. The brigadier inspected the map, realising that Bracken was in deep thought and unlikely to be shaken out of it by anything less than the recapture of Nasoud. The soldier had shaken off his own depression, and his enthusiasm for the hunt was now redoubled. They were close to the Arab now and the little, bluff soldier was determined that he should not escape.

Bracken had told him about his wife. The brigadier, whose own wife had faced the Mau-Mau with him and the shifting, drifting existence of a soldier's wife with equanimity, was unlike the woman Bracken had married, who had upped and left him when the going got tough. The brigadier was unable to comprehend the vagaries of a woman like Alison Bracken, but he understood and respected the fact that Bracken, whom he had come to like, loved her. If the little soldier could influence the outcome, Bracken should have Nasoud on a plate to present to his precious friends at Heathrow, in exchange for his wife.

The brigadier's cough hardly impinged upon Bracken's awareness as he turned to the sergeant and said, 'Well – where is the blighter heading?'

The sergeant came eagerly round the table and looked at the landscape of the map.

'He knows now that all the farms are guarded, sir – and he's in the trees at the moment. Taken to the water again, according to the radio. I don't think he'll stay there – he was making for Cheltenham and that's still his best bet. He's moving south, or south-east now, and he'll want to break cover before long to get some kind of bearing.'

The brigadier clicked his tongue against his teeth. 'You love making a meal of things, Porson. What is your diagnosis?'

'Sorry, sir. I think he'll come out about here, somewhere along here, anyway.' His finger tapped at the map, along the north-eastern edge of the wood.

'What's to attract him there?'

'One farm – and the lights of Withington, sir. I don't think he'll be very interested in either. He's bound to have some vague notion, at least, that he'd be doubling back into our arms if he moved north.'

'Hm.' The brigadier rubbed his chin thoughtfully. Then he said, 'Then we'll make him turn north, towards that farm. Put out a call to all units in the area and to Major Anderson's reserves, especially choppers, and get them to beat that wood, from the south, so that he has to turn north and come out where you suggest. Not only that, but he has to keep moving north. Get the men at that farm – what is it, Highgate Farm – get them to turn all the lights on, make it look like a Christmas tree. I want him to feel that it's the only alternative he has.'

'Right-oh, sir. Mason is plotting for me on the big map inside. I'll get everything I can into that area, as soon as . . .'

'Sooner, sergeant.'

'Sir.'

Porson climbed into the helicopter and his voice, issuing the necessary orders, could be heard faintly.

The brigadier stood in silence for a moment and then he said, 'All right, my boy?'

'Mm?'

'Are you all right?'

'Oh! Yes, Brigadier. Sorry . . .'

'Quite all right – quite understand, my boy.'

'You do?' Bracken sounded genuinely surprised.

'Quite. Wouldn't wish to lose Margaret, myself – my wife, you know.'

'No, sir. And . . . thank you.'

'Think nothing of it, my boy.' The brigadier's voice dropped to a confidential whisper. 'We'll get him – don't worry about that.'

'I wish I could be as sure as you seem.'

'God is on the side of the big battalions, Bracken – even if luck does not seem to be! And that's what we've got – a battalion. I'm a Montgomery man myself. Can't lose eventually if you've got superiority of numbers and supplies. Unless you've got a bloody fool for a C.O. – and we haven't!' Spencer-Handley laughed and Bracken, out of his withdrawn mood, smiled.

'I'm sure of that,' he said.

'We had word from Anderson just before we touched down. They've withdrawn all personnel from the vicinity of Chedworth, and from the farm where the blighter stopped for a rest. They're aboard assault helicopters now, and airborne. We'll put them down on the south side of the wood he's in and drive him north. Over there . . .' His arm extended to the south. 'I think we ought to be airborne, too. Ready for him when he pops out!'

Bracken was silent for a moment, then he said, 'Very well, Brigadier – let's get off the ground.' Silently, he wished he shared some of the soldier's confidence. As it was, a creeping fear possessed him, a sense that things would not unravel cleanly.

The two tankers were parked still in the shadow of the tower, out of sight of the 707. Latymer had checked that all the hijackers were inside the aircraft before he gave the order to start engines. The silence of the airport seemed suddenly overwhelmed, stunned, by the noise of revving motors. His eye glanced at the driving cabs and then slid along the gleaming flanks of the two vehicles to the men suspended like trapped flies in the webbing fitted to the rear of each tanker.

He pressed the walkie-talkie to his cheek and said, his voice almost drowned, 'Very well. Pull out in front of the tower – show yourselves. My agreement with Mr Packer is that he be allowed to inspect you for traps before you start. Good luck to you.'

The huge vehicles pulled round past him and he and Seaborne followed in their wake, until they could be seen by Packer, using field-glasses from the steps of the 707, as two brightly-lit spots. Asif was at his side at the top of the gangway and behind them the girl, gun in hand, waited with impatience to use the binoculars.

'Well, Packer – what in hell is going on?' she snapped.

'Shut up, baby – I'm looking,' Packer said without turning to her or taking his eyes from the magnified tankers in his vision. His hands moved the glasses delicately. He inspected the tankers as he might have studied the body of a loved woman. After some twenty or thirty seconds, he seemed to be satisfied and passed the glasses wordlessly to the Arab beside him. Joanne Fender fumed silently behind them.

When Asif had finished his inspection, he said, 'I think we can tell them to approach.'

'Good. Lady, get those passengers down on to the tarmac . . .'

'Yes, boss!' she snapped and turned away from Packer's back. 'Outside, all of you!' she ordered and stepped aside, gun pointed, so that the first of the passengers came out into the cool night air, and tremblingly pushed past Packer and Asif and headed down the gangway.

Packer watched them go, lack of concern evident on his features. Asif, professional and undistracted, watched the slow approach of the tankers.

The girl pushed past him, jogging his arm, and he heard her say to Packer, 'I'm going down on the tarmac, Packer – I don't want any foul-ups this time!'

'Suit yourself, baby,' he said with a grin. 'Don't catch cold.'

She glowered at him and passed through the line of passengers until she stood at the foot of the ladder, gun pointing back in their direction. One by one they passed, like the weary survivors of some disaster; they straggled out on to the tarmac, away from their duralumin prison, not daring to hope, deadened by disbelief, hand-luggage trailing from their hands.

The tankers approached at the same deliberate speed. Joanne Fender began to watch them, intent and suspicious, but she was unable to see the tension on the faces of the men in the cab of the leading tanker, nor could she hear the driver's conversation with Latymer.

'The girl must be killed,' Latymer was saying. 'There is no need to fire through the fuselage, unless she regains the cover of the aircraft. You're sure she doesn't have the bomb with her?'

'Quite sure, sir. Just the hand gun.'

'Good. But – no relaxation, no delays. It is still of the utmost importance that you adhere to our timetable.'

'Sir.' Mercer, the driver of the leading vehicle, stop-watch slung from his neck, turned to Sanders seated next to him and observed, 'Christ – how does he keep his cool, that bloke?'

Sanders smiled thinly and kept his eyes on the nearing aircraft.

'He's so bloody worried about the bomb they've got on that plane, I think he's forgotten the bomb we're riding in!' he said.

'He hasn't forgotten – just ignored it. There's no other way. We wouldn't get near them any other way.'

The neon landscape through which they were crawling was peopled with the wan, tired faces of the passengers, whose interest in the tankers was fitful, abstracted. Mercer watched the white, dead globes of the faces as they floated past the windows. Then they were gone, and the landscape was filled with the slim, pale fuselage – the lights bleaching the scene.

Mercer shivered involuntarily and Sanders said, 'Not an inspiring stretch of country, is it?'

Mercer looked in his wing-mirror at the retreating passengers. 'I hope to God one of them doesn't turn round and point!' he muttered. 'Keep your eyes on them in your mirror.'

Mercer pulled the tanker round in a gentle curve, so that it puled in under the wing. According to the rehearsed moves, the two men hanging on to the rear should have climbed down and concealed themselves behind the flank of the vehicle. Mercer looked out of the driver's window – yes, they were there. The other tanker was alongside him, in file, and he saw that its two passengers were also hidden from view.

Then he saw the middle-aged man, with very white hair and a silver-grey suit, who had been watching the tankers, his mouth open. He was running back towards the aircraft, his hands waving. Mercer did not know it, but the element of surprise was about to be taken from him. The man, an American, had been forced to leave his wife on board the aircraft. The sight of armed men clinging to the backs of the tankers had terrified him. He had only one thought in his mind, that the wife he had been forced to leave, who had made him go, overwhelming him with guilt as he stepped from the plane, was in danger. He called out, waving his arms, and Mercer, transferring his gaze to the steps, saw Packer stiffen and level his gun on the approaching figure. The girl, at the foot of the ladder, had turned her attention to the tankers, as though she realised the cause of the man's actions.

'For Christ's sake – that silly bugger's going to ruin everything!' Mercer exclaimed. He leaned out of the cab, and yelled, 'Go! Go!' He pressed the button of the stop-watch.

Sanders, on the side of the tanker closest to the passenger steps, opened the door and dropped to the ground, went on to one knee, his gun trained on the girl. There was only one job now, to kill her. He saw the white teeth bare in a savage grin and squeezed off three shots. Less than ten yards separated them and one of the shots tore into the girl's arm, flinging her heavily against the ladder. She seemed surprised by pain,

184

and the gun dropped from her hand as she buckled against the passenger gangway, her absorbing interest seeming to be the blood welling over her fingers as she clutched her shattered elbow.

Other shots rang out. Mercer, down on the blind side of the tanker, crawled round the radiator and saw the Arab tumble down the steps. The man was obviously dead.

'Go, Sanders!' he yelled, over the bonnet. 'For God's sake, get on with it!'

Packer was in the act of closing the door. There was nothing final about the action, since the hatches of the 707 could be opened from outside and could not be locked from the inside. But it would mean delay, the clock would tick on. He saw White detach himself from the belly of the tanker and sprint for the ladder, ducking low. The door was still open a crack, and then Mercer realised that Packer was using it for cover. Flame spurted from the shadow of the doorway and White, his lean figure shaken by the impact of the bullets, halted in mid-stride and toppled sideways. The girl was out of sight of Mercer, having gained the gangway, and was crawling up the steps, clutching her shattered elbow.

'Shoot that bloody girl, one of you!' he yelled, moving out of cover. Sanders, unhurt, was ahead of him, easing his way across the light-splashed yards between the gangway and the tanker. 'Get on with it! Get on!' Mercer shouted, and then experienced the peculiar sensation of the concrete rushing at his face. He tried to put out his hands to stop his fall, but they were a long way away. The ground flew into his face, but his eyes were closed with a sudden pain before the impact.

Sanders turned in the direction of the new shooting. The door of the second-class had been opened and he could see the face of the negro peering round above the barrel of the machine-pistol. He skipped to one side, as bullets puckered the concrete at his feet. Two men were on the gangway ahead of him taking the steps at a rush, when the door opened and Packer, at point-blank rage, opened fire again. As the door opened, Sanders could see the girl, lying on the floor through Packer's widespread legs, and then the falling bulk of the man ahead of him knocked the breath from his body and he tumbled backwards down the last few steps, jarring the elbow of his gun hand on the tarmac. The Smith & Wesson flew out of his grasp, skittering across the concrete, as the dead weight of Rickards subsided on top of him. The door, he could see helplessly, had closed again and the other man was a terrible shapeless lump, dead at the top of the passenger steps.

As the feeling returned to his arm, he heaved at the bulk of Rickards and rolled out from beneath him. He glanced in the direction of the other door, from which the cross-fire had come and saw that that, too, was closed.

On the tarmac were the bodies of White and Mercer. He had not known that Mercer had been hit, he had assumed that he was somewhere behind him. Slowly, with the blood still pounding in his ears, he eased himself away from Rickards, sliding on his belly across the tarmac to the shelter of the tankers.

There were four of them left, he saw, a huddled group behind the leading tanker. White, Rickards, Gunter and Mercer were dead. Bolt had a shoulder wound which was causing him considerable pain, but the other two were unharmed, like himself.

'Fucking never stood a fucking chance!' Bolt muttered through clenched teeth. 'Fucking waste of time – where's that bastard who warned them we were hanging on the backs of the tankers?'

Sanders looked over his shoulder and motioned with his thumb. 'Poor sod's dead,' he observed. Their eyes followed his gesture. The silver-grey suit lay crumpled around the patch of white hair on the tarmac. The hijackers had shot him out of hand, assuming that he had been part of the attack upon them.

'Good bloody riddance!' Bolt said.

'We've got to get out of here,' Sanders said. 'We can use the cover of the tankers until we're out of hand-gun range. Ready?' They nodded – anger, frustration and defeat crossing their faces. 'Let's go, then.'

Once inside the fuselage, Joanne Fender had dragged herself to her feet and now her hands were clenched round the bomb which she had taken from beneath her seat, her mind oblivious to the pain of her wound; rather, like something innocent that has been hurt, she had been stung into reaction. There was a balm for her hurt and that balm was beneath her seat in the first-class – the balm was now in her hands.

Clay's strong fingers closed round her wrist, causing her to cry aloud with pain as the wound in her elbow throbbed anew. She looked up at him, and cried, 'Get your hands off me, nigger!'

'You ain't blowin' me to hell, baby – just stay cool!' Clay replied, his fingers tightening on her wrist until she wanted to shriek. She stared into his face, then, sucking her dry cheeks, she spat into it.

'Stay cool, soul-sister,' he warned, as the pressure of the grip tightened to the extent that the bomb had to be held impotently in one hand.

'What in hell's name is going on?' he heard Packer ask, from the aisle behind him.

'Soul-sister wants to start the glory-train right here and now,' Clay replied, without taking his eyes from Joanne's face, or letting go of her wrist. As if to punish her for spitting on him, he twisted the arm slightly, heard the shattered elbow grate and smiled as she cried aloud in pain. Her head dropped into her breast and she appeared almost to have fainted. Clay took the bomb from her lap. Packer grabbed her by the hair and yanked her head up, so that she stared into his cold eyes.

'Listen to me, Miss Home-and-Beauty – you got bombs on the brain! You wanna die, go out there and let those guys blow your head off! Only don't try to take us with you, you bitch!'

He let go of her hair and her head fell weakly forward again. Packer grinned at Clay, his lips shaking slightly with relief, as if he had just become aware of how close they had been to disintegration.

'What's the count?' Clay asked.

'Four of them dead – and Asif. They got Asif,' Packer said. 'And lady here – she got wounded, didn't she?' He grinned.

'Why, man – why? Why they try it?'

'For Chrissake – why in hell should I know, man?' Packer

replied. 'That crazy bastard Latymer – I gotta talk to him. You keep an eye on her.' He nodded at Joanne Fender, who was clutching her elbow, nursing it in her good hand and moaning softly. 'And for Chrissake don't let her get near that bomb again!'

'Sure thing – you gonna talk to this guy Latymer?'

'I said!'

'Man – what happens now?'

'Now? Now we get Nasoud for certain, man! They won't try anything else now – got no cover, no surprise . . .'

'Man – we just killed four of their pigs. They gonna let us go after that?'

'No choice, baby!' Packer was smiling. 'We still got all these good people here.' He raised his voice. 'Rice! Come here!'

Rice appeared through the curtain that separated the two passenger sections.

'They've headed off towards the tower again,' he reported.

'O.K. Now, you get these bird-flyers down on the tarmac and make them fill their own tanks for a change. I gotta talk to the man!'

Packer walked off down the corridor to the flight-deck and the radio.

Latymer watched the four remaining men straggling away from the bulk of the tanker, a sick feeling in the pit of his stomach. Two of the bodies were hidden from him but he could see the other two, and the body of the passenger who, for some unaccountable reason, had tried to warn Packer and the others. He felt unable to face Seaborne. It had been he who had cajoled and persuaded him into finally agreeing on the wisdom of a frontal assault, and now the regrets and frustrations picked and nagged at him like hot needles. Men were dead, Packer and the others alerted, made less likely to trust him, less likely to agree to any deals. . . . It *was* his fault, he realised, though the reasons which had prompted him to that course of action still seemed valid.

The whole affair had been so brief and bloody it appalled him. It had been so senseless, the way in which blueprint had failed to become fact. It had been no sort of climax, merely a silly, fatal little episode in the chain of events. It was not important, because it had achieved nothing. His men had gained the steps and been unable to enter the aircraft. In a matter of seconds, almost within the timetable limits, four of them had died and the other four had found the doors shut against them. It had taken more than an hour to plan – and it had taken less than fifteen seconds to fail.

He turned to Seaborne and saw that the big policeman was staring ahead, out through the windows of the 'Greenhouse', deliberately avoiding his eye. His face was stony, grim. Latymer felt like a child who has failed a stern but loving parent in some important way. He feared Seaborne's displeasure and his veneer of calm cracked for perhaps the first time. He wanted to apologise, to be forgiven, to make amends. Yet he knew that the brute facts were all that he was left with.

Seaborne, aware of his intent gaze, turned to him and said, 'I'd better get a report from Sanders, don't you think?'

'Clarence . . .' Latymer began. Seaborne's unwinking gaze disconcerted him, and he faltered.

'Too late to feel sorry about it, isn't it?' Seaborne asked with a grim sneer in his voice.

'Nevertheless, Chief-Superintendent – I am sorry for what has happened.'

'Would you like to tell that to the widows and kids, sir?'

'No – no, I would not. Look, I realise that you must be feeling the same kind of regrets as myself . . .'

'No, sir – not the same kind as yourself. You're "Rat-catcher", after all. You've the power to send my men out to die – without remorse, if required.'

Latymer was aware of the hostility around him. The team had been with him until that point. They had assumed that the plan would work, that it would not end in the futile deaths of four of their colleagues. Now they blamed Latymer. It was his idea, his fault. They silently echoed Seaborne's strictures.

'Not without remorse,' he said softly.

'It didn't work!' Seaborne exploded. 'It didn't bloody well work!'

'There was no other way – I couldn't find another way . . .' Latymer said. Then his voice seemed to gain in strength and confidence. 'The safety of the passengers is our concern, Clarence. Not the safety, in the first instance, of your men.' His mouth was a compressed line in the silence which followed and his eyes were hard. Seaborne looked at him for a moment, his face a mask of contempt and then he turned on his heel and left the room.

When he had gone, Latymer returned to his contemplation of the tarmac. It had been pointless, the whole thing. Yet there was no time for regret. Seaborne could perform his self-laceration on his behalf. He had to concern himself with the safety of the passengers, now and forever, amen. So far only one of them had died, because his motive in warning Packer had been misinterpreted. He had received a report that the other eleven passengers were safe. Alison Bracken had not been among them.

He fell to thinking of Bracken, and looked at his watch. It was after ten-thirty. Bracken's last report had been cautiously hopeful – yet Latymer knew the pressure of self-deception under which his assistant would be functioning. He could not accept what he said without qualification. There, too, the death toll was mounting with the frightening normality of road accident figures. As the hours passed, a death and another death and another, added here and there, slipping under his gaze like blank statistics. He shrugged off the thought. He would have to bargain with an hysterical, enraged Packer for more time – but only after he had recovered, if he could do so, from the disadvantage under which the abortive attack had placed him.

He recognised that the girl was now doubly dangerous, wounded as she was. She would want revenge now, revenge for her pain and hurt. *She* was a bomb now, and she was armed and ready to explode. He wondered whether he had not already triggered her . . .

He wondered whether Packer and the others could keep a sufficiently tight rein on Joanne Fender. He profoundly hoped that they could.

He had not decided on his course of action when the R/T

blurted into life and he heard Packer's angry cry ring through the control room.

'Hey, Latymer-man – you still there? C'mon, man – talk to Packer!'

Latymer crossed to the R/T and flicked the switch. He paused for a moment and when he spoke his voice was heavy with defeat, with a subtle sense of horror at what had happened.

'Yes, Mr Packer, I'm here. You – wish to speak to me?'

'What in hell's name are you playing at, Latymer – you crud? You send men against me, when I said no tricks.'

'I – I thought that I could get away with it,' Latymer said slowly, as if the words were difficult to pronounce.

'Man – you wanna learn the hard way? Just send some more! This is the twentieth century, man. Pigs don't frighten us!'

'I realise that, Mr Packer – now. Of course, there will be no more tricks of that kind.'

'Man, you got your fingers burned, surely! You're too damn right there won't be any more tricks. I ought to fade some of your precious passengers – just to teach you a lesson!'

'No! You must not, Mr Packer. You must listen to me ...' Someone behind Latymer, convinced by his performance, let his breath escape in a long, derisive snort. Latymer squeezed obsequiousness into his voice. 'Listen – I was ordered to do what I did – it was against my advice. Do you understand, Mr Packer – I tried to stop it ...'

'You're the *man*! Don't give me that hoss-shit, Latymer – you ordered the attack!'

'No, really I didn't – I was overruled. You must believe me.'

'Who overruled you?'

'A senior member of our security services – a spy-catcher, Mr Packer. Apparently, he's causing trouble for *us* ...' He left the emphasis on the last word to impinge on Packer.

'What trouble?' Packer was attentive, convinced – on the hook. Latymer pressed on, in the same tone, spiced now with eagerness to be believed.

'He thinks Nasoud is sufficiently important to be worth more than the lives of the passengers.'

'The hell he does!' Packer exploded.

'I tried to convince him . . .' Latymer pursued. The fiction of his own weakness and the superior orders he had acted upon was, he knew, his only chance to persuade Packer to take no action in reprisal against the passengers. He had to whine, to wheedle – to convince Packer that they were, in reality, on the same side. He had convinced the men in the tower, many of whose stomachs he had undoubtedly turned. Now he had to convince Packer. He played him on the hook.

'Let me talk to him!' Packer said.

'I'm afraid he's already been summoned back to Whitehall, Mr Packer – it appears that the Home Secretary considers him to have exceeded his authority. I hope you understand that I couldn't avoid what took place?'

'Are you in full control *now*?'

'Yes. I have been granted full authority to patch up the affair. My superiors wish to ensure the safety of the passengers and they wish you to understand that they regret what has happened. The trade will, of course, take place at midnight, as arranged.'

'With *my* say-so! Don't forget that, Latymer. I hold all the cards.'

'I haven't forgotten that, Mr Packer. I'm not likely to. You – do still hold to our agreement?'

There was a silence. Latymer felt the beads of perspiration standing out on his forehead, felt the dampness of his shirt beneath his arms. Everything now depended on the psychological condition into which he had manoeuvred Packer – had he made him feel sufficiently appeased, sufficiently superior and powerful?

'You've been a very bad boy, Latymer,' Packer said. 'You got Asif killed, and I don't like that . . . and my little friend, the girl – she's wounded. There's a price to pay, Latymer – there's always a price to pay.'

Latymer noticed his knuckles, white where he was gripping the edge of the console.

'You must release the passengers, Mr Packer.' His voice

was almost a whine. He was calculating, so finely, on the sound of Packer's voice, on his slender knowledge of the man from his file, from their conversations. He knew, with terrible clarity, that he could be wrong. In the utter silence of the 'Greenhouse', he could hear the faint hiss of background from the R/T and the humming of the electric clock on the wall.

'No deal!'

'What . . .?'

'You heard me – no deal unless . . .'

'Unless what, Mr Packer?' Latymer said eagerly. 'What else do you want from us?'

'You, man!' Packer laughed loudly, the harsh braying sound echoing over the R/T. Then he added, 'You come along for the ride, when we fly outa here!'

Latymer understood what was being asked of him. He knew that Packer, to slake the thirst of his ego, wanted Latymer physically as well as morally, completely at his mercy. He hesitated only long enough to appear frightened by the prospect, then he said in a small voice, 'Of course, Mr Packer.'

'Midnight – come midnight, I wanna shake hands with my soul-brother Nasoud, and be wavin' to you and the ambassador! See to it, Latymer!'

There was a click and Packer was gone. Latymer flipped his own switch and straightened up. He had done it. In terms of the safety of the passengers, he had recovered the disaster of the attack. He heard the relief in the exhaled breath of one man, the muttered words of another. Perhaps they had been impressed by his agreement with Packer's suggestion, or perhaps they understood the play-acting. It did not matter. One man whispered an insult and Latymer ignored him. He watched the flight crew handling the heavy, reluctant serpents of the fuel lines, tiny figures in the white light of the arc lamps still out on the tarmac.

He needed, he realised, another report from Bracken. He had re-established a queasy equilibrium at Heathrow, but it was now utterly imperative that Nasoud be recaptured and returned to Heathrow as close to midnight as was humanly possible.

He wished he were standing alongside Bracken, somewhere in the Cotswolds, seeking the fleeing Arab. The 'Greenhouse' had the appearance, more than ever, of some unfinished, abandoned task. And Nasoud was still running . . .

9: The End of the Hunt

Nasoud crept forward, sensing rather than seeing the trees thinning about him. Starlight and moonlight began to wash the ground at his feet, unnoticed since his eyes were sweeping the trees and open places ahead of him. Unknown to himself and to the hunt, he was approaching the road running south from Withington towards the main Cheltenham-Cirencester road. Because he had moved swiftly, with the elation of killing, imposing his will to survive, he had passed across the face of the hunt which was beating north through the woods in an attempt to drive him out.

Car headlights, seemingly inside the wood, flashed glaringly across his eyes, rushing from right to left. Then they slowed, halted and he froze. He could not see the vehicle, but he knew that it had stopped. He cast about him for cover, then the headlights moved away again and gradually faded, while he rubbed at his eyes to rid them of the ruinous light. He heard no sound. He paused in the shadow of a tree and waited for the return of his night vision. It took a minute or two, by which time the startled pulse and heartbeat had steadied and he was able to appraise what he had seen.

There had to be a road, just a little way ahead of him, running parallel with the original course he had taken through the wood, therefore north to south. It had seemed a narrow road and there had been other trees massed darkly on the far side. The woods, apparently, did not end at that point for there was another spur, stretching cover further to the east. But why had the car stopped?

His problem, he decided after minutes of straining his hearing for the slightest sound, long after the engine of the car had faded into silence, was to cross the road. He waited patiently as unguessed minutes went by and no more traffic

195

came up or down the road. Yet he sensed that the road was guarded, because the car had stopped. Or had been stopped . . .?

He was terrified of bumbling childishly and ridiculously into the hands of a foot patrol, of being caught again like a moth on a pin in the glare of sudden penetrating head-lights. There was something of a stubborn pride in his reaction. He had proved himself a worthy opponent for upwards of a thousand men for many hours. He had no intention now of calmly walking into a trap.

The past was no longer real to him. To think of the girl, of the camps, of the black-garbed Arab woman who had been his mother; to think even of the atrocities he had witnessed, or had performed; all this demanded an effort of mind which he could not make, as if he feared the concentration of thought might cause him a migraine. No, there was only the present now, the moment-to-moment existence he had experienced on only a handful of occasions. All of them had been times when he had been on the run, or engaged in the activities of some attack or raid. The last occasion had been those terrible moments at the airport, with the suitcase full of guns and the men closing in, and then the attempt to escape . . .

Even that occasion was difficult to recall, since it was irrelevant to his present circumstances. That was it, he thought – everything *was* irrelevant to him now, except the hours immediately in the past, and the moments of waiting behind this tree . . . and the very distant prospect of escape, real escape, so that he could stop running. He did not think about death. The prey is not subject to fatalism, and neither was he. Nor is the hunted animal much given to optimism. It merely exists. So Nasoud merely existed, in the moments of time he was given. He was not greedy for time, like a thirsty man for water – he merely passively accepted and recorded the moments as they passed.

He decided that it was time for him to move. Whatever lay ahead of him on the road, he could no longer merely antici-pate it. When he got to the road, he would decide whether to follow it, at least for a time, or cross it, seeking the cover of the trees on the other side. Or . . .

He heard voices, and this time he carefully lowered himself to one knee at the base of a trunk, and turned his head like some inquisitive bird so that he might pinpoint the direction and number of the voices. He was now on the edge of the road, as it ran a little below him like a black, tarred stream, reflecting only in its deeper blackness the moonlight. He could see trees on the other side, dense, tall, leaved. Safety.

He had little need to decipher the noises he heard. An owl called, hunting like the men below it. There were three of them, gathered round a Land-Rover with its bonnet open. One of the men, a sergeant – he could see quite clearly in the moonlight the stripes on his arm – was smoking, standing a few yards from the vehicle, his rifle slung over his shoulder. He was, supposedly, guarding the two men bent over the engine, heads submerged in the intestines of the vehicle. The dialogue was desultory and consisted, so far as he could translate the contemporary service argot, of blasphemous encouragement on the part of the N.C.O., to which banter the two privates, tinkering with the vehicle in the glare of a spotlight clipped to the open bonnet, replied with a casual mixture of vulgarity and technical comment.

Nasoud, at first, reacted unconditionally to the situation in which he found himself. He would move back into the trees very quietly and take a southerly direction for some hundreds of yards, until he could cross the road without being observed. The N.C.O. seemed unconcerned that he might be anywhere in the vicinity, and would be unlikely to see him from a distance, a shadow flitting from shadow to shadow. Then he began to consider the circumstance of the vehicle with a cold, inhuman logic. A plan formed in his mind.

Slowly, he began to realise that he had been presented with a great and valuable prize yet, at the same time, a prize that was useless to him.

'Do I 'ave to call the piggin' REME wallahs up here just 'cos you two can't put a little problem like that right?' the sergeant drawled.

'We don't need our noses picked, sarge,' came the muffled reply from beneath the bonnet, followed by: 'Get out of the fuckin' light, you soft turd!'

Nasoud listened, but did not gather what was wrong with the vehicle. He understood only that the two men working on it had refused help, presumably of an expert kind. This either meant that the fault was slight or, simply, that the three soldiers did not mind spending some time under the stars on a warm summer night, rather than rushing about the countryside.

What should he do? He could not wait indefinitely. When he failed to emerge from the wood, then the patrols would backtrack, the helicopters would be overhead once more and the men below him would be put on alert. How long did he have? How much time could he allow in the pious hope that the men down there were really attempting to repair the Land-Rover? He did not know, but was loth to leave.

It was a little less than ten minutes later that the two men straightened, with exaggerated stretchings and complainings, from under the bonnet, to which complaints the N.C.O. did not deign to reply, and announced that the engine was as good as the day it left the factory.

'Will it work, though?' the N.C.O. observed. One of the temporary mechanics snorted by way of reply, while the other clambered into the Land-Rover and pressed the starter. The engine coughed and then roared into life, shattering the nocturnal calm of the wood.

Nasoud grinned to himself, teeth bared. His problem had been solved, and long before the deadline he had given himself for moving on and crossing the road. Now he knew what he had to do.

He had enjoyed the time he had spent watching the soldiers at work, watching the N.C.O. patiently, aloofly smoking, enjoyed the small sounds of metal against metal of the repairs, the scuffling of boots, the desultory conversation. He had enjoyed it because the men not twenty yards away from him were oblivious of his presence. He had been secreted like a child eavesdropping on an adult conversation. He had, for the first time since the aircraft had crashed, felt superior to his enemies. These three men were in his hands and he savoured each moment of their unguessed peril.

He had decided, as his own sense of danger had receded,

198

lulled into the background by the evident peril of those around the Land-Rover, that all he had to do was to kill the three men and commandeer their transport. One of the men, the one who had started the engine, was closest to himself in build. Nasoud had even decided exactly the manner in which each member of the trio should die – a bullet through the brain to preserve untorn, unbloodied the uniform of the man like him in build ... the other two should die as quickly and effectively as possible. He had weighed the positions of each man. The other two had lit cigarettes now and the three of them were standing in a tight group, solving his problem of drawing three separate beads. All that concerned him was the state of the uniform of the smallest man.

His mind made a sudden, daring leap into the perspective of the future. As if drawing aside a curtain, he had seen the miles unroll and the hours pass with himself seated, in British army uniform, in the Land-Rover. The image had excited him, as if it had been sexual, catching his breath, stirring him.

There were two problems, one hypothetical, the other real. What if a vehicle passed along the road during the shooting, or just afterwards when he was busy concealing the bodies? There was no guarantee that a vehicle would not pass, and there was absolutely nothing he could do to ensure it. It might even be another army vehicle. The other question was, more correctly, a statement of fact. When he killed the three men, and he had no doubt that he could kill them, the noises of at least three, and possibly more, shots would undoubtedly carry to enemy ears. He would be calling down or himself at least some portion of the forces ranged against him.

He listened. He listened for the sounds of a vehicle. Also he listened for the noises of the airborne search which might cover the explosions of the SLR. The helicopters had retreated, moved northwards, away from this corner of the woods. He thought it unlikely that gunshots would be heard by the crew of a helicopter above the noise of the rotors, however low they were flying, but he would have preferred one at a slight distance which would lay down a blanket of sound between himself and the forces mustering to the north-west on the edge of the wood.

He waited, the tension seeping back into him, the sense of wasted time becoming stronger. The three soldiers, as if accomplices in their own murder, were content to remain in their tight group, unmindful of any danger. For them, Nasoud had moved north, ahead of the search-parties from which they had become detached.

Just as he was arriving at a moment of decision, the noise he had hoped for occurred. He knew that it must mean that the search was beginning to cast about for him again, the renewed aerial activity signifying that they realised they had lost him yet again. Nevertheless, he was grateful. The helicopter seemed to be moving on a course that would carry it slightly to the north of his position, and the position of the soldiers who idly turned their eyes to the sky at the sound of the rotors. Slowly, carefully, flicking sweat from his eyebrows, he raised the gun to his shoulder, and the stock fitted snugly there, and against his cheek.

The gun hovered round the heads of the three soldiers, and his aim narrowed to the shortest man, still smoking, and he saw a smile on the man's face in reply to a remark by the N.C.O. Then he squeezed the trigger. The head disappeared from sight, tugged out of his view along the barrel and he swung the gun, squeezing the trigger another four times, more indiscriminately, into the other two bunched masses of khaki. Then he lowered the gun and stood up, moving only a few feet from the tree-bole which had hidden him. The three bodies lay sprawled on the road, separated by the impact of the bullets. He watched for any movement, listened for any sound. Nothing.

Carefully watching the three bodies rather than his feet, he scrambled down the bank, jumped across the narrow ditch at the side of the road and walked over to the victims. He turned the N.C.O. over with the toe of his shoe, the SLR staring down into the dead face. Then he checked the second man and the splash of darkness on his tunic-breast told him he was dead.

He crossed to the third man, the selected target, the little man who had started the car, and whose uniform would fit him. He was lying, legs flung out into the road, head over the lip of the ditch. The army beret was wet, Nasoud noticed with irritation. He bent down and tugged at the blouse, pulling the body sideways into the road. Then he inspected the remainder of the uniform. He was again irritated when he saw the stub of a cigarette, still smouldering, beneath one arm. It had burnt a hole in the fabric of the sleeve. Apart from that, as far as he could tell, the uniform was perfect and would fit him.

He laid down the gun and dragged the other two bodies off the road, hauling their dead weight up the bank and into the trees. He was sweating profusely by the time he returned to the third man. He began to undress the body, realising that he could not drag it into the trees, since that would dirty the uniform. He dragged it into the shade of the Land-Rover, hands beneath the arms, holding the body half-erect. Then he closed the bonnet of the vehicle. If another vehicle passed, he did not want attention drawn to the Land-Rover.

When the man was in his underwear, and Nasoud was sweating with haste and with fear, he began to undress. He stripped off his own clothes, grabbed at the uniform and climbed up the bank, leaving the soldier lying whitely in the shadow of the Land-Rover. Behind a tree, he swiftly donned the uniform, taking pains with the webbing and the puttees. The belt he buckled on last and then, as if before a mirror, straightened, posed and climbed back down the bank.

The dead man looked ridiculous now in vest, pants and the sodden beret on the head that had leaked darkly. Nasoud bundled him into the ditch, realising that he should have concealed the body before putting on the uniform. Now, like the most fastidious of bachelors, he would not touch the man with anything but the toe of his army boot, in case he somehow soiled his uniform. The blouse and trousers fitted, but the boots were too large. But he decided he must wear them.

His hand brushed through his hair. He saw that he had left the beret of one of the other two men lying prominently in the road. He tried it on. It was a little small but he arranged it as it might have been worn by its owner.

He picked up the SLR and dumped it in the back of the Land-Rover. He checked the pockets of the uniform for identification and found the necessary documents. He was relieved there was no description, no photograph.

He cocked his head, listening. A distant drumming of rotors headed away from him westward. That was all. He got into the Land-Rover and fired the starter. The engine roared comfortingly again, and he checked the fuel gauge. More than half-full. He had no idea of the capacity of the tank but he assumed that he could get well clear of the area, well clear, before he needed to concern himself with fuel. He went through the gears, following the pattern etched in white on the gear-lever. He found reverse and spun the wheel. The Land-Rover backed until its rear wheels overhung the ditch, then he changed gear and turned the wheel to opposite lock. He was intending to head south. There would be soldiers there, he knew, but fewer than threatened to confront him if he took the direction in which the vehicle had originally pointed, north.

He pressed his foot on the accelerator and the Land-Rover moved away. To anyone in another car, he was obviously a soldier driving an army vehicle, like many they would already have seen on the road engaged in the hunt for the escaped terrorist. He smiled, enjoying the sensation of safety promised by the uniform – safety, at least, from any civilians. Behind him, to anyone passing in a car or truck, there were no signs that anything untoward had occurred. The small amount of blood on the road would hardly be noticed in the light of headlamps. Only from the high cab of a heavy truck might the white, dead soldier in the ditch be spotted.

Before he had gone half a mile he passed an isolated pair of houses on the left. The wood had thinned and disappeared and the road ran alongside the brook down which he had previously waded, now flattened and shallowed into a ribbon of water. He drove at no more than thirty, despite the urgency he felt, despite the overwhelming desire to press his foot down hard, use the powerful engine to take him further and further from the scene of the murders as quickly as possible. Then the road petered out ahead of him becoming little more than a track, while to the right, turning west, it seemed to continue. There was a signpost, and he fished beneath the dashboard until he found a torch. He got out of the Land-Rover and inspected the signpost. The village of Colesborne was announced as being less than a mile along the road, while the town of Cirencester lay seven miles away and Cheltenham eight. He was aware that Cheltenham must still lie away to the west, but he had no idea about the direction or size of Cirencester.

He returned to the Land-Rover. Cheltenham was probably out of the question, so it would have to be Cirencester. He started the engine and turned right. Rounding a bend, he was aware of light traffic clipping past ahead. He realised he was about to join a main road, and his first thought was that it would undoubtedly be patrolled. He looked at his face in the mirror – he was unmistakable, surely. Hope seemed to drain out of him, the disguise seemed to become a futile, shallow impersonation. He braked gently.

He fished in the pockets of the tunic and found a packet of cigarettes and the box of matches that had rattled as he had put on the blouse. He switched off the headlights and sat, smoking, drawing deeply at the smoke, thinking. He was, however, unable to arrive at any decision. He got out of the Land-Rover, crushed out the cigarette and, keeping to the grass verge of the road close by the hedge, he crept forward until he arrived at the junction. A car passed, lighting him up and he started back against the hedge. He listened as its engine-note slowed and the car drew to a halt. It had been heading north. He saw from the sign across the road that Cheltenham meant a right turn, while Cirencester lay to the left. Cautiously, he peered out into the main road, wary of betraying headlights.

The road was patrolled. There was a police-car parked someway further down, less than twenty yards from the turning. Why they had not straddled the junction he could not at first understand, until he saw the humped shape of the army truck parked in the lay-by next to the police-car. There were red and white bollards set in the road and every vehicle, from either direction, was channelled into the verge, and the vehicle and its occupants inspected. Nasoud watched the car that had been stopped pull away and the lights die until the police and soldiers were all that was visible. Those, and the yellow, flashing light atop a tripod almost in front of him.

He peered to the left, southwards along the road. Then his heart leapt. It appeared that the road was clear. The junction was not, apparently, the cause of the road-block. He could hardly believe his luck. If he approached quietly, while a vehicle was moving up the main road, he could turn left and be away. Undoubtedly they would spot him, but they would be unable to detain him if he were quick.

He jogged along the verge back to the Land-Rover. Then he waited. The first car that approached allowed him to fire the starter and to creep, headlights off, to the junction. Then he waited again, engine switched off. He had to wait for four minutes, though to him it seemed like hours, before a car approached. Then he realised it was travelling in the wrong direction, coming from Cheltenham. Its engine noise would never cover the firing of the starter. He cursed, volubly, under his breath.

Suddenly he realised his luck. All he had to do was wait, wait for this car to pull away, so that it was a shield for him. They would not dare to shoot at the Land-Rover with the car between them and their target.

He listened, ears cocked, for the pick-up of the accelerator. Then he heard it and pressed the starter. He pulled blindly out into the main road and was immediately dazzled by headlights coming towards him, heading north. Then, quite suddenly, there was a soldier at his side, staring up into his face.

'Christ, mate! Where you come from?' the soldier asked. 'You almost run over my boots!'

The Land-Rover now firmly blocked the southbound lane of the road. Nasoud, helpless and sweating, realised that the junction was guarded, though he had not seen the soldier. Probably the man had been having a smoke or relieving himself. The ludicrous explanations flashed across his mind. Then, he was suddenly ice-cold, logical, even daring.

'Sorry, mate!' he called down to the soldier. 'In a hurry.'

To him, his voice sounded hopelessly inadequate, unmistakably foreign.

The guard at his side smiled.

'Bloody makin' us jump through 'oops, the bloody lot of 'em!' was his comment.

Nasoud continued staring down at the man's smiling face. He was unable to grasp that his disguise had worked, that he had been taken for a soldier and by, of all people, another soldier. The car blocked behind him pulled out and he glimpsed an irritated face at the window of a large sports car.

Then he heard the soldier say, 'Pillock! See the tart with 'im? I could take 'er 'ome and find a use for 'er, couldn't you?' Then he laughed uproariously.

Nasoud attempted to laugh and managed a feeble smile. Then he glanced in the mirror. He saw that the appearance of the Land-Rover, no longer masked by the sports car, was attracting attention. A light, carried at a soldier's side, was wobbling down the road towards him. He smiled again at the soldier, and then waved his hand and pressed the accelerator.

He pulled away, watching in the mirror for signs of alarm and pursuit. Yet there seemed to be none. He settled thankfully back in the seat and pressed his foot down harder. He could see the red tail-lights of the sports car ahead of him, further along the straight stretch of road. He blessed the car and its occupants. Though he had not realised it at the time, the woman in the passenger seat had saved him from careful scrutiny. Nasoud had not even noticed her, not even when the car had overtaken him. The soldier, on the other hand, had continually darted his eyes behind the Land-Rover during his conversation with Nasoud, looking hungrily at the woman.

Behind him, the corporal carrying the light had reached the guard. He stood watching the tail-lights of the Land-Rover.

'Was that a Land-Rover, O'Neill?'

'Yes, corp. Just one up.'

'Who was it?'

'Christ, corp, I don't know – one of us.'

'Name – unit? What were they?' the corporal snapped, looking with hard eyes at O'Neill, who began to shift uncomfortably on the spot.

'Dunno,' he muttered.

'You what? What did you do – pass the bleedin' time of night with him?'

'Yes, corp.'

'You birk! You were looking at the expensive tart in the Ferrari, weren't you?' O'Neill's smile seemed to enrage the N.C.O. He snarled: 'What the hell's one of our blokes doing tear-arsing down the road to Cirencester – did you ask yourself that? The search is thataway!' His arm extended, indicating the north. 'What did he look like?'

'Little bloke – dark . . .' O'Neill's mouth dropped open and he was unable to speak. The N.C.O. smelt his breath as he noisily exhaled, and realised why the soldier had been talking through compressed lips.

'You turd! You bleedin' lump of dog shit!' the corporal bawled. 'You got a bottle hidden here somewhere, and you're too pissed to spot a bloody Arab when you're standing next to him!'

'No, corp, it wasn't him . . .' O'Neill faltered.

'I bloody well hope not – I bloody well hope not, for your sake! If it was, I'll have you digging latrines from now until 1984!' He turned on his heel, face dark with rage, and began to run up the road, calling out as he did so.

Bracken stood next to Spencer-Handley in the rocking, shaking din that was the helicopter, as it cruised above the woods. Nasoud was late, and he and the brigadier and Sergeant Porson were all aware of that fact. Nasoud should have emerged from the trees more than a quarter of an hour before since the first troops were already breaking cover. The narrowing horns of the crescent were apparent as they drew together on the ground blow.

The fields beneath them were full of men – two armies, it might have been, drawing together for battle, except that they were both intent on one tiny figure, one fly that had not been drawn into the trap. Bracken forebore to comment. He looked instead, for perhaps the fiftieth time, at his watch. Ten thirty-four. Nothing. The radio-crew were monitoring the sections of the patrols as they reported to Stanton, Anderson and Mayhew who were all foregathered below them, complete with the group of command helicopters that had airlifted them and their staffs from the airfield at Chedworth. The brigadier would also have been there, had it not been for Bracken's insistence that they remain airborne.

When the message came, Bracken heard it with something like relief. He knew, then, why he had requested that the chopper should remain aloft. He had feared another escape, a furtherance of the pursuit, an enlargement, violent and eruptive, of the complacently closing jaws of the search. He listened as the radio operator relayed the message from the road-block on the A435, just east of the village of Colesborne. The map-sergeant, Porson, placidly fiddled over the OS map with his pins.

The brigadier said to the operator, 'Ask Major Anderson whether there are any reports of a Land-Rover being sent south – I want to know what vehicles are in the area of Colesborne Park and the eastern side of these woods as soon as possible.' As the man relayed the order, Spencer-Handley turned to Bracken. 'You heard that report, my boy?'

'Yes – is it him?'

'Don't know. Something about a soldier being on guard, drunk, and a Land-Rover appearing from this side road here . . .' His finger tapped at the map. 'And pushing off south towards Cirencester . . .'

'How far?' Bracken looked at the map intently.

'From here – oh, a couple of miles, no more.'

'We can go there?'

The brigadier looked thoughtful. He was not, by nature, an impetuous man. He heard the voice of the radio operator.

'Major Anderson says they're calling in, sir. Can't raise one of the Land-Rovers at the moment – they were on that road, stopped with engine trouble, dropped off as a rear guard as a result . . .'

'That's it!' Bracken said. 'That's it!'

The brigadier's face darkened, appeared troubled. Then he said, in a curiously strained voice, 'Request Major Anderson to put down a small chopper at their last reported position, as soon as possible! I want to know where they are.' He turned to Bracken. 'We couldn't put down this flying office on a minor road, even if we wanted to . . .'

'Do you need to check it out?'

'Yes – dammit!' Spencer-Handley snapped. He stared into Bracken's face with hard blue eyes. 'This is a *costly* little venture, my boy – very costly!'

Bracken flared up: 'That bloody road-block must have been sited by an idiot . . .' He was silent for a moment, seeing the look on the brigadier's face. Then he added, 'Can't we . . . ?'

'Yes,' the brigadier replied grimly. 'I think we'd better.' He looked round at the four soldiers seated in the rear of the helicopter, armed, patient, waiting. He said to one of them: 'Tell the pilot to head for . . . reference, Porson?'

'132 002, sir.'

'Sir!' The man laid down his rifle and passed them, pushing into the cramped flight-cabin. In another moment, the helicopter was swinging to starboard as it altered course. Bracken and the brigadier waited, each looking at the map unfolded on the table. The red line of the A435 stretched thinly to the south, through North Cerney and on to Cirencester.

'Pass this message via Major Anderson to A.C.C. Maxon,' Bracken said to the radio operator. 'Army vehicle, identified as a Land-Rover, heading south on the A435. Intercept before it reaches Cirencester, but don't necessarily *expect* trouble. Warn all police mobiles in the area of North Cerney.'

'Sir.'

'A little strong, Bracken?' the brigadier asked.

Bracken was about to reply, when the radio operator said, 'They've put a Scout down on the road, sir. Have found a man in a ditch and two more in the trees. All dead. The man in the ditch has had his uniform removed, and Nasoud's clothes have been found . . .'

'It *was* him!' Bracken said, and the brigadier looked at him harshly for a moment. He sensed the delight in Bracken's voice. Nasoud, at the end of the long day, had broken cover at last.

The brigadier said, tiredly, 'Very well. I want as many mobile units on that road as possible. Get Major Anderson to commandeer whatever he can find in the Cirencester area. Confirm the ident. with A.C.C. Maxon and warn him that the man has killed again, and is in army uniform.'

'Sir.'

Bracken was looking at the OS map. There were a number of side roads, too many, which could take Nasoud off the A435. Yet Bracken was certain that he would use none of them. The man had only recently killed three soldiers and had stolen a vehicle. He estimated the man's state of mind. For the first time, he would be able to move swiftly and the desire to do so, Bracken hoped, would prove overwhelming. If they could get to him before he reached the outskirts of Cirencester, then they would find him still on the A435 And now he was obvious, easily identified, even if he reached Cirencester – he was in army uniform.

Bracken looked out of the window. There were lights below him, a mere couple of hundred feet below, the headlights of cars moving along the invisible ribbon of the A435. Nodding to the brigadier, who spread his hands in a gesture which signified that Bracken was now in effective command of the helicopter, Bracken pressed his way into the flight-cabin.

He tapped the pilot on the shoulder, and yelled, 'Get down lower, can't you?'

The pilot looked at him, grinned, and said, 'This is the twentieth century – ever hear of high-tension cables?'

'Don't give me that – they're marked on the map!'

'Telephone wires, would you believe?' the pilot said, dropping the nose of the helicopter, seeming to ease the flow of lights up at them. Then he levelled, at less than a hundred feet, and Bracken slipped into the empty seat next to him. The pilot nodded, grinned again and indicated the headphones and mike dangling from the dual controls in front of him. Bracken reached for them and slipped them on. The drone of the beating rotors went away.

He began to search for vehicles heading south. As they overtook them, he attempted to identify type and make. It was difficult. Had they been driving without lights, the moonlight would have betrayed the shape, the outline, would have told him whether the vehicle was open or possessed a roof, perhaps the make and model. But, behind the white beams of the headlights, each vehicle was a dark bulk. Bracken felt something rubbing his knee and looked down. The pilot was pushing a map under his gaze.

'Not trying to touch you up,' he said, as if Bracken's thoughts lay open to him.

'Thanks. Where are we?'

The pilot leaned over and, as if the map were some braille construction, tapped at it, his finger tracing the route of the road below, without his eyes moving, apparently, from their scrutiny of the night ahead of them. They were following the road as it passed through one spur of Penhill Plantation, north of where it by-passed the village of Rendcombe. Bracken adjudged the accuracy of the pilot's tracing finger. He picked out the dark mass of trees below and the lights of the village away to the left. Two more cars passed beneath them, both of them saloons, moonlight shining back from their roofs; then he tapped the glass in front of him. The pilot dropped dangerously low, and then lifted again. Bracken had seen an open vehicle, but it had been nothing but a small sports car.

Behind him, in the command area, he knew the brigadier would be establishing the search proper, in consultation with Anderson, Mayhew and Stanton – probably also including Maxon via a radio link. They would all be engaged in the desperate attempt to encircle the speeding Nasoud. The brigadier had given over the use of his helicopter to Bracken because it in no way interfered with his organisation of the search.

'I *am* enjoying myself!' the pilot remarked cheerfully. 'Really super stuff, this – eh what?' He grinned. 'When do we get to spot the murderous little bugger?'

'Can you put down on the road in front of him?' Bracken asked.

The pilot looked scornfully at him.

'Not a chance, old son! Mustn't get the Brig's best airborne command-post dented. Besides, I'm not insured for main roads!'

210

'You mean that?'

'Couldn't get her down, I don't think. It's not wide enough – too many trees, too many hedges. We can sit on him, though, if you like, keep him in sight as long as you want – or you can dive out of the door and into the Land-Rover, like a modern Tex Ritter.'

'You're giving your age away!' Bracken said. 'All right. It'll have to do.' He sounded disappointed.

'He was always jumping off his horse on to the chief crook,' the pilot said regretfully.

'Who was?'

'Tex Ritter.'

'That's why you're just an army helicopter-pilot – too much television in your youth.'

'Probably – if I'd worked really hard, I might have become a policeman!'

Bracken realised that the excitement had infected him, the emotional stimulus of the chase, and it had also infected the pilot. He smiled. There was a comfort in action, an emotional charge that elated . . .

'There!' he said.

The nose of the chopper dipped and as it flashed over the vehicle below, Bracken caught the details – open vehicle, army, one occupant in uniform. He looked across at the pilot.

'Already doing it – throttling back.'

Bracken looked down. The headlights nosed from beneath the shadow of the helicopter and the Land-Rover seemed to speed up, leaving them for a moment.

'It's him,' Bracken said in a choked voice. For the first time, he had caught a glimpse of the white moonlit face of the quarry.

'Putting his foot down,' the pilot observed. 'Does he consider us a threat, I wonder?'

'Keep him in sight,' Bracken said, getting out of his seat, laying the map and the headset down. He pushed his way out of the cabin and the brigadier looked up from the OS map on the table.

'We've got him,' Bracken said.

The brigadier smiled with an almost cruel satisfaction and said to the radioman, 'Put that message over, will you? Porson, give him the references. We'll keep him in sight, and tell Major Anderson to stand by for any orders, any changes of direction.' Then he joined Bracken. 'We'll not lose him now,' he said. Bracken saw the determination in his eyes.

'No,' he said. 'We won't lose him.'

The helicopter slewed hard to port sending Bracken against one of the windows in the fuselage.

'What's going on?' the brigadier asked.

'I don't know!' Bracken snapped, brushing past him and pushing into the flight cabin. 'What's up?' he asked, his tone indicating his fears.

'Our pal just turned off. He's heading for Woodmancote, on a side road.'

'Shit!' was Bracken's comment. He looked down. The helicopter was keeping pace with the racing lights below as they flickered and winked through a grove of trees. If he stops, or gets out, we've lost him, Bracken thought. He picked up the map and the headset, and settled himself in the co-pilot's seat. The lights were fifty yards ahead and below, but the pilot kept at that distance to compensate for any sudden changes of speed and direction by the Land-Rover.

Bracken studied the map. Three roads, apart from the one they were following, led out of the village of Woodmancote – no, four, he corrected himself as he spotted the white line of a farm track, leading south-west from the village towards Cooles Farm. Which one would Nasoud take? Would he enter the village? Would he . . . ? Bracken preferred not to think what might happen if Nasoud became sufficiently rational to see the hope that lay in taking another hostage.

The lights of the village glowed ahead. Bracken felt a tap on his shoulder and turned. It was Porson.

'Any orders to be relayed, sir?' he asked. 'Brigadier's had Nasoud's new position sent back and Major Anderson's telling him what the coppers – sorry, sir – what your lot can put in the area, sir.'

'Nothing, yet. Thanks, Porson.' Bracken returned to the

map. Then he spoke to the pilot. 'Can you set down ahead of him, so that we've time to set up a road block or an ambush of some kind?'

'Not before he reaches the village.'

'Damn!'

Bracken watched the lights of the Land-Rover merge with the lighting in the main street of Woodmancote. The outline of the vehicle became visible, blocked in, and the hunched body of the driver could be clearly seen. The helicopter lifted slightly, to avoid any aerials or wires, and Bracken watched the Land-Rover career through the village. The pilot overshot, and the scene below was dragged away from beneath Bracken's gaze for a moment, and then it returned, minus the Land-Rover.

'Where's he . . .?' he began.

'Taken the farm track, old son – no sweat!'

The helicopter settled on its new course, the night darkened, and the merging beams of the Land-Rover's headlights gathered strength. Nasoud was driving like a maniac, like an enraged animal fleeing from a maddening insect, like something running before a forest fire. Bracken felt a fierce, revengeful delight in the speed of the vehicle, its careering passage along the bumping farm track, a pleasure deep and strong in the waving and leaping of the lights. Nasoud was really afraid, was *really* running . . .

The thought that the man might kill himself sobered him. He was driving with a total disregard for his own safety. Ahead of the Land-Rover and its airborne shadow, the bird of prey hovering above it, the lights of Cooles Farm could be seen.

'Can he see those?' Bracken asked, pointing ahead.

'I should think so – the farm's in a hollow, if you look at your map.'

'Then get ahead of him – he musn't get to the farm first!'

The headlights disappeared beneath the belly of the helicopter and their glow was left behind. The lights of the farm solidified into square buildings and light spilled from a doorway, as the chopper circled once and began to descend. The pilot was settling the helicopter on to grass, just short of the walls of the farmyard.

Bracken left his seat and went to the brigadier's side.

'This is it!' he said. 'You men – on your feet!'

The soldiers were at attention in a moment and one of them dragged back the door. The helicopter settled, rode and seemed to collapse on to its undercarriage. The soldiers were through the door before Bracken could detect any change in the dying note of the rotors. He went through the door after them and the headlights of the Land-Rover glared in his eyes. The up-draught from the rotors plucked at him. The vehicle was less than forty yards away, swinging wildly to the left, veering towards the gate of the farmyard, as Bracken yelled out.

'Put a bullet in the engine-block – stop him!'

'I'll do it!' the N.C.O. snapped.

He was on one knee and the Land-Rover was broadside-on to his aim. Nasoud was obviously intent on reaching the farm-house where cover and hostages both lay. The gate of the farmyard was wide open and Bracken wished that the pilot could have blocked it off with the bulk of the chopper.

'For God's sake, don't damage the driver!' he yelled, and then the rifle spurted flame twice. The noise of the engine ceased almost at once, as if the ignition had been switched off. Then, in appalled slow-motion, Bracken watched the Land-Rover veer away from the gateway and drive itself into the low stone wall. Even as the car's speed, more than forty miles an hour, was transferred into Nasoud's unbelted body, Bracken knew what was going to happen. The man flipped like a dummy out of his seat, bounced on the bonnet of the Land-Rover and jack-knifed into the top of the wall. He slid slowly, sack-like, over the wall, and disappeared.

Bracken was running, knowing that the man would be dead, that the impact with the bonnet and the wall would have killed him, killed Alison two hundred miles away . . . It had all come to nothing, the whole, elaborate thing had come to this – a shot, a split-second, the noise of tortured metal, and a broken neck . . .

When the brigadier came up to him, he was bending over the body of Nasoud, the lolling head cradled in his lap, while he sat in the mud and mire of the farmyard, his back against the wall, staring at the dead face of the Arab terrorist.

It was ten-fifty-seven by the brigadier's watch.

10: Liebestöd

The clock in the 'Greenhouse' announced that the time was thirty-one minutes past midnight. Hilary Latymer, silent, stony-faced, was standing at the window staring at the distant shape of the airliner. The arc-lamps still whitely illuminated the ribs of the 707 and the two fuel tankers, emptied of their payloads, were parked fifty yards from it. There was the generator, the fire-tender with its ladder still extended, and the obscene litter of the abortive attack – the dead Special Branch men and the body of the passenger. Asif, the Arab, had been hauled inside the aircraft. Only to him had the necessary decencies of death been extended. No shots had been fired as the body had been taken aboard. Latymer had not dared to exacerbate the situation.

The silence and emptiness of the great airport now seemed its natural condition. It was almost as if Latymer expected to see grass and weeds forcing their way through the concrete of an abandoned wartime airfield. The scene depressed him profoundly and yet it exercised a fascination over his eyes and his imagination. Activity seemed to be held in suspense. There was nothing else to do but to stare out at the wreckage that surrounded the aircraft, human and mechanical, and to reflect upon the wreckage of so much else that had occurred since the summons to the scene of the hijacking had reached him.

Bracken had arrived a little after midnight, flown to Heathrow in an army helicopter. He had made his report and received from Latymer an account of the events since his departure. He had lived vicariously through the dangers of each separate manoeuvre and the threat each had posed to Alison; now, however, he had subsided into a profound and futile reverie. Everything had now sunk beneath the surface and the scene at the airport was no more than an empty ceremony held for the dead.

For Alison was dead. It was true that by some ghastly immoral joke she was still out there, a physical presence still bodily alive, but he accepted that there could now be no reprieve for her. He did not feel guilt or failure. He understood and believed that he was responsible for her condemnation, but his mind buried the growing flood of guilt for the moment, even though the pressure was building-up like water behind a dyke wall.

Latymer turned from the window and looked at his assistant, at the spars and flotsam of feeling still visible in his face. Bracken, he understood, was in an emotional limbo at that moment and he preferred to leave him so. For himself, it was as if his official function would not let him rest, though it was now rendered purposeless by Bracken's news. He continued to function as the Executive Officer, even though he knew that in the minds of his masters, he no longer bore that title – except for the performance of one last task. The Home Secretary, in two telephone conversations, one in the wake of the attack and the other after news of Nasoud's death, had given him a last task. He was to persuade the hijackers to accept any deal, *any* deal in order that they leave without Nasoud *and* without the passengers.

Latymer smiled thinly to himself. He, Hilary Latymer, was still in effective command – because the Home Secretary was nervous of his political future if seen taking command of, and responsibility for, a disaster. It was because he was still in command that he had overridden, less than ten minutes before, the accumulated feeling of the 'Greenhouse' team that Packer would accept the money waiting in a security van downstairs. Latymer knew he would not, despite the fact that the van contained close to three million dollars. Seaborne and the others, no longer spellbound by his narrative concerning Marie, had been almost unanimous in deciding that Packer and the girl could be persuaded to take the money, and leave the passengers. Latymer knew they would not – especially the girl. He had called a halt to the discussion, and he knew that he had been staring out of the window merely in order to allow

217

a decent interval in which to accept that he had to put the offer of the money. Whatever his feelings, there was no other road to take.

At two minutes past twelve, Packer had called Latymer over the R/T, demanding fulfilment of the midnight deadline. Latymer, sweating visibly, his body hunched over the instrument, knuckles whitened with the pressure of his grip, had bluffed for the last time. The Lebanese ambassador had not arrived — a technical hitch. Packer had blustered and threatened, but Latymer had won more time.

In fact, the Lebanese ambassador had arrived before the news of Nasoud's death had reached Heathrow. It had taken a great deal of hard bargaining and, Latymer suspected, pressure from guerilla groups based in the Lebanon, before the Lebanese government had agreed to endangering the life of His Excellency.

When he arrived, the little man with the shiny bald head had been bravely talkative and obviously nervous. However, when the news that his services would not be required had reached him, he had been plainly relieved. However, Latymer admitted to himself in fairness, the little man had volunteered to stay on in case he might be required in any capacity other than hostage. At the moment, he was sitting across the control room from Latymer, talking in a low voice in Arabic to the young man of good family who was his private secretary.

Latymer's thoughts returned to Joanne Fender. If he had offered Marie three million dollars in 1944, had he guessed her intention, she would not have taken it. To have offered it would have been the final insult, to attempt to place her back within the class she had rejected and which she wished to wipe from the face of the earth. He dare not, he realised, offer money in Joanne Fender's hearing to Packer for the release of the passengers.

The P.M. and the Cabinet considered the persuasion of the hijackers to accept a large sum of money as a simple task. Money would be the guarantee, the elixir — the panacea. The nightmare would go away and become the problem of the Lebanon. They did not believe him about Joanne Fender —

yet she was the rock on which their frail craft would founder, tear itself to pieces.

Unless, he realised, Packer could silence her completely and effectively, she would destroy the aircraft. Latymer had known that ever since the memory from thirty years before had slipped like a blade into his mind.

Detective Chief Superintendent Clarence Seaborne wrinkled his nose at the fragrant smoke emanating from the ambassador's cigarette, and thought about Joanne Fender. True, Latymer's feeling was not his own, and he was still holding out against offering the money – but Seaborne knew he had nothing else to offer and that it was just a matter of time until Latymer spoke to Packer over the R/T. Seaborne had encountered fanatics before, amongst the Provos as well as Arab groups and the 'Angry Brigade'. He did not believe in a breed that was not open to some, *any* kind of reason or bribe. Money was convertible – in this case into heroin, guns, bombs. Seaborne's stomach turned at the thought of his government handing over the means of so much misery and death to people like Packer, but he understood the necessity of the action. With Nasoud dead as a doornail, they could offer nothing else.

Latymer's story of 1944 and the French girl had receded in his mind. It was the impression of one man, to which that man was giving far too much weight.

He sniffed. The effeminate cigarette smoke irritated him. He glared balefully at the ambassador who conversed obliviously with his secretary. Seaborne yawned. Suddenly, he felt very tired. He looked again at Latymer. What the hell was the man going to do, and when was he going to do it?

The ringing of the telephone cut across his thoughts and was amplified in the sudden silence of the room. The noise seemed to catch them all unprepared. Then McCarthy leaned over the central dais and picked up the offending receiver.

'Yes, he's here – but . . . yes, sir.' McCarthy put his hand over the mouthpiece and said softly: 'It's A.C.C. Maxon, sir – from Gloucester. Wants to speak to you.'

A glancing, fierce irritation crossed Latymer's features, and then he relaxed, and held out his hand.

219

'Excuse me, Clarence, gentlemen – this shouldn't take long . . .'

He put the receiver to his face, and said: 'Good morning, Mr Maxon, how good of you to call . . .' He listened and as he did so, his eyes widened and his mouth dropped open, slowly. Maxon had called him merely to report the withdrawal of all units from the area of the search and to give his opinion of the handling of the whole operation by Bracken and Brigadier Spencer-Handley. Latymer's rage mounted as he listened, until he was furious with the pompous, unimaginative, petty clown at the other end of the line. However, he merely muttered acknowledgements, speeded the A.C.C. through his recital, and waited for the man to have done.

It was ten minutes before Maxon appeared to be satisfied and wound up his monologue with what Latymer supposed was an attempt at humour.

'And that chap, the dummy Arab you wanted despatched from Dartmoor by car – he's reported in, too. Says he was nearly arrested by the army. They didn't believe his story and they thought the officers with him might have stolen the uniforms and the ID cards.' He ended with a flourish of derogatory comments on the army.

'Thank you, Mr Maxon. Thank you very much for your report. Goodbye to you.' Thankfully, Latymer put the receiver down.

Seaborne watched Latymer's face, as he had done almost continuously while he was in conversation with Maxon. He smiled to himself, knowing Maxon and being able to guess at the churning frustration and anger that the call had generated in the unflappable Latymer. Then he saw the man straighten, become almost rigid, and his face take on an abstracted look. When he turned to face him, Seaborne was shocked at the determination that had appeared on his features.

'Clarence – gentlemen. I have a possible solution to our problem!' His voice betrayed his excitement. 'What would you say was our most pressing need at this moment? What do we *really* need?'

There was a silence, and then someone said, 'A clear shot

at Joanne Fender – and Packer!' There was a small ripple of laughter and then again silence.

Latymer waited, calculated his moment, and then said, 'What price the resurrection of Mr Nasoud? What would you give for that?'

It was Bracken who answered him, without humour, without exaggeration.

'My right arm,' he said softly. Latymer looked at him. 'But he's dead,' Bracken added, his face despondent.

'Who knows it?' Latymer pressed.

'Half the British army . . . us . . .'

'Who *doesn't* know it?'

'The great unwashed British public – and our friends out there.'

'Exactly!' Latymer was almost grinning. 'In fact, they confidently expect to see him and be reunited with him in a very short time from now – do they not? Now – what if the longed-for event were to happen – or, at least, *appear* to happen?'

'Appear?' was all Seaborne said.

'Yes. Mr Maxon, of interminable breath and little sense of the time, has just reported that the dummy Arab we sent from Dartmoor by car this afternoon has just reported in, finally . . .' He paused, then said, 'Don't you see it – can't you see where I'm leading?'

There was a silence, and then Seaborne said, 'No! Christ, no! You'd never get away with it!'

'Are you sure, Clarence? Are you absolutely sure?'

'The money's safer!' Seaborne countered.

'Not if it's a trigger – and you yourself admitted that she'd be interested only in the original exchange . . . well, then? Let's make that exchange.'

There was a mutter of sound and Latymer left them to it for a couple of minutes. In his mind, he anticipated their objections, examined the dangers and flaws of the idea. He was not a man given to rash and impulsive ideas, and this one had leapt on him wildly, unexpectedly. He imagined it was spawned by his very desperation, and that made him suspicious of it. Nevertheless, he had had to persuade them to take it seriously. His excitement had been genuine, the elation of relief, but he had added to it, made it more impressive. It was a hare-brained scheme, he knew, and it posed the most grave dangers for the passengers. Unless he had been firmly and irrevocably convinced that to offer Joanne Fender the bribe, to get them to go away, was to seal the fates of the four dozen passengers on the aircraft, then he would never have voiced it.

'How can we fool them, sir?' McCarthy said. 'They *know* him, for God's sake!'

'Yes, indeed,' Latymer said softly. 'We could never let him board the airliner – whoever our impersonator might be – could we?'

'Then how the hell will it work?'

'Clarence – use your imagination! We get the passengers off the aircraft *before* we hand him over – *we* make that part of the deal, for Heaven's sake!'

'And when they discover what's happened – what happens to the flight-crew?'

There was another silence, a long and heavy one. They realised that Latymer had already considered that objection.

After a while, he said, 'They might well have to die . . .' He raised his hand to still the appalled mutter of reaction. 'But they need not do so – we are not *necessarily* signing their lives away by taking this course. Let us examine what we might gain from this deception . . .'

'There's been too much deception, Latymer!' Seaborne burst out, stilling the room. His words choked off, as he saw the darkening anger on Latymer's features.

'That, Clarence, is my job,' he said through clenched teeth. 'I may like it as little as you do – but my unofficial title, the one that tells the truth, is "Executive Liar in charge of Hijackings". I'm sorry that it offends you, but I must persist in fulfilling that function, in spite of your own blunt honesty!' The silence that followed would have persisted for a long while, had he not added pleasantly, 'As I was saying – let us examine the possibilities. It is night and the light would be behind the impostor – he's been on hunger-strike and his features would be altered. His clothes would not necessarily be his own. His voice . . . we would need to have someone,

222

not necessarily the same man, who could speak Arabic, and impersonate the tone and colour of Nasoud's voice. Aubrey's tapes of Nasoud's interrogations would help us there. Now, I agree that all of this takes us only so far as perhaps thirty yards from the steps. They have glasses on board and our man would have to be lucky to get that far without being rumbled. But, if we agreed that the change-over should take place at some half-way point on the tarmac, so that both sides could be guaranteed safety, then all the passengers would be sufficiently close to here to escape the blast should our deception not please Miss Fender. In fact we might, just *might*, get them to agree to hand over the bomb as part of the deal.'

He paused, letting his final statement sink home. Heads, he could see, were beginning to nod, to signal agreement with his thinking thus far, signalling pleasure at his last statement. He continued. 'Now, providing that all those stipulations can be met, what do you feel about the idea?'

He left them to their deliberations. They had begun to draw together into small knots and groups, all except Seaborne, who kept his eyes doggedly on the ground.

Latymer crossed to Bracken, and said, quietly, 'Well, Philip — what do you think? Are you in favour?'

Bracken looked up at him, his face troubled. 'I want to be, sir. But it seems so much more . . . so . . .'

'*Insubstantial,* you mean? Alongside three million dollars, you think?'

'Yes, sir. That's just it.'

'To you — yes. Even to me. Because we would have a use, even perhaps a desire, for that kind of money. And in ninety-nine cases out of a hundred you would be right to think that of others. But, in this case, I'm convinced you would be mistaken!'

'But why, sir — why is *she* so different?'

'She possessed once, free, gratis, and for nothing — a great deal more than three million dollars, Philip. But it's not that. Do you know what she would do if she found out that Alison was on board that aircraft? I am convinced that she would shoot her in the back of the head and make you watch it through binoculars!'

Latymer hated what he was doing to Bracken, but he needed allies. He could no longer count on Seaborne, and he needed support. He did not have to justify his scheme to the men now discussing it. If he ordered it, they would carry it out. It was merely the illusion of democracy they were enjoying at the moment. But with Bracken – with Bracken, he wanted agreement, even if he terrified him into giving his support. Perhaps, he reflected, it was because he was afraid to have Alison's death on his hands, without Bracken's consent.

Bracken recovered from the nauseous images that had overwhelmed him and said, 'You're *sure* – you're absolutely sure?'

'I am – yes.' Latymer did not have to lie.

Bracken looked thoughtful for a moment and then he said, But you can't guarantee anything, can you? Nothing. The flight-crew, for instance . . . she could kill them, even if she couldn't blow them up.'

'If the others let her – but if she hasn't the bomb, then it takes time to shoot people – enough time for someone to put a bullet in her, which I am convinced any of them would, if she threatened their means of escape – the crew – now that they're so close to being safe. They think they're winning. They won't let anyone stop them now – not even her!'

Bracken was appalled. 'My God, but you're cynical!'

Latymer winced. 'It's merely that I'm aware – more aware then some of the Special Branch seem to be, in this matter,' he said flatly.

He looked at Bracken for a long time, and then the younger man nodded his head and said, 'I suppose you're right – it is the only hope . . .'

Latymer turned away and saw Seaborne on his feet, facing him. There was a tense silence between the two men and then the policeman, with poor grace, said, 'The first thing we'd like you to do is to talk to Packer, Mr Latymer.'

Latymer nodded.

'Naturally – we have to be clear about the matter of the bomb. After that, I leave it up to you to find the impostor!'

Detective-Sergeant Henry Currie had an incipient dislike of make-up and the more effeminate appurtenances of disguise.

The man fussing with his face and hair at that moment, in the ground-floor Alpha Group room in the control tower at Heathrow, was a policeman himself but that in no way made his attentions any less unsettling. Currie's real irritation, however, related to the girl he had left, warm and naked, in his bed at the flat. One o'clock in the morning was really no suitable time for members of the Special Branch to be knocking at one's door and demanding that one accompany them to Heathrow.

He had sat in the helicopter from Battersea, silently fuming. The two men who had collected him and dragged him almost literally from the girl, had been totally uncommunicative. When he had arrived, he had been introduced to Seaborne, the senior detective, and then to the civilian, the man Latymer whom he now knew to be 'Ratcatcher'. In minutes he had been appraised, like some prize exhibit at a cattle-market, and then the make-up man had been loosed upon him with a free hand. He had discovered, to the consequent unsettlement of his stomach and nerves, that he was to impersonate the escaped terrorist, Nasoud, who had been killed a couple of hours earlier with the army's heavy-footed help.

His hair had been trimmed, the afro-style that was of such help to him in his undercover role with the Drugs Squad of the Met., removed so that now his hair was merely untidy, shorter, fuzzy. The drooping moustache had also been altered in thickness and line. Then, of all things, his skin, normally sallow, had been carefully stained. This had been followed by the gum-padding inside his mouth, to fatten his own cadaverous features slightly.

He followed the operations of the make-up man and compared the alterations of the face he thought he knew by looking in any one of the battery of vanity-mirrors ranged on the table opposite his chair. Alongside this, erected on easels, were blow-up photographs of the dead man taken after his original arrest. Nasoud was his build and there was some superficial resemblance, he admitted. In fact, he considered, there had been more resemblance before the make-up man had started than there was now. Henry Currie, to his own eye, looked rather ill, very tired and certainly not capable of looking after himself. Had he applied for the police force looking as he did now, he would most certainly have failed the medical.

Latymer stood looking at the small wiry individual in the chair. After his plea with Packer for more time – coupled with his desperate appeal for the exchange to take place half-way between the Tower and the 707, together with assurances that the bomb, in Packer's possession at the head of the convoy of passengers, would be handed over to Special Branch experts immediately – after that tense, wearing dialogue, Seaborne and his team had wasted no time in ransacking the police files, by proxy. It had taken them less than twenty minutes, such was the urgency with which they worked and the manner in which they were driven by Seaborne, to come up with Currie's name and address and photograph, and merely an additional ten minutes for him to be collected and on his way to the airport.

Seaborne, it now seemed to Latymer, was convinced of the rightness of the course upon which they had embarked. Reluctant, even truculent at first, once Latymer had removed, by Packer's word, the danger of the bomb, he seemed like a man possessed, willing and driving his men to accomplish his side of the bargain he appeared to feel had been struck. They would not fail because of Seaborne's part in things.

Latymer continued to watch, intently, as the substitute Nasoud took shape before his eyes. The body of the real Nasoud, if required for consultation by the little man fussing round Currie, was in an adjoining room, lying on a narrow bed. The make-up man, Melluish, had refused to even look at the body since, as he pointed out to Latymer, the man's features in death would bear no relationship to the image that Latymer had already planted in the hijackers' minds.

Latymer looked at his watch. The time was one-thirty-six. The transformation of Currie, now almost complete, had been achieved in twenty minutes. Latymer went over again in his mind the details of the operation that he had sketched in consultation with Seaborne and Bracken. It could work – looking at Currie, he felt it had a good chance of working. They had the substitute, and they had another man upstairs in the 'Greenhouse' who spoke Arabic and who, after listening to recordings of Nasoud's interrogation was, at that moment, talking as much like Nasoud as he could into a tape-recorder. If Packer wanted to talk to Nasoud, he would in fact be talking to this man. Aubrey and his department of the SIS had not been at all pleased at the idea of allowing material of such confidentiality into Latymer's hands, but they had delivered the tapes when impressed with the urgency of the matter. So – Nasoud could walk and he could talk. All that remained was hope, fervent hope, that Packer could, and would, keep his side of the bargain.

Bracken stood at Latymer's side, chin cupped in his hand, watching Currie's face with a disconcerting stare. The make-up man stepped aside and wiped his hands on a towel. Then he looked round at the two men who formed his audience, as if for their judgement. Latymer looked at Bracken, who had seen the face in the moment after it had died.

He was silent for a long time, and then he said; 'It's good – very good. If the man I saw had been ill – hadn't eaten, it would be him.'

'Thank God,' Latymer breathed. Then, in a more business-like tone, he addressed Currie. 'Right, young man – let's get you dressed, shall we, for your big part?'

He smiled. Currie suspiciously, critically, inspected himself in the mirrors, and then said, 'Are you really serious, sir? You think we can get away with it?'

Latymer looked at him, the smile becoming slightly strained. He said, 'If we don't, young man – I don't care to consider the consequences of our failure – do you?'

He waved Currie past him to where another policeman waited beside a bundle of clothes spilling from a suitcase. Currie, shrugging his shoulders, crossed the room and disappeared in company with the man and his suitcase into an adjoining room.

'It could work . . .' Bracken said, attempting an encouraging tone.

'Mm. He *looks* the part, I agree – even under this lighting. He should be more convincing out there, with the light behind him, even through field-glasses.' Latymer paused, then added, 'It's that bloody bomb that worries me, Philip! I can't stop thinking about it. The results of an explosion would be . . . horrible.'

'But the girl won't have it, will she, sir?'

'I hope not. But if Packer has it, and he discovers our little subterfuge before we can get to him, and he takes it into his unstable brain that he's been fooled one final time . . . what do *you* think he might do?'

'I see what you mean,' Bracken said after a pause. 'It might be very nasty.' His voice became throaty as he again envisaged the possibility entirely in personal terms.

'Indeed.' Latymer straightened himself. 'We're committed now, Philip. Too late for second thoughts. I have to see His Excellency now and coach him in his part. We don't want to have to find a second substitute, at this late stage, do we? And then we have to teach young Sergeant Currie how to walk properly if he is to give a convincing performance!'

Smiling, he passed out of the door on his way to the room where His Excellency the Lebanese Ambassador had been comfortably ensconced – SATCO's office. Bracken, looking after him, realised that Latymer had plunged himself into this last act of the drama, as if to forget the past and to ignore the future. Bracken was sure that Latymer would lose his job as Executive Officer as soon as the aircraft took off, as soon as the dust settled. He wondered where the man would go – Cambridge again? He did not think Latymer would be willing to accept any alternative employment in a Whitehall department, and he was dubious about his joining any of the branches of the security services.

Suddenly Bracken was filled with regret for what would be bound to happen to Latymer. He liked and respected his chief, and what would be done to him, by the Cabinet and the press, would be totally unjustified. As Latymer had said, no one really understood the kind of people they were dealing with out there on the tarmac, what they were capable of . . . He wondered whether, by now, Alison understood them. He bit his lip and prayed that she, at least, might be spared.

Alison Bracken looked at her watch. It was one-forty-eight. She wiped at the corner of her mouth with the damp, grimy handkerchief screwed into a ball in her palm. She now felt nothing more than a desperate tiredness, as if her nerves had been stretched to breaking point. The grimy handkerchief in her hand was a geological specimen, representing a past era of her life.

There had been delays, a reprieve, and now it seemed they were to be released. Some people in the compartment had stuttered into a babble of subdued excitement at the news, as if they had managed to retain their ability to respond; as their terror had been constant, so their relief had been evident. For herself, she no longer cared. The abortive attack had roused her, temporarily, hideously, from her torpor of mind and heart – but, as the wounded and the survivors had been seen from the window dragging themselves away, she had sunk back into her lethargy. Her eyes had watched things happen, she had heard words spoken, but it had all happened at such a terrible distance. The tower, and her husband – they were light-years away, and not at all real to her.

She gave no thought to what Bracken might be feeling, or even to whether he would be waiting to meet her. It was as if she had walked through a door as final as divorce, or even death.

Packer entered the first-class, a grin on his face, one which might have expressed relief as well as sadistic pleasure. He said, addressing them all, 'Ladies and gentlemen – British Airways apologises for the delay in disembarkation. If you'll collect your hand luggage and remain in your seats, we'll be releasing you real soon now.'

'Thank God,' someone muttered.

'Not Him, lady – just thank the Latymer-man!' Packer replied. 'He's seen the light at last. He just called to give me the O.K., that the Lebanese ambassador has arrived, and I've just spoken to my soul-brother, Nasoud, so you sit tight, all of you.' The voice became the familiar, harsh thing they were accustomed to hearing. 'And then, when I'm satisfied there are no tricks, we all take a little walk. And don't forget to wrap up real warm, folks – you can't trust the weather over here one little bit!' He grinned, confident, pleased in his last exercise of authority over them. Then he passed through into the second-class to repeat his instructions, and his humour. Alison had collected her hand luggage together by the time he passed through the compartment again and opened the passenger door. The night air outside seemed fresh, and surprisingly cold after the foetid atmosphere of the aircraft. She breathed deeply and the air in her lungs seemed to stir something within her. She began to quiver, a tremor that had nothing to do with the slight drop in temperature. She saw her hands were shaking. She had begun to hope again, and fear had come, as the inseparable ally of hope. She was afraid, very afraid that something would go wrong, that she would die after all . . .

Packer stood at the top of the passenger-gangway, the field-glasses to his eyes. He had given Latymer precise instructions that he was to be able to get a clear sight of Nasoud. True, he had already spoken to him over the R/T, but he would only trust his eyes in this matter. He wanted to see Nasoud, the Ambassador and Latymer himself before he would give the order for the disembarkation of the passengers to begin. He watched the tower, anticipation twisting in his stomach. He began to feel the tension of relief, the weight of the long hours in the plane stretching behind him. He realised he had been living on his nerves, and on heroin, since they had hit London. The toll was beginning to tell. His legs felt weak and his mind was a spinning, jumbled mass of images. He was tired and he wanted to sleep. He knew he was in bad shape as he tried to shrug off the heroin haze that surrounded his thinking. He had to clear his mind for the next few minutes. When they were in the air, with Nasoud, Latymer and the Ambassador on board, then he could relax, go to sleep – and wake up free in Beirut.

At that moment, his resentment against Mr J. back in New York reached a peak. At the moment when it appeared that things were going to pan out and on his side, he hated Mr J., the man who sat in his office and who gave the orders – the man who had put him on the spot here. He had no idea how Mr J. had become involved in terrorism, or why. He had little idea about Mr J. and the workings of his mind. He tried not to think of Mr J.

Then the field-glasses picked up the small group of figures detaching themselves from the shadows at the base of the tower. Yes, there were the demanded car headlights and the group of figures pausing in the light thrown on their faces. The little man in the expensive overcoat, that had to be the Ambassador – the tall, grey-haired figure of Latymer. Packer smiled. Latymer appeared not to be very happy about the situation – he looked beaten. There were others, behind them, police? He did not fear a trap now, it was too late to expect such a thing to work, too dangerous . . . Yet he decided to send Clay at the head of the file of passengers.

He focused the glasses as finely as he could and concentrated on the figure in the centre of the group. He was astonished at the change that had come over Nasoud. Latymer had not been lying when he had talked of a hunger-strike. Even allowing for the bleeding of colour from the face because of the white headlights, Nasoud was not a well man. But it was him. That was Nasoud. He raised his arm and waved it slowly back and forth over his head, to signal his acceptance of the arrangements. The three figures began to move, ahead of the lights now, Nasoud walking slowly, supported it appeared on Latymer's arm. Smiling to himself, he continued to watch for a few moments, then he turned back into the first-class compartment and called to Clay.

'O.K., superfly – get the show on the road!'

Clay grinned at him, the relief he felt evident in his face. Packer nodded and drew his gun. The first passengers joined him at the head of the gangway, Clay alongside the fat bitch he had frightened with the gun. For a moment, Packer felt a surge of anger, as physical as nausea, at the idea that these people were walking away free.

Then he nodded again to Clay. 'Take 'em down, Clay!' He hefted the airline bag from his shoulder and passed it to the negro. Clay took it gingerly.

'We can't leave this for her to play with, man!' he said. Then he grinned. 'I wanna bird to come back to, when I de livered these cats.'

'Sure, man. Keep your eyes peeled. They won't try anything with the passengers around, but just watch it, uh? We'll cover you from here, man.'

'Right on, brother! Keep me a seat on the glory-train, 'cause I'm gettin' outa here tonight! He turned to the knot of passengers in the doorway. 'Come on, people – the black Moses gonna lead you to the Promised Land!' He went down the steps cheerfully, machine-pistol riding on his hip, airline bag slung over his shoulder, and waited as the first passengers began to descend.

Packer watched as the file grew, as the last of the second-class passengers drew slowly away from the bulk of the fuselage. He felt a moment's resentment, and nervousness, as if he had thrown away his armour, but then comforted himself with the thought that he still had the flight crew, guarded by McGruder at their stations on the flight-deck,' as well as the stewardesses. There would be no slip-ups, no double-cross . . . and no explosion. The bomb was gone, slung over Clay's shoulder in the airline bag. He looked round to check on the whereabouts of Joanne Fender. She was no longer behind him. He grinned. Sulking, because he had taken away her nice new toy, he thought.

Joanne Fender watched the last of the passengers leave with a furious, cold rage that obliterated the bandaged, biting pain in her arm. Rice had tagged on the rear of that herd of complacent, vicious, hypocritical animals, sleek, well-fed, going not to the slaughter, but going on to be the kind of people they had always been. Packer was congratulating himself on making the exchange, but to her he had capitulated – he had had those people in his hands, and he had allowed them to live when they had no right to life. Her rage against him, against them, was so deep and so pure she was almost in tears, the tears of a child.

She returned to her seat in the first-class, cradling the damaged elbow, and gingerly and with difficulty she reached up with her good arm to the rack for her second bag. Then she sat in her seat, holding the bag in her lap. She tugged the zip open and reached into it with her good hand. She drew out a small box, apparently a box of chocolates. She held it lightly in her hand. There was no anger, no frustration now, merely a feeling of elation, a calm, leisurely elation. Packer had taken the bomb, the one that had been designed to destroy the plane and its entire passenger-manifest, if that had become necessary. But he hadn't known about the second bomb, the one in the box of chocolates. It wasn't a big bomb – it would hardly tear the fuselage. It was an anti-personnel device, hardly more powerful than a brace of grenades. But it was enough – for what she had in mind, it was enough. Smiling to herself, eyes closed, she hugged her shattered elbow and rocked to and fro in her seat. humming tunelessly, softly to herself.

And there was Packer, she thought, standing on the gang-way, with field-glasses, watching the passengers escape, watching the animals crawl away . . .

Captain Burgess sat in the pilot's seat, looking straight ahead into the night. They were ready for take-off, as soon as the tower gave him the all-clear. Despite the armed man at the rear of the flight-deck, he felt a breath of normality for the first time since the lights had indicated that he had engine trouble, just before they had landed. He was back on his flight-deck and the controls were in front of him – normality. He was desperately tired, too tired to be allowed to take off in normal circumstances . . . nevertheless, he felt a certain qualified lightening of the heart. There was a time-limit, it seemed, on hell itself. The time-limit was the duration of the flight to Beirut. He knew, and believed, that everything had been cleared and he no longer doubted his eventual emergence from this affair. The Lebanese Ambassador would be on the flight and that was a guarantee that nothing dangerous would occur.

He looked across at Hislop, who was staring silently out of the window, watching the exchange that was taking place out there, the nearing of the two groups. He felt sorry for Hislop – he had been through a worse nightmare than any of them. Twice, Packer had been within an ace of blowing him to kingdom come, egged on by the girl, the murderous little bitch . . . Burgess put out of his mind the too-vivid images of the Russian roulette Packer had played, the gun against His-lop's temple, until Hislop had begged and whined for his life . . . just for the amusement of the hijackers. Hislop was

233

in no shape to fly the 707, and Burgess knew that the strain of the flight would fall entirely on him. As if in answer to that demand upon himself, he squared his shoulders and began his pre-flight checks.

Clay, at the head of the passengers, held up his hand and halted the column. The group ahead of him, now less than thirty yards distant, had also halted. He stood looking at them for a long time. There were the three men in front, the Ambassador, Nasoud and the Latymer-man, and then the group behind them, armed policemen. Clay did not expect trouble. All he required now was Nasoud to walk forward and he would give the word for the passengers to move ahead. Then they would head back to the plane, keeping an eye on the hand-guns the police were certain to be carrying.

'O.K., man – come ahead. Walk away from them, baby!' he called.

Currie glanced once at Latymer and the man nodded, his face grim. Currie swallowed. He had a gun in his pocket, in the pocket of the old overcoat they had given him, and his hand closed around the butt, finger seeking the trigger. Slowly, stumbling slightly as he had been instructed to as Latymer's supporting arm fell away, he moved towards the negro. Behind him, Bracken moved up to fill the gap between Latymer and the Ambassador.

'And the Ambassador – now him!' the negro called. Clay then moved to one side, exposing the leading passengers. Bracken felt an anguished lump in his throat, his stomach churned, as he saw Alison at the head of the file. He realised, with a huge shock, that she was pregnant. Suddenly he was trembling with fear for her safety.

'Just take a couple of steps forward, Your Excellency,' Latymer murmured. 'Please move in a line directly ahead so that you do not block our view of the negro.' The little man nodded, and swallowed. He had regretted his decision to acquiesce to Latymer's earnest request with every step he had taken across the tarmac. It had been a selfless decision, in response to the plight of the passengers, one that he knew, on all official grounds, he should never have taken. But he had never imagined that it could have been like this, these endless moments of sheer terror.

He stepped forward.

'Hey, man – how you doin'?' Clay called to Currie, who nodded and tried to appear to be concentrating all his energies on putting one foot before the other. He was no more than fifteen yards from the negro now, well within the range of accurate fire from the wicked-looking machine-pistol at the negro's side. It wasn't trained on him, he saw, but it would take only a split-second for Clay to loose off enough lead to bring his existence to a summary close. The girl in his bed seemed an impossible distance away. He knew he was sweating and hoped the dye on his face was waterproof. His mind screamed to him that the disguise was transparent, that at any moment he would be recognised as an impostor.

The passengers had begun to pass him now, away to his right, staring curiously at what they assumed was the cause of their recent misery, and now their release. They had been directed to move in an arc, spread out, so that they did not interfere with the exchange and so they presented the easiest target to Clay, and to the other man, Rice, now at his side. Fourteen yards, thirteen, twelve . . . Then it happened.

'It's not him – that's not him!' Rice yelled, and the machine-pistol swung without hesitation. Currie felt a tearing ache in his stomach and chest and saw the ground, at a great distance, rushing up at him.

Bracken knew what had happened. He had forced himself not to look at Alison, as she led the crocodile of passengers in a wide arc to safety. He saw Rice stiffen, saw his mouth open, knew the words that would emerge and was already on the move, his revolver drawn. He had covered yards of the distance that separated him from Rice and the negro before Currie's body hit the ground. He dropped to one knee and, as Clay swung, enraged, blind to his own danger, to draw a bead on the file of passengers, the last of whom were no more than five or six yards away, Bracken fired three times and watched the big black man spin away, arms comically thrown up, limbs rubbery as he fell.

Rice, the passengers forgotten, everything forgotten except the safety offered by the 707, began to run towards it, waving his arms, shouting insanely that it was a trap, that the man was not Nasoud. On the gangway, Packer had seen the distant body of Nasoud fall forwards, shot by Clay, and then he had heard the percussive noises of the machine-pistol. He did not stop to consider what had happened – his single thought was that the flight-crew were his only hope, that Latymer had fooled him for the last time. He did not see Rice's lifeless body fall wearily on the tarmac, shot by Bracken in a merciless, cold revenge for what Alison had almost suffered, and in a purgation of his own emotions.

Joanne Fender was in front of Packer, the door to the flight deck open so that he could see the faces of the crew, turned to look back, surprise and shock on their features. McGruder, he saw helplessly, was a humped, dead shape in the corridor. Joanne had something in her hands, a box, and she was laughing . . . He tried to cry out, to stop her, his desire for revenge suddenly overwhelmed by his terrible fear for his own life. He had not, he thought ludicrously, even heard the shot that had killed McGruder. She did not even look at him, as the fingers of her undamaged hand fiddled awkwardly in the box. Then Packer's world exploded in flame and noise.

Latymer saw the canopy of the flight-deck bulge, then shatter; he saw the roar of flame and then, lagging behind, arriving at the same moment as the first sensations of horror, he heard the noise of the explosion and the heat burned on his face. He looked at the group gathered round Clay, defusing the bomb he had carried, as if what he had just seen was a fiction, a trick of eyesight. Then his gaze returned to the 707. The girl had achieved her Liebestöd, he realised. There had been a second, secret bomb, and she had detonated it. He felt sick. He was unable to take his eyes from the orange flames of the fire, now licking round the ruined crater of the flight-deck, the heat driving back the huddled passengers, and the only sound he could hear was the wailing of the fire tenders as they pulled out across the tarmac.

He did not see Bracken holding Alison, shaking with re-

236

action, in his arms. All he could see, until it filled each of his senses, was the orange glow from the 707. It was something, he knew, which would remain with him for the rest of his life.

It was one-fifty-six in the morning.

*And don't miss the new INTERNATIONAL
SUPERSELLER from CRAIG THOMAS*

WOLFSBANE

For almost half a lifetime ex-agent Richard Gardiner has
buried his searing memories of treachery and torture, of that
nightmare time in the bloody cellars of the Gestapo. And
the hideous sick double-cross that followed when freedom
appeared to be within his grasp.

Now 1944 seems a long time ago. Until skilled
manipulators, playing on the horrors of Gardiner's wartime
experience, squeeze the trigger that lies deep within him.
Turning him into a merciless killing machine: hunter – and
hunted – in a tangled web of retribution and death that is
to decimate a whole branch of British intelligence.

The killing-ground is among old friends and enemies. The
search is for the man who always betrayed and murdered by
proxy. The man known as WOLFSBANE . . .

ADVENTURE/THRILLER FICTION   0 7221 8455 7
£1.25

And Craig Thomas's supersonic superthriller

FIREFOX

The Soviet Mig-31 is the deadliest warplane ever built.
Codenamed FIREFOX by NATO, it can fly at over
4,000 mph, is invulnerable to radar – AND HAS A
LETHALLY SOPHISTICATED WEAPONS SYSTEM
THAT ITS PILOT CAN CONTROL BY THOUGHT-
IMPULSES. There is only one way that British
Intelligence and the CIA can counter the threat it poses:
a scheme more desperate and daring than any undercover
operation since the Second World War –
HIJACK THE FIREFOX!

"Simply won't allow you to put it down until you reach
the last page"
      JACK HIGGINS, author of *The Eagle has Landed*

"Sensational . . . all too real"
WILLIAM STEVENSON, author of *A Man called Intrepid*

ADVENTURE/THRILLER FICTION   0 7221 0520 7
                                                              £1.25

A selection of bestsellers from Sphere:

Fiction

THE WOMEN'S ROOM	Marilyn French	£1.50	☐
SINGLE	Harriet Frank	£1.10	☐
DEATH OF AN EXPERT WITNESS	P. D. James	95p	☐
THE VILLAGE: THE FIRST SUMMER			
	Mary Fraser	£1.00	☐
BLOOD OF THE BONDMASTER			
	Richard Tresillian	£1.25	☐
NOW AND FOREVER	Danielle Steel	£1.10	☐

Film and Television Tie-Ins

THE PASSAGE	Bruce Nicolaysen	95p	☐
INVASION OF THE BODY SNATCHERS			
	Jack Finney	85p	☐
THE EXPERIMENT	John Urling Clark	95p	☐
THE MUSIC MACHINE	Bill Stoddart	95p	☐
BUCK ROGERS IN THE 25TH CENTURY			
	Addison E. Steele	95p	☐
BUCK ROGERS 2: THAT MAN ON BETA			
	Addison E. Steele	95p	☐
DEATHSPORT	William Hughes	95p	☐

Non-Fiction

NINE AND A HALF WEEKS	Elizabeth McNeill	95p	☐
IN HIS IMAGE	David Rorvik	£1.00	☐
THE MUSICIANS OF AUSCHWITZ	Fania Fenelon	95p	☐
THE GREAT GAME	Leopold Trepper	£1.50	☐
THE SEXUAL CONNECTION	John Sparks	85p	☐

All Sphere books are available at your local bookshop or newsagent, or can be ordered direct from the publisher. Just tick the titles you want and fill in the form below.

Name ....

Address ....

....

Write to Sphere Books, Cash Sales Department, P.O. Box 11, Falmouth, Cornwall TR10 9EN

Please enclose cheque or postal order to the value of cover price plus:
UK: 22p for the first book plus 10p per copy for each additional book ordered to a maximum charge of 82p
OVERSEAS: 30p for the first book and 10p for each additional book
BFPO and EIRE: 22p for the first book plus 10p per copy for the next 6 books, thereafter 4p per book
Sphere Books reserve the rights to show new retail prices on covers which may differ from those previously advertised in the text or elsewhere, and to increase postal rates in accordance with the GPO.